The Clash of Queens

Emma Bradley

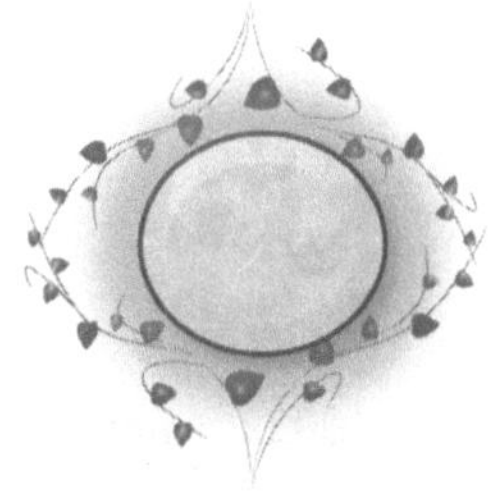

WATCH. LISTEN. LEARN.

ISBN: 978-1-7398180-4-3

DEDICATION

For those who have come on the journey from book 1 to book 4
– I promised everything would be okay, so here it is!

CONTENT WARNING

This book features some emotional scenes involving building
trust in the aftermath of mental manipulation and also the
suggestion of one or two physically intimate scenes (mentioned
in scene but not shown graphically).

CHAPTER ONE
At The Queen's Court

It wasn't the talking wardrobe's fault.

A tiny voice in the back of my head reminded me I'd not even bothered to ask her name the last time we'd met, or this time, but all-encompassing grief had eclipsed everything around me.

Now, I stood in 'my' room at the Queen's court, facing a mirror with a dark scowl on my face.

Someone had taken the trouble to update my room since I'd been there last, but I didn't know who to thank and couldn't find the effort to ask anyone. Where before there had been fabrics and furnishings in various shades of plain cream, now the fabrics were evergreen and muted browns, from the curtains and the bed covers to the fluffy rug on the floor.

I guessed someone had tried their hardest to pick out things I'd like, to make this room feel less like a prison, but I couldn't dredge up any gratitude.

I'll be gone by tonight anyway. Back to a home that doesn't feel like home anymore. Not without Taz.

I pushed aside the frantic stab of grief to my chest that threatened to knock me over and focused on my immediate problem. The dress.

"I'm not wearing it," I muttered. "I look like a whore."

The responding huff from the talking wardrobe did nothing to calm my anger.

Two days had passed since we'd arrived at the court, and today was the morning of Taz's funeral. I'd spent most of the past forty-eight hours either holed up here in my room or inside the conservatory that had been Taz's twelfth birthday present from the Queen.

I hadn't seen her since arriving, but now I wondered if perhaps she was avoiding me. As Taz's mother, she'd shown so little grief when she told me he was gone. Then again, I would have avoided someone if I was expecting- no, *forcing* them to turn up to their boyfriend's funeral in a dress that barely hid their underwear.

Even my friends, Ace and Milo, had understood my need for solitude the last couple of days. No doubt they'd been coping with the entrapments of the enchanted house and avoiding Taz's awful sisters by themselves.

I faced the mirror again.

The enchanted brushes were cautiously trying to get my black curls into some kind of order, but since the news about Taz even the oil-slick colours in my hair were dull. Lifeless. But even though I was heartbroken, it didn't mean I had to take the dress situation without a fight.

It was a deep purple with shimmering golden threads, Taz's court colours, but the respect for him stopped right there. There were slits up both sides of the flimsy skirt, and one very wide one right down the front of the halter-neck bodice.

"Problem?"

I turned my glare from the mirror to the doorway.

The Queen of Faerie, also Taz's mother, stood there with a firm frown on her face. Even looking at her now hurt, her hair the same honey brown shade as Taz's. I could see minor similarities in the shape of the nose as well, although she didn't have his freckles or his turquoise eyes.

"It's too revealing," I bit back. "It's disrespectful."

The Queen's expression flickered. "It's elegant, and we have no time to procure another. This is Faerie, and things such as modesty are not relevant."

I ignored that, knowing that I couldn't exactly do anything like blast her across the hall without incurring a similar reaction. That and she could probably take me easier than breathing in a straight fight.

"Modesty's not relevant at a fu- on a day like today?" I couldn't say the word 'funeral' without breaking down. "Your resilience astounds me."

The Queen's jaw twitched, but she didn't rise to the taunt.

"You are princess consort in the eyes of Faerie and our folk now. That cannot be undone, so you must act like one."

I opened my mouth to tell her where she could shove her titles and the whole of Faerie, but memories swarmed of every time Taz had called me princess and I couldn't find the words.

"Your companions will be along in a minute to escort you down," she added. "I take it we can rely on you to not cause any kind of commotion?"

I gritted my teeth and nodded. As she walked away down the hall, I realised that this hostility was probably the only thing holding either of us together right now.

I rushed across to push the door shut.

No commotion, my arse.

I pulled the ties holding the top of the dress around my neck, shivering as the fabric dropped and chilly air hit my skin. Taz's t-shirt, the one I'd worn for the past three days, was lying on my pillow. I grabbed it and pulled it over my head.

With the top of the dress secured again over the t-shirt, I was ready. Not actually ready, because I'd never be ready to face today, but I would do it without causing a scandal.

I owe him that much at least. Although, in Faerie wearing a t-shirt is probably more of a scandal than me turning up completely naked.

"Well, you'll make a statement, dear, if nothing else," the wardrobe sighed.

I looked at her, the small whorls in the centre of the door that formed a face of sorts.

"I never asked you for your name," I told her, as if she didn't already know.

A pause, then, "Cynthia."

Not the name I would have thought of for a talking wardrobe, but I managed the barest of smiles.

"Thank you, Cynthia."

I curled my nails into my palms, squeezing tight as someone knocked on the door. It opened a moment later, and I moved across the cold stone floor to meet Ace and Milo.

Ace wore a smart suit in a dark blue that complimented his black skin and hair, while Milo was in a stiff grey shirt and black trousers that made him look like a bulky, pale vampire. I noticed he'd not managed to rake his messy brown hair into tufts yet, possibly because Ace would have kept smacking his hand down away from his head when he tried.

At least I still have them, even if I don't have... I choked down a strangled sob.

"Um, Dem, is that what you're wearing?" Milo asked, chewing his lip.

I nodded, forcing myself back under control. Waited for some kind of argument. Before either of them could say a word, my mentor Petra popped up behind them in a black t-shirt dress that fell to her ankles.

See? Her dress is fine. Casual but dignified.

She eyed me up and down with a grimace.

"If you're going to make a scene, Demi, at least put some pants on to go with it. Here, I'm packed to go home already but my leggings should fit you."

She dug around in the rucksack hanging off one shoulder, twisting like a pretzel to reach it. She threw some charcoal grey leggings at me, and I tugged them on beneath my dress.

She nodded. "Better. Come on."

Revulsion swelled, burning acidic in my throat. I managed to breathe through my nose, but if I opened my mouth, I worried I'd never stop spewing. I stayed where I was, the ragged breaths hissing through my nostrils.

Ace slid an arm around my waist, Milo's settling slightly higher from my other side. I let them support me, both of them bulky enough to basically hoist me out of the room and into the hall without any assistance from my legs. I hadn't been eating more than a few mouthfuls since Taz had died, too morose to be hungry and too listless to look after myself. The brushes in my room had sorted my hair, but I knew Cynthia would be quietly bemoaning how my unwashed skin was dirtying what was no doubt a priceless royal dress.

My revenge-fuelled determination to go and hunt Taz's killer was still simmering, but I couldn't do anything until this cursed day was over.

We walked, or got led in my case, down the sweeping staircase toward the main hall. I barely noticed the branches of oak amid the gold and purple floral arrangements. I listened instead to the dull roar in my ears, clinging tight to the knowledge that once this was over, I could let rage lead me on to destroying our enemies.

The doors to the hall were open, but I recognised the faces gathered on either side. Beryl, Meryl, Cheryl, Hutch and Harvey, Petra, Trevor with his family, and most if not all of Arcanium were gathered in silent support as we passed.

I tried to find some strength inside me, a last vestige of effort to make my legs do the work as we entered the hall. My feet pushed against the floor, a lame attempt, but when I saw the ornate wooden coffin decorated with acorns, my knees buckled.

Ace and Milo held me firm like a rag-doll between them, guiding me forward. The Queen stood at the very front beside the coffin and a large portrait of Taz. He would have hated all the pompous ceremony, but I couldn't find enough breath to say it out loud. The Queen's eyes flashed over my body, but I couldn't even dredge up any spark of delight at having won the dress argument.

Go numb. Stop listening. Stop feeling. Detach.

I counselled myself with the same words over and over as Ace and Milo drew me into the front row of chairs, physically sitting me down on one. Even then, they kept hold of me, arms around my waist.

I stared at the coffin, drowning in my cowardice. The lid was fixed down now, but earlier it would have been open, surrounded by people swarming to pay their respects and to say farewell. But I couldn't bring myself to do it, to see with my own eyes that he was really gone.

"Did you…" I couldn't say it, pointing with a shaking hand to the coffin.

Ace shook his head. "The Queen wouldn't let anyone in. Said it had already been closed."

I nodded to show I'd heard but couldn't dredge up any effort to respond.

Exactly like her to deprive everyone else of the chance.

I barely noticed Milo's worried hiss fill my ears.

"What are they doing here?"

"It was unavoidable, apparently," Petra answered.

I turned to find her seated right behind me. I hadn't noticed her hand on my shoulder until now but it was there, holding tight.

I eyed the crowd and saw who she meant. Filling the front row on the opposite side of the aisle to us were the Apocalyptians, their bodies covered with hazy glows of innate power.

Anger slammed through me so fast I couldn't move, stealing my breath away.

"To not invite them would have made too much of a stand," Petra continued. "Their arrival at Kainen's court was made known to the whole of Faerie after the battle, and the Queen can't risk showing her hand too early and making enemies of them. Beating them outright isn't likely to be an option, so the plan is to be sneaky about it."

"The Queen can't be seen to have a hand in what happened at the Court of Illusions either," Milo added. "If they knew the whole of Arcanium were abandoning missions to find a way in, it'd be chaos and Arcanium would be rui-."

"Ouch," Ace hissed.

He and Milo had to remove their arms from around me as my energy gift spiked, zinging from my skin, but I was too busy eying the enemy to apologise.

Eleven of them, not Twelve.

I scanned their faces, then the room. The Apocalyptians were talking amongst themselves as though they were waiting for a play to start at the theatre. One of them was even fanning herself with what looked like a programme. But of the fourteen Apocalyptians that existed, three were missing. We'd captured Lust and Chastity at the Court of Illusions three days ago, but in my grief I'd not thought to ask Ace who he had given them to.

And Fury was absent also.

"Even she wouldn't be stupid enough to come here today," I ground out. "Not after what she- not when-"

Not when she was the one who killed him.

I tried to fight the memories, the battle at Kainen's Court of Illusions, Apocalyptians fighting us for stealing two of their kind and sealing them in vials. But they were the enemy, and the all-powerful essences of vices and virtues. They were working with Elvira, who wanted to bring us down. Taz hadn't even been anything to do with what happened there, but he'd paid the price for it.

As did I, with the nightmares that stalked me every time I managed a few short snatches of sleep.

I shook my head and glimpsed the only other person that could set my anger firing.

Kainen Hemlock was dressed in a black suit with his brown hair slicked back, as if he were truly here to mourn. My rage boiled over as he rose out of his seat behind the Apocalyptians and slipped toward a side door.

I forgot about the funeral, about the grief and my own wretched existence. If Kainen hadn't tricked me into things, if he'd told me what was happening around me, then Taz might never have had to come and rescue me. He'd still be alive, and I wouldn't be here.

He's going to pay.

Kainen was the one who'd tricked me, he was the one who'd been working with the enemy despite promising us he'd turned to our side. No matter the sob stories he'd told me while his mistresses discussed ways they should torture me, and who should go first.

"Demi, sit down!" Petra hissed.

I ignored her and slithered over Milo's legs, my eyes flickering with the tell-tale burn that meant they were glowing red. Another mark Fury's meddling had left on my life.

Milo didn't try to grab me. Perhaps he didn't dare.

The Queen was deep in conversation with Queenie, Taz's aunt and the Director of Arcanium. Queenie had once told me that she chose her name to intimate that although she was the Queen's sister, she had ideas above her station. It was all a ruse to keep Arcanium, and Taz, safe.

They failed.

Neither of them noticed as I powered past them at the front of the hall.

My brain awoke from its fog of grief, the sharp clarity of rage sending me through the door after Kainen. The Apocalyptians could follow me, anyone could, but I didn't care.

Let them come. Let them try me right now.

Perhaps a fight was what I needed, to slam and smash and hurt until there was nothing left of me and the pain could finally go away.

The door led onto a narrow hall with only one arch at the far end. I saw the back of Kainen as he disappeared through it and powered after him, not bothering to even put up a warding.

Make it hurt. My new motto danced in my head. *Make it hurt. Make them pay.*

Even though I wanted nothing more than to burst in there and kill him dead, I had enough vengeance to keep me back. If I struck him now, it might make capturing the Apocalyptians more difficult later if he knew things that we didn't. I wanted them all to suffer, not just him.

"…not much longer," he said. "I'll confirm the status when done."

I stuck my head through the archway in time to see the pearly grey vision of a familiar face looming out of Kainen's communication orb.

My blood seethed. *Traitors, all of them.*

Emil's face disappeared, the call over. He was the right hand of the enemy, the wannabe-queen Elvira, and he had killed my old mentor. I owed him double pain for that.

I thought Kainen would come back toward me, but he slipped his orb into his pocket and turned toward a huge brown vase in the corner, the kind with two handles on either side. It was bigger than him by several feet, dwarfing the entire room. He ran a hand over it and I was sick of waiting.

"Traitor." I strode into the room. "Not satisfied with your lot killing my boyfriend, you have to come and taint his memory?"

Kainen span around, his dark eyes wide.

"Demi." He hesitated. "Please, I don't know how much you remember from your time at my court, but it's not what you think-"

I didn't care, even if it was the exact opposite of what I thought. If he'd done better, Taz might still be here.

I sent my energy gift out and he crumpled over, clutching his stomach where it had hit him.

I pulled back, wanting it to last. A tiny voice in my head screamed that this wasn't the way to settle things, it wasn't who I was, but she was a tiny soul drowning in fury and grief.

Kainen lifted his head, his eyes watering.

"Don't make me have to defend myself. I don't want to fight you."

I laughed, raw and dark. "Defend yourself? I dare you, try it. You're a traitor and you're going to die for it."

Before I could issue another shot, a hand clamped on my arm. I tried to shake it off, but the fingers tightened.

"Demi, leave it." Petra was somehow fighting against the residual energy crackling out of my skin. "It's not worth it. *He's* not worth it."

I ignored that tiny voice in my head that was getting louder and saying Petra was right. That voice was the one that did the grief and the crying. Right now, I was the part of me that wanted to slaughter every last enemy I had.

"He was talking to Emil, right? Just now." I snarled at her. "A traitor. We should kill the lot of them where they stand."

Petra held her ground, her unerring calm battling my fury although I noticed now that several strands of her hair were dishevelled, which always happened when she was stressed.

"Any other time I'd join you," she said. "But not today. Any day but today, and there will be countless days for you to hunt them down one by one. Not today."

The grief-stricken part of me found a crack in my anger. I slumped, my connection leaking back down inside me, exhaustion needling over my skin.

I let Petra lead me out of the room without a backward look at Kainen or his giant pot. People stared as we crossed the hall, but Petra passed me off to Ace and Milo and they clamped onto me again, pressing me down into my seat. I ducked my chin against my chest, determined to pretend this wasn't happening. It wasn't goodbye.

It can't be goodbye.

I managed to drown out most of the eulogy, but I couldn't ignore the Queen's commanding voice calling my name, or Ace and Milo gently shaking me.

I fought the wave of compulsion that shot through to my bones, but my mind was so wrecked that my body obeyed the summons despite my resistance to compulsions. I rose out of my seat and stumbled to the front of the hall.

"Demi, it's customary for you to say a few words," the Queen murmured.

I stared at her in horror. I would plead, I would beg, anything to avoid having to face this.

"I can't."

The Queen glared at me. "You have to. You'd dishonour his memory by not even speaking up for him?"

The ache grew inside me, nails of grief clawing and gouging against the faint screaming growing in my head. I could see the crowd clearly, not a sea of faces but a horde of Fae waiting for my inevitable failure.

I took a ragged breath. Then another. Even the Apocalyptians leaned forward, several of them sniffing with intrigued eyes, their hunger for draining emotions latching onto the tantalising torment of mine.

How can I even begin to say anything? I owe him so much more than a simple few words.

"Taz was…" I hesitated. Gulped. Started again. "Taz was an absolute pain in the arse. He was moody, and insufferable. But he was also the best person in the world, everyone's friend, always helping others. When I first met him…"

My knees buckled and this time nobody was there to catch me as my knees smacked onto the marble. The anguish tore through me like rabid animals, the ache in my throat stealing my breath away.

A vague awareness hit me that I was in danger, urging me to run, but I couldn't lift my head. Waves of power surrounded me, familiar like a tsunami of emotions, and I focused my eyes on the multi-coloured haze shimmering in my eyeline.

The Apocalyptians were swarming me before I realised what their behaviour meant.

They're feeding off my emotions.

I felt the stab of laziness hit me, no doubt Sloth trying to urge me to feel more of his essence so he could drain more of mine.

I couldn't make out the differences between them, each attack against my emotions hitting and tearing at me as the others rounded into me at the same time.

"Stand, Demerara!" I heard the Queen's voice puncturing through the agony of feelings. "Fight!"

I would have ignored her, ignored the compulsion and her using my full name. I wanted them to drain me dry, take away the grief and the sheer agony of having to keep going without him.

But then I felt *her*.

The attacks from the other Apocalyptians ceased, until all that was left inside of me was that familiar sear of unending rage.

I found the hard marble floor with my palms. I pushed, gritting my teeth as my legs slithered beneath me. I found my footing and stood to face Fury.

Her red robe flickered with flames and anger, the part of her essence she left lodged inside me responding with a feral roar.

Fury gave me a smug look, the hint of a smile. With a roar, I sent every element of my energy gift at her.

She dodged it, but barely. Her eyes widened as one of the vast marble columns behind her splintered into shards. She swept them aside with a wave of her hand, but I'd managed to catch her out at least.

I sagged, breathing hard. That had taken nearly every ounce of me, but either she would die today or she would kill me trying.

The Queen and Queenie stood beside me now, the three of us forming a protective arc around the coffin as the Apocalyptians fractured to swarm through the frantic crowd now fleeing in all directions.

Pride stalked up beside Fury, his eyes gleaming with intent as he smiled at me. I focused on gathering everything I had left, dredging all the pain and anger and grief inside me to fuel this one last shot.

I lifted my aching arms, but the energy brewing on my fingertips never left me.

I flinched and twisted around as a loud bang echoed at my back and the coffin lid sailed sideways.

CHAPTER TWO
Demi Runs on Instinct

I let out a whimper as Taz's torso lurched upward like a grotesque mimicry of a horror film.

Someone shoved me to the side but I had no hope of knowing who as a shot of boiling water shot through the air where I'd just been standing.

Taz blinked several times as if the light was blinding him, one hand lifting to shade his face.

Then the screaming began. I had no idea, but I think I it was coming from me.

Shouts came from nearby, yelling and shrieks of confusion filling the air as the room burst into battle.

The energy I'd gathered to attack with was still roiling inside me, clawing to be released. I sent it out flying toward Pride in the absence of Fury, who'd vanished again, but it was pure animalistic panic now rather than a targeted attack. The blast lifted the Apocalyptian into the air, slamming him onto a pile of chairs. He got to his feet, but I couldn't cope with this any longer, my hands slamming to my head.

I eyed Taz up and down, taking in the pale complexion and the entire aura of him, his gaze roving over me in return.

It was all a trick. He's alive. He's alive. He's not dead. It was a trick, and he must have been in on it. He knew what this would do to me, he must have known.

I backed away as he stumbled to get out of the coffin. Gifts were zinging all over the place, the Queen's great throne room a smoking scene of utter destruction with huge gouges in the marble. Even her throne was on fire.

One group of FDPs managed to trap Sloth, his snarl shrinking as he was sucked into a small blue Selessium vial. Their movements were organised, coordinated.

They planned this. Used me for it.

I knew it then without needing to ask.

The Queen, Queenie, even Taz, they used my grief to draw the Apocalyptians here, to get them distracted enough to attack so we could capture them.

Kainen was nearby now, the huge vase towering over the remnants of the ridiculous coffin. Memories swarmed, of him tricking me into thinking he was Taz and kissing him, of Elvira pretending to be someone I'd trusted to coerce me into doing her dirty work.

Even Fury. If Taz is alive then she didn't...

I stared around the hall, stuck rooted to the same spot even as Petra darted in front of me to absorb an attack sent my way and turning the glass shards into petals.

The Selessium bottles holding Apocalyptians were being thrown into the vase and I thought I heard a smash through the cacophony of fighting.

Taz finally managed to lever himself out of the coffin and find his feet, his eyes fixed on me. I stumbled back.

Even he tricked me. Used me. Is this payback for what happened, for what Kainen did to me at his court?

He stopped limping toward me when he realised that I was trying to get away from him, his urgent expression falling into a mask of horror.

I had no idea how many Apocalyptians were getting trapped in the mayhem, but the remaining few of them vanished into thin air one after the other. With nothing left to fight, the chaos settled in moments until only tense silence remained.

"We did well," the Queen addressed the crowd. "Eight out of fourteen, over half. We will need to be vigilant now. As you can see, the prince is unharmed as part of our plan to ensnare them, so we will understand that you wish to depart quickly."

It wasn't a generosity on her part, but a command for everyone to get out of her court. She stalked off toward a side door and I recognised Sagar and Eldrich, her two bodyguards, flanking her as they carried away the huge vase.

Most of the Fae in the throne room fled in seconds, but I noticed our friends were hanging around with varying expressions of shock and wariness.

Were any of them in on it too? How could they do it? How could they watch me unravel, knowing he was alive? How could he?

Queenie appeared beside me and it took all my effort not to swing a punch at her.

"I know what you're thinking," she said.

I stared up at her, eyes burning, my chest heaving.

"No, you really don't."

She sighed. "Your grief had to be real to entice them to you so that they could be captured. Only such an explosive range of emotions, linked as much to your human side as your grief, could have drawn so many of them to the funeral, otherwise they may not have bothered. Only that could have distracted them enough to give us the time to attack. They all took great interest in you before by all accounts."

I'd guessed all that. I didn't need to be reminded.

I stared at Taz as he approached me, his steps now hesitant. I couldn't tell if he was walking slow because of my reaction or a lingering injury. I eyed him up and down, checking him over for damage even now. His side, the one Fury had all but gutted a handful of days ago, was covered by a black shirt, but his arm hung there like no damage remained.

The sound of Queenie's voice vanished, although I think her lips were still moving as I forced myself to ask him the question.

"Did you know?"

He grimaced. "Dem, I-"

"Did you know I'd think you were dead?"

He crossed the space toward me. "Technically yes, but-"

I shoved my hands into his chest and whirled away from him. *He knew. He used me.*

I ignored him calling my name, pacing away from him. I could hear him chasing after me, but the crashing sounds and the frantic squeaking of his shoes on the marble suggested he was having trouble coordinating himself.

I can't go back home. He'll know every single hiding place there. I looked around the now almost empty throne room while still powering toward the exit. *I can't go to Mum's house either, not with my sisters there crowing over me. I'd probably annihilate them.*

"Demi, please! Just let me explain!"

I increased my pace.

There's nowhere here I can hide either, even if I translocated up to my room. Keesley would lock the door if I asked him, but Taz would find a way in, or his mother would overrule me.

Sickness rose up in my gut, burning through my chest and tearing at my throat. I needed somewhere safe, unknown to anyone.

I couldn't think, couldn't get my head straight.

He knew.

An image filled my head then, of safety and shelves full of books. Nobody in Arcanium would think to look there, and Mum probably couldn't reach it.

My translocation gift won't work that far though.

I burst into the hall, frantically trying to think of someone who could realm-skip me back to Arcanium so I could grab some clothes and my chameleon Leo and flee up to the human world.

But getting away was the only thing I could hope for now, before Taz or the Queen or Queenie or Petra or someone else found a way to contain me and trick me into believing them again. Ace would look after Leo for me.

I stumbled toward an oak sapling growing by the stairs, reaching out for it as I sprawled in my panic and lost my balance, tumbling into the branches.

"Please." I didn't even know who I was begging, but I couldn't stay here. "Please, take me away. *Please.*"

I pressed my hand to the trunk and closed my eyes, sending the plea right down to the roots dug right through the flooring as I imagined the only place I could think of that was still safe.

Please.

A whimper caught in my throat, making me choke as a soft breath of air caressed my face. The silence that followed a second later slammed into me and I started to cry without daring to open my eyes.

Moments passed. No shouts behind me, no noise.

I opened my eyes and huffed a relieved breath. Someone, and I could take an educated guess who, had heard and honoured my pleading.

The shelves were lined with books old and new. The desk underneath had been tidied bare. I recognised the worn blue sofa, as much as the potted plants that were now dead from neglect and accompanied by a stench of dust and roots rotten in soil.

My old mentor's cottage had always been a safe haven for me, a place where for two afternoons on the weekend I could avoid my sisters and dream of a different life.

Xavio had been unfailingly kind, and I wished he could be here now to give me some of his wisdom drenched in not-so-gentle sarcasm.

I tore off the dress first, leaving it in a crumpled pool of fabric on the edge of the sofa.

"Taz is alive," I murmured.

Somehow speaking out loud gave my adrenalin reserves a dash of calm. Even so, I started to pace to settle my pounding nerves.

"He's alive and that's a good thing. But he used me. They all did. I can't forgive that. I can't go back, at least, not yet."

There were also still six Apocalyptians out there in the world, Fury among them. Dealing with Taz's supposed death had shown me that there were forces out there that could wipe us all from existence as easy as sneezing.

I eyed Xavio's overstuffed bookshelf.

Perhaps this is exactly where I need to be. I can research the Apocalyptians if there's anything in these books, and calm down properly.

I knew that part of my sanity returning, and the ability to think of sensible things rather than just wanting to murder ancient essences and traitor Fae, was because Taz was alive.

Perhaps someone tricked him into disappearing, into playing dead.

I shuddered. Either way, there was too much for my weary brain to unpack.

I'd spent days at the Court of Illusions being tortured and having my mind warped. I'd been tricked by Kainen into kissing him, thinking he was Taz. I had that guilt laying on me, as well as the agony that I'd not been able to save Taz from dying. Even though that now technically wasn't relevant because he was very much alive, the sensation of betrayal lingered.

I hadn't eaten or slept much during my time at Kainen's court either, or since then.

"I'll do some research here," I told the house. "I'll cool off first, then I can think about whether I want to go back. I don't have to decide now."

Chilly in just the t-shirt and Petra's leggings, I found a musty blanket and wrapped it around myself. The kitchen had been emptied of all perishables and I wondered who by. Xavio hadn't ever mentioned any family, but then I'd only been thirteen when I started going to his with the other local fairy kids for lessons.

Memories of Xavio coming to the Queen's court during Taz's birthday surfaced, and I wondered if she would think to look for me here. Probably not. Perhaps she'd even be glad that I'd disappeared.

None of that would feed me or let me rest though, and that had to come before anything else.

I survived sixteen years with my sisters.

I survived the battles at Arcanium, the Fae at Gallow's Oak, almost dying twice.

I survived the Court of Illusions, barely.

I can do this again.

I would need to glamour myself and go over the border into the human world to get fresh food, and I didn't have my bank card or anything either, but I'd deal with that later. For now, I wanted to sleep off the weary fog clouding my brain.

I peered out of the kitchen window, able to see the main road in the human world. I'd always wondered why Mum never came into Xavio's house, or even got out of the car. No doubt she hadn't wanted to cross the border into Faerie like I did every weekend.

It was still bright daylight in Faerie, but now I could see the glimmer of the human world in night-time darkness, as if through a television screen with no frame.

I had no way of getting a message to anyone back at Arcanium either, not after my orb was destroyed at Kainen's court. That stuck me here because without the orb I couldn't even call Trevor to come and get me when I was ready to go home. But I had to let them know not to worry or look for me somehow. Even with everything that had gone between us, Taz would be going mental, and Ace and Milo would be sick with worry. Petra might decapitate someone.

That thought alone made me smile. The action hurt my cheeks, but I let it reign over my face for several seconds anyway. While digging through the kitchen drawers in the hopes of finding some non-perishable food that had been forgotten, I came across an ancient mobile phone.

If the phone was a contract one, I'd likely bring all hell of a communication company down on the cottage, but then it was a human phone vs. a house in Faerie. I decided to risk it.

I pressed the power button, marvelling that the screen was literally just black and green pixels when it lit up.

Odd, I thought they ran out when left alone for ages.

The possibility that I was still being manipulated, that someone would know I might come here, occurred to me. But I wasn't in a position to be picky and nobody had come knocking or bursting in yet. Even if they did, I would be ready.

Luckily, I knew Ace's human number off by heart, one of the benefits of being able to remember information easily.

I glamoured myself into Petra, because she was the first person I thought of, and took the phone with me to the front door. I remembered the door didn't auto-lock without a key, but a quick search suggested there was no key just lying around.

When I tried the door, it opened without complaint.

Security hazard, but it'll have to do.

I'd set something in front of the door later so I could hear if anyone opened it while I slept. At least that way I'd be able to translocate behind them and flee into the human world if anyone tried to creep in.

I wandered down the path, noticing the blessed warmth of sunshine. I couldn't remember the last time I'd noticed anything natural like that, what with Arcanium being wholly indoors in the mid-space between Faerie and the human world. I forced myself not to think of the time I'd spent in Kainen's court either, all underground.

I pushed open Xavio's gate and stepped through.

Ah. I recognised that tiny breath of air now, the suggestion I'd just moved through a skip-way. *To think I never realised that when I was a kid.*

Standing in front of the gate, I could hear the wholly average sounds of the human world. The quiet hum of traffic on the roads nearby, the sound of someone's television blaring through an open window. The lights in nearby windows illuminated the quiet street.

I typed Ace's human mobile number into the phone.

What do I even say? I'd keep it short, to the point.

> "Hi Ace, it's Demi. I'm fine, but I need some time to myself. Don't worry, and don't bother looking for me. I'll come back when I'm done."

And send.

I didn't bother waiting for a reply, knowing he'd most likely not get it for ages anyway as mobile phones didn't work in Arcanium or in Faerie.

It was a cowardly move, but Ace would tell Taz about the message and Taz would insist on tearing the human world apart to find me and demand answers, and dealing with everything that had gone on recently…

I need sleep before anything else.

I left the human world and went back into the cottage, throwing the mobile phone back in its drawer in the kitchen. I'd check it again in a while. If they messaged me, they might try to guilt trip me to go back and face everything.

I couldn't, not yet.

One final dig around in the sitting room produced an old bottle of cherry bubble juice, no doubt left over from fairy lessons. I also found a packet of Jelly Babies, Xavio's reward system of choice, and a pile of crisp packets. It would do for now.

I couldn't manage much, but I ate until I felt queasy. Once my security system, a tower of old paint pots, was in place, I wandered up the stairs. It felt a bit like trespassing, but I found a small, tidy bathroom and two bedrooms that had been stripped of possessions, although the bedsheets were still there and looked fresh.

I washed up but couldn't bring myself to undress and shower. Instead, I collapsed onto one of the beds and closed my eyes.

I will go back eventually and sort things out with Taz. But not yet. He's alive, and that's enough for now.

CHAPTER THREE
Fae Boys Never Give Up

Two days passed. Two days of being too cowardly to check the phone. Two days of eating leftover junk food and pretending that I was doing important work by trawling through Xavio's copious and really boring textbooks.

I missed Leo and my room. I knew Ace would look after him, as he often did if I got sucked into FDP assignments, but I missed the natural hubbub and chaos of Arcanium too. I missed my friends. I didn't even have any clothes to change into, but I did my best to stay clean.

The other possibility was going to my mum for a visit and seeing if she'd loan me some money for food to tide me over, but every time I thought about that option, I remembered my sisters and went off the idea. Taz might well have called my mum in desperation to find me as well, so each time I considered it, I backed out.

By the time the second night came around, I knew I had to do something. I'd finished the food and was a third of the way through the books. The only option was going to Mum for help, and I really, *really* didn't want to resort to that. So instead, I sank back into the piles of books like a coward. I even managed to find some interesting information about Apocalyptians during the last age, but nothing ground-breaking we didn't already know.

As the darkness fell outside, I sat on the bed I was using with several hefty books open around my legs, scanning a rather unsettling paragraph. It had nothing to do with the Apocalyptians, but I couldn't tear my eyes away.

"Anchoring is rare," I muttered the words aloud into the silent room. "It can be broken, but a true anchoring gives both strength and weakness to the linked Fae. Weakness during separation, strength when paired, there are many variations of how deep anchoring can run."

Old Tara had told me a while back that I was Taz's anchor. He'd confirmed it, but I hadn't dwelled too deeply on what it meant until now.

I thought it was like some kind of Fae sweetheart thing, like a magic crush or emotional promise ring.

I shook my head and read on, my heart beginning to thud.

"Many seek it and fewer find it, but when the anchored pair learn to work in harmony, few can break them. There is no way to force an anchored link, or conjure one. As previously mentioned, an anchoring can be broken, either before the anchoring sets or after a great severing, and it can be one-sided. One can choose to disown and sever their side of the connection, but there are less than a handful of examples of this known throughout history."

I rubbed my eyes and slumped back on the pillows.

So, if I'm Taz's anchor, us being together makes him stronger. Another nauseating wave of guilt crashed through me. *And he's mine, my anchor, because of course he is. I almost went mad when I thought he was dead.*

The realisation hit me hard, all but punching the breath out of me, so much so that I almost didn't hear the noise downstairs.

The crashing and rolling thuds of paint cans falling.

I struggled to pull my legs out from around the books, the blankets swamping me and getting in the way.

I eased my feet onto the floor and tiptoed toward the open door. Doubling over, I peeked through the top of the banister to see the front door still open. A moment later, the sounds of someone rifling around in the kitchen floated up the stairs.

I found my fairy connection and threw up a protection warding, trying to keep my feet silent on the steps as I went downstairs, avoiding the middle one that creaked. With my energy gift ready to zap whoever was breaking in, I rounded the bottom of the stairs.

And froze.

"What are you doing here?" I squeaked.

I stared at the boy in the kitchen doorway, even now sweeping my gaze over his face to make sure he was okay.

Taz looked like hell, his eyes ringed with shadows and his clothes crumpled, but somehow he was here. Before I could reason with myself, the anger sparked inside my chest. He was here, but why? I'd told Ace I needed space. And Taz had tricked me along with the rest of his family. Used me.

"How did you find me?" I demanded, my tone fiercer than before. "Are you really here? Really you?"

He eyed me with wariness clouding his face. In dim yellow light from the table lamp, I could see his exhaustion, and even his curls were hanging lifeless despite signs he'd been raking his hands through them. He looked flat and sad and worn out, and my insides ached raw.

"I'm really here, and it's really me." Even his voice sounded faded. "Ace did something complicated with the message you sent him. He managed to trace the location, I think he called in some family favours, but we couldn't find you anywhere. I even checked your house-"

"You spoke to my family?"

"No, just waited outside until it was clear you weren't there. Then Milo suggested you were probably dipping between Faerie and the human world, so I asked Old Tara. She told me where you were so I came straight here. Apparently, she was the one who heard you pleading and helped you cross half of Faerie to run away from me."

I couldn't let myself dwell on the image of him running around two worlds trying to find me. I was still too angry, too grieved.

Too guilty.

The bare face of my cowardice over the past two days revealed itself. I felt too guilty to face him, to own up to what had happened at Kainen's court.

He stood there, his turquoise eyes wide and expectant like he expected me to say 'oh, okay then' and forget everything. He'd known what I was going to go through, the grief, the pain. I hadn't even had time over the last week to process the guilt I'd been carrying about what happened with Kainen either.

But anger, that I could fall back on easily.

A book was in my hand before I could check myself. It flew through the air a second later, not at him but as a hopeless attempt at a warning.

"Why are you here?" I screamed. "You and your family aren't using me for anything else, I'm done."

Taz turned the next book into liquid, and the television remote, splatters marking the walls. Even as I screamed inarticulate words at him and threw random objects, he was taking steps toward me. I tried to control myself; I wasn't the kind of person who threw things at people, at least not anyone who wasn't already attacking me, but the volatility gift Fury had saddled me with seemed to be taking control.

"Demi, please, just listen."

The pleading tone in his voice punctured a tiny hole in my anger, and suddenly it was zapping away fast. My limbs ached with tiredness and the natural deprivation of sleep. My head had a fuzzy sensation to it that I'd been carrying around for days and only now recognised, like my awareness of myself was somehow linked to Taz's re-existence. Or his proximity to me. But even without Fury's volatility powering me, I was still angry.

"You have sixty seconds."

He bit his lip, hesitating.

"Fifty-five."

He rolled his eyes with a weary huff. "Okay, look, the Queen did tell me the plan, but I wasn't going to go through with it. I lost consciousness for a while, but when I came around Marthe had fixed my side. I was up and about to find Milo to take me back to you, when she stopped me and asked me to play dead. I told her I'd consider it but that I had to get you first, so she put a sleep on me."

My inside writhed in knots, barely daring to believe him. A traitorous stab of relief threatened to unravel my anguish, but I couldn't get my head straight. He couldn't lie to me, assuming it was really him, because Fae and fairies couldn't lie. But even so, this was too coincidental, too easy.

Sensing I might be thawing, or at least able to hear sense, Taz inched a step closer. If I reached out, I could touch him.

He might be an apparition, or I've finally gone mad. But I can't touch him. I don't know if I'm going to slap him or hug him.

He sighed. "The next thing I knew, I was waking up in a coffin with a note from Queenie on the lid about keeping quiet until it was opened. I heard voices, then yelling."

I rubbed my face, my legs beginning to wobble. With one hand on the back of the sofa, I gulped against the catch in my throat.

"Then I heard someone shouting your name," he continued. "So I busted out. I would have said as much but the whole situation was completely bonkers, and you just disappeared."

He folded his arms and I realised then that he was mad at me too. Mad at me for not trusting him, mad at me for running away without finding out the truth first.

No doubt mad at me for what happened with Kainen too.

I pressed a hand to my forehead, knowing I owed him an answer at the very least.

"I'm not sure what to feel." I hurried on as he frowned. "I'm fine, you're alive, that's great, but it might be best if you go. There's so much still outstanding, and I can't-"

What do I do? Hug him like everything's okay? Apologise? I can't cope with this now. I'm not ready to face telling him what I did.

His face burst into a furious scowl. "I'm not going anywhere. I've only just found you, I've barely slept and neither have you by the look of it."

"I can't-"

He dropped his arms to his sides as I snuffled and wiped my nose with my arm, only then realising that my face was soaked with tears.

"I get you need time, but I'm not leaving," he repeated. "We sort this out together. If you- if you've- if there's someone else now, I'll handle it. I know things happened with Kainen, and I can deal with that. But when I thought I was dying after being at his court, I only thought of you. Before I could find a way back, or even leave the room, the Queen asked me to pretend to be dead. I said I'd think about it and let her know after I'd brought you back safe to get myself out of there but she jumped me. Look, you might not want me anymore, but I'm not leaving until I know you're going to be okay."

His chest was heaving by the end. His eyes looked watery, and his lips pressed tight as silence blasted the room.

He thinks this is about me wanting Kainen instead?

I shook my head, anxiety clawing out of the roiling pit of agonising emotion. If the Apocalyptians were in the room with us they would have had a field day and emotional indigestion for afters.

"I don't, I mean, not him- the whole time at his court, the whole time anything remotely happened, I thought he was you. Ace should have told you that."

I folded my arms, mirroring him to cling onto the last shred of holding my nerve. Taz stalked into the kitchen, robbing me of any chance to read his expression. He had a rucksack on his back, hitched on the ridges of his wings under his t-shirt, and I watched him wriggle out of the straps with my heart in my throat.

"He did but I had to hear it from you," he said. "I don't care what happened between you there, only if anything's going to happen between you now. I deserve to know. Do you want a drink? I bought a couple of cherry bubble juices."

I gripped the hem of my t-shirt in a tight fist, agony swelling. His head popped around the kitchen doorway before I could find a single word in reply.

"I mean it, Dem. I don't care what happened when you were being influenced, it's like being drunk on *Beast*. You had no say in what happened, and I swear to you now, if you don't love him, don't want him, then I'll curse him for the both of us. But I'm not leaving now, whether you want me to or not."

I caught his eye and noticed his fingers gripping the doorframe firmly, his shoulders sagging with exhaustion.

"Are you still injured?" I asked.

A flicker of a smile. "Just a bruised ego and possibly a broken heart, we'll see. Marthe fixed the physical stuff."

"Faerie gift her," I mumbled.

"What was that?"

I glared at him. "Nothing."

We stared at each other, the tension thickening until I was scared that I'd never be able to find my voice again.

"I don't love him," I whispered. "I don't like him. Maybe I don't even hate him now. You're alive, and he's less than nothing to me."

He tilted his head.

What if he thinks I'm just rejecting Kainen because he's back now, or that it's because I'm more interested in a prince than a court lord?

The thought was ridiculous, but I couldn't risk even the weirdest or most stupid of misunderstandings right now.

"I mean, I wanted revenge on him, I almost killed him at your- at the Queen's court." I still couldn't bring myself to say funeral. "But now, I don't even want to think about him ever again, unless it's skewered on the end of something sharp."

Taz leaned into the kitchen for a few seconds, then approached me with a bottle of cherry bubble juice held out, a second one in his other hand. I ignored those and gawped at what he had hanging under one arm instead.

"Oh, Leo!" I smiled then, relief overtaking all else.

Guessing he must have been in Taz's rucksack this whole time, I moved to take him. He mashed his gums at me in delight but Taz twisted so he was out of reach.

"Take the drink, but you have to talk to me before I hand him over. Can you at least tell me where I stand right now?"

Aware he was essentially holding my pet to ransom, I took the bottle and set it down on the desk. Now was the time to be brutally honest. To tell him I loved him more than anything in the world, in Faerie, in existence. That he was my weakness and my anchor and my everything, and I would do anything for a chance to earn his forgiveness.

I gulped. "I-"

A hammering noise outside almost made me scream. Leo grumbled, his tail beginning to flick. Taz's face scrunched with fury and he stormed to the door, clearly not caring that this wasn't his house.

"Well?" I heard Ace's disgruntled voice from the other side. "I take it you found her, given the fact you're not storming out issuing orders?"

Taz swung the door open and stalked back toward me with a scowl. I took the opportunity to grab Leo as he passed, settling the uneven mass of lizard bulk onto my shoulder. I'd missed Leo almost as much as I'd missed Taz, which was saying something.

Milo and Ace wore similar expressions of disapproval as they stamped into the cottage, but their faces weren't anywhere near as mutinous as Taz's.

"You were meant to let us know you'd found her," Ace muttered. Then he smiled broadly at me. "How's the holiday, Dem?"

I folded my arms. "Fine, until everyone decided to barge in."

Milo ambled up to me and I froze as he tugged one of my cold hands free and encased it in his huge warm ones.

"I just want you to know that I had no idea," he insisted. "No part in any of it. Nor did Ace. The moment I dropped Taz off after the fighting, the Queen dismissed me. Petra didn't either. You should have heard the things she called Queenie."

I squeezed his fingers. Even in my grief, I'd never truly blamed my friends for any of it.

"I'm still half angry," he continued. "I felt so guilty for leaving afterwards when I found out- when I thought Taz was gone, but also I'm relieved that the Queen knew I'd put our friendship above the potential future of Faerie. I would have told you straight away if I'd known."

I opened my mouth to reassure him, but Milo's eyes glazed over and his fingers dropped away from mine.

Ace rubbed his forehead and rolled his eyes as Milo spotted Xavio's bookshelves and started inching toward them with undisguised greed on his face, all thought of me instantly forgotten.

"I'm going to be hideously antisocial, but we've been working late a lot to find you," Ace said, his gaze sweeping briefly over Taz. "Is there a room we can use? If not, sofa's fine."

I nodded. "Up the stairs and go to the one on the left. I've been using the one on the right. Bathroom's in the middle."

Ace gave me a fond smile then, as though seeing that I was still functioning had loosened some of his stress. He grabbed the back of Milo's hoodie on his way toward the stairs and tugged him away from the books, ignoring the feral hiss of protest.

Leo jumped off my shoulder and went skittering across the coffee table toward the huge potted fern in the corner. I hadn't even noticed in my previous anxiety, but that plant was the only one still alive, and it was thriving.

What chances are there that big pot has no bottom, and there's no floor beneath it, and the roots of that plant go right down to Old Tara?

Securing that suspicion for assessment later, I waited as Milo and Ace walked up the stairs, their heavy footfalls filling the cottage with something I'd been missing, the sounds of people. I couldn't bring myself to look at Taz, overcome by how much I ached with the sheer confusion of it all.

"I won't pressure you for answers," he said quietly. "I'm not leaving you, but I won't push you either."

I bit my lip, relieved. "Okay. If you need to sleep, and no

offense but you look like you need it, take the room I've been using. I've got some things to finish up here, stuff I've been looking up, but I can sleep on the sofa if I crash."

Taz eyed me up and down, no doubt taking in my unwashed hair, ghostly skin and dull eyes. I wondered if I looked thinner as well. I couldn't remember when I'd eaten the last of the leftover junk food, but my stomach had been growling on and off for hours.

When he moved toward me and sat on the sofa, his stare defiant as he watched me, I realised he meant he literally wasn't intending to leave my side.

"What is this place, anyway?" he asked.

I frowned. "It belonged to Xavio. I translocated here I think out of instinct, but then there were loads of books and I wanted to find something to kill off the Apocalyptians once and for all."

"And you didn't think to let me know?" he asked, his tone icy. "You didn't even consider how awful I'd feel, or think I'd need to at least explain my side?"

I perched back on the edge of the desk.

"I needed time. I sent Ace the message-"

"You basically said 'I'm safe, don't come looking for me'. How the hell am I meant to interpret that?!"

He exploded off the sofa, his eyes tumultuous and dark with pain. A second later in the silence that followed, a sad little ripping noise like Velcro preceded the emergence of his wings as they broke through the back of his t-shirt.

"I was angry," I mumbled. "I thought this had all been part of some big game, some strategy with me as the pawn."

Taz folded his arms. "It was, but not by me. I thought you could at least trust me enough to give me a chance to explain."

I grabbed handfuls of my hair, aware that the tears were leaking free again.

"I spent a week being manipulated by Kainen, having my head messed around. For all I knew, this was all part of some elaborate super plan, or that he'd finally gotten back in my head again, or broke me completely! For all I know, it still is."

Taz froze. He opened his mouth to speak, but seemed stuck for the actual words.

"I was grieving," I whispered, the ache pouring out of me as a strained whimper. "I thought you were dead. Then you weren't. I couldn't even think, let alone think straight. I still have Fury's gift muddling my head, making me angry. I felt so guilty about what happened at the court, what we- *did* when I thought Kainen was you, it was easier to be angry. I want her dead. I want Fury dead for killing you, and I want him dead for tricking me."

Taz's frozen expression seemed to sag then, his entire body tumbling downward a few inches.

"Technically she just injured- okay, okay." He held his hands up hastily as I glared at him. "How about now? How about you talk to me now. Tell me what you need to get rid of. I'm here, and I'm not going anywhere."

I pressed my hands to my face. It would be easier if I couldn't see how heartbroken it made him.

"We kissed. A couple of times. He was pretending to be you, glamouring the whole thing. He stopped the orb messages coming through, I think. Then I couldn't orb out. Even Ace was taken in. The moment I found out, I kicked him and Ace threw him off a balcony. But I felt so guilty, and we were still hunting the Apocalyptians. Then you were dead, or I thought you were, and I couldn't bear it."

Silence drifted between us. I couldn't bring myself to look, petrified at the thought of seeing his heartbroken face. I knew he needed the confirmation, that I owed him this information, but speaking it out loud hurt.

I wouldn't blame him for leaving, and I had no idea how much of it he saw on the Ogle before Kainen locked down the court. But I owed him the truth and there it was.

I couldn't stop a sniff escaping as I waited for the inevitable rejection. He might placate me, or he might simply leave. But as he took a deep breath, I tensed every single cell I had.

"I heard you blew up half of Queenie's hallway."

CHAPTER FOUR
Homeward Bound

I flinched at the sound of Taz's voice now perilously close to my face. When I peered over my fingertips, I found him right in front of me, mere inches away.

"I can't tell if you're real or not," I mumbled. "They screwed with my head, and I'm scared I won't ever be able to know what's real again."

I expected his face to fall, but instead he looked at me with rising determination pinching his brow.

"Do you love him?" he asked. "Have any residual feelings for him?"

My insides curdled with nausea. "No, of course not. Other than I want to punch him a lot until he's very, very dead. I never did have feelings for him, ever."

Taz didn't smile, his mouth twisting with anxious expectation.

"Then all I ask is don't send me away. Don't ask me to leave again. Give it time, with our friends. I can tell you anything you need me to, about us, memories, how I feel. I promise, I don't care how long it takes, we will banish any thought of him until there's just you and me again."

That was more than I thought I deserved. More than I could have hoped for. Even then, the doubt crept through me, that this was too easy, too much like exactly what I wanted. Kainen had given me exactly what I wanted last time as well.

Before I could answer, Leo swung out of the fern. He made a solid thud on the floor, his claws clacking as he plodded around the edge of the sofa toward Taz. I watched as he gave me that withering lizard stare then started trying to climb Taz's jeans.

Animals can't be affected by visual glamours alone, and he'd smell straight away if something wasn't right. I don't think he's ever even met Kainen properly, and he's picky about people.

My pulse picked up at the sheer drop of hope he was giving me. Taz leaned down and picked Leo up, righting him on his legs and plonking him onto the sofa. Leo gave him a look until Taz pulled a random piece of lettuce out of his pocket, throwing it to the other end of the sofa to get rid of him.

I might not be able to trust myself, or what I see, but I can trust Leo.

I could trust the tiny scratches on my arms from his claws as well, the sheer reality of it that Kainen probably wouldn't have thought to create. Even when he was torturing me at Fury's request, I'd been able to cling to tiny inaccuracies like the shadows not being cast quite right, or the ripple of water not moving at the correct speed.

It was the only way I'd known there was a chance that the torture was being projected into my head instead of really happening. Kainen had forgotten to include the micro-specifics that a lot of people wouldn't even take notice of.

Even if Kainen was glamouring Leo now, he wouldn't ever think to have a piece of lettuce in his pocket for him. He wouldn't have thought to conjure that sort of thoughtful kindness into his visions.

"Demi?" Taz's voice was soft, but I heard the undertone of anguish there.

"Okay." I nodded. "Okay. I'm so sorry."

He held one arm out, giving me the choice. Such a simple option, an invitation rather than a manipulation or a demand.

I inched forward and let the agony tumble out as his arms closed around me.

"You have nothing to be sorry for," he murmured into my hair. "Nothing except running away when I could have explained it to you then and there, could have looked after you. But then, you never did need looking after. Also, you seem feistier since that volatility gift thing."

I veered back and gave him a look, the disapproval somewhat ruined what with my cheeks being soaked with tears.

"Well, you don't have to be here to put up with it, but you insisted on staying."

A grin of pure sunshine broke across his face, his gaze flicking over me.

"I did insist, and I will, forever if you'll let me. You were always like this though, it's just more intense now. Luckily, I happen to think your dramatic side is one of your attractive points."

I snorted in disbelief, but his mere presence was now melting a large chunk of my anger. So fast that the overwhelm threatened to bowl me over.

I changed the subject.

"I found some interesting information in these old books about the last time they were rampaging though, the Apocalyptians I mean."

His smile softened. "Show me?"

I found the book in the pile and flicked through the pages.

"Here, it says that to contain them, they need a vessel. Ace and I found out that you can use a special vial to trap one, but we still don't know how to finish them all off."

"I think there's a plan for that, but I doubt my mother will tell me now."

I scowled. I didn't want to so much as think of the Queen

because that still made me very angry very quickly. So I ignored that and continued explaining.

"Historically people see a vessel as like a holding object, but in old lore a vessel literally means a case for the human soul. So, I think to actually get rid of them they need to collectively be possessing someone who then gets killed, or contained somehow. Ace and I thought that might be how they were contained with the Old King the first time he was dealt with."

I babbled on out of sheer awkwardness until I literally had no more words left in my head that weren't embarrassing declarations.

Taz raised an eyebrow. "I'm not offering and neither are you."

He didn't mention who we were no doubt both thinking of offering up instead. I managed a weak smile.

"I wasn't planning to. But it's information we can take with us at least when we go back."

He lifted his hand as if he wanted to squeeze my shoulder or brush my hair back but thought better of it. I *hated* that hesitation and watched him walk toward the stairs with part of me crying out to follow him.

"Okay, princess, I'm going to get some sleep," he said. "Your choice. Take the book up with us, or stay here and I'll have a quick nap on the sofa. Oh, one more thing."

He looked so lovely as he glanced back, despite the sunken eyes and lank, dull hair. The mere mention of upstairs, being beside him, possibly even being able to curl up next to him, made me smile.

"Yeah?"

He grinned. "You can keep the t-shirt, looks better on you anyway. Might want to give it a wash though."

I looked down to see his *Demon Babies* t-shirt, stained and beyond stinky since I hadn't changed since before taking off the awful dress two days ago. It also reminded me that I was currently in nothing but that and Petra's ragged leggings. As I looked down though, my eye snagged on the page of the book.

"Wait, Taz, come here a minute."

He appeared at my side instantly like he'd been waiting for that very summons, his arm brushing my shoulder as he leaned close.

"Always. What, you want a hoodie to go with it? You've stolen most of them already but I can risk a couple more before I freeze to dea- before I run out."

I ignored the fickle attempt at bribery and raced past the near mention of what I'd thought had happened to him.

"No, look at this."

His eyes scanned the page, reading that the Apocalyptians were known to leak out of vessels or prisons by possessing people with strong enough natural desires, if not all of them had been captured and the vessel sealed.

"Who's guarding them?" I asked. "We know some weren't captured. How bad is this?"

Taz grimaced. "A partly empty vessel guarded in a court full of Fae? I'm surprised the world is still here by now. I'll wake Ace and Milo and we'll take this straight back home."

He ran toward the stairs, then hesitated at the bottom.

"You are coming back, aren't you?"

I nodded. It was time to stop hiding, and Taz's beaming face in reply was all the incentive I needed.

I packed up a couple of the books, not even flinching when Milo appeared beside me and wordlessly started packing the whole lot into a huge suitcase. I didn't ask where he'd found the case, and didn't mention that we probably should find out who the books belonged to now before we nicked them.

Ace and Milo disappeared outside to realm-skip back to Arcanium, and I glanced up to find Taz giving me a searching look.

"I'm still a bit mixed up," I admitted. "But I don't want you to think I don't care or anything. I just- time, you know? To recover, get myself back to normal."

When he leaned forward and kissed my forehead, I closed my eyes and let the simple blessing of it relax me. Even his fingers on my left hand turning my newly-marked wrist upward to show the fiery orb tattooed there didn't startle me away from him.

"You've got my artwork on you and you're wearing my t-shirt, Sparky. I'm not worried." He turned his right arm and showed me a fresh tattoo of his own, the orb he'd designed in icy blue. "I had to wait around while Ace was doing his thing with your message and Hutch told me. He said he'd do mine but then the freebies are over if we want any more."

I reached out and traced the unharmed skin around his tattoo. In marking himself, Taz had done the one thing, other than bringing Leo, that could have persuaded me he was really him. A Fae or fairy could easily glamour any visual they chose, but the chances that Kainen had delved deep enough into my mind to drag these tattoo designs out, considering I'd only found them after leaving his court, it was all but impossible.

"You haven't said you forgive me," I whispered.

I imagined Milo, huffing to himself outside as he waited for us to finish so he could skip us back home, giving us time. I didn't let that worry me, focused only on the subtle dip between Taz's eyebrows.

"Of course I forgive you. I'd probably have run away myself after what you went through. But you should have let me explain, let me run away with you."

"I know, and I'm sorry I didn't." I shook my head. "But I meant what happened at his court. You haven't said you forgive me for what I did. I know that maybe you can't yet, but I have to hope you can someday, that I haven't completely ruined this."

Taz groaned, both hands coming to cup my cheeks. I blinked back at him.

"My sweet, wicked princess, you're an absolute idiot sometimes. There's nothing to forgive because you didn't do anything wrong. You were influenced and tricked, it's not the same as doing things by choice."

When it seemed like I might not believe him, too shocked to react, he growled and pressed a light kiss on my nose.

"Please try to hear me," he insisted. "What he did is one of the worst things anyone can possibly do to a person, and worst of all, he did it to *my* person. I will make him suffer one day, but you need to get this idea out of your head that it was your fault. It wasn't. He manipulated you, twisted your head, and gave you no choice about what happened. You say you thought he was me, and I believe you. You have nothing to be sorry for."

Each word wiped away another splash of my guilt. Something Ace had said to me at the Court of Illusions resonated then, strong and pure, that I wouldn't treat a friend the way I was treating myself.

If Taz had been coerced into kissing someone else, thinking it was me, would I hold it against him?

No, of course not. It would hurt, but it would be the person who manipulated him that I would blame.

I nodded. "Okay. We should go though, Milo stole half the books but he's probably halfway through them by now while he's been waiting for us."

Taz chuckled, but he still didn't let go of my cheeks.

"He's not coming back for us. I told you I wasn't leaving

you, but when you're ready to leave, I go where you go. I can realm-skip us straight back to Arcanium if that's where we're bound, or we can start walking."

I frowned. "When did that happen? You used to only be able to skip back to your mother's court, and from there to Arcanium."

He grinned. "I had to do something while you were on assignment. Tormenting my mother to give me extra allowances seemed like a good idea at the time."

I found a real smile then as Taz grabbed Leo under one arm and slid the other around my waist. I wrapped my arms around his neck, pressing my forehead into his shoulder.

"In that case, take me home."

I felt the brush of air caress my face almost instantly, and Taz's quiet "thank Faerie for that" was lost into the ether.

I didn't want to open my eyes, but I couldn't stand here hugging Taz forever, although he made no move to let go or step back. A second later though, Leo squirmed with a lethal lash of his tail and ruined the moment.

"I thought I'd bring you back to the scene of your triumph." I could hear the laughter in Taz's voice now. "I was furious when I got here, but even I had to stop and take notice."

I opened my eyes and stared around at the hallway, just recognisable by the pictures of landscapes half-hanging off the walls and Queenie's office doors with the Arcanium emblem on at the far end. The walls were scorched in many places, smashed completely to rubble in others. The rubble had been cleared but the walls were boarded up rather than re-panelled.

"I did this?"

I had a vague memory of all-encompassing fury, the Queen realm-skipping me to a desolate strip of rock and then back to my bedroom, but not this. In that short time before going to the

Queen's court, I hadn't ventured up here as Queenie had come to find me.

"You did." Taz sounded insanely proud. "You also blasted a huge hole in my mother's favourite brooding spot apparently. She's probably more likely to crown you heir apparent than me or any of my sisters after that."

I groaned, the heel of one hand landing without any real strength against his shoulder. He hesitated as I turned away, but I stayed close to him. As we started walking toward the lift, his arm gradually tightened around me again.

"Don't say that. I'd make an awful queen."

Taz waited until we were in the lift with the grill closed before laughing.

"You would make a fearsome queen, but maybe not just yet."

I scowled. "I don't want to be fearsome. Or a queen."

"You don't have a choice, my wicked princess. Hell, she'd rather choose you over any of my sisters right now, she said so."

I frowned, aware of Leo now snoozing like dead weight flopped over Taz's arm as the lift shot upwards.

"Luckily for me, that's still a 'you' problem."

The lift stopped and I put a hand out to open it, before realising Taz was staring at me with a startled look.

"Oh." He hesitated. "Um, you won't have heard. I abdicated."

"You *what*?"

"I abdicated. I got back from trying to find you, made Ace do the human phone thing, and I need to apologise to him about that actually, I was kind of rude and might have threatened to kill him a little bit. Then I realm-skipped to the Queen's court, announced my abdication in front of her war council, told her she was dead to me and skipped back."

The lift pinged, desperate to get on its way again, so Taz slid the gate open and jostled me out with a sheepish grin.

"I think the only way I avoided her finding me when I got back here was because I was with Hutch getting tattooed while I was waiting, then we were off to the human world looking for you. I'll drop Leo in your room, shall I?"

He was off surprisingly fast for someone who claimed he hadn't slept properly in days. I didn't have the strength to race after him, but reached my room to find Leo already back on his logs and Taz sitting tentatively on the edge of my bed.

"You abdicated?" I couldn't believe it.

He rubbed the back of his head. "Yeah. Did you not want to date me anymore then, now I'm not all political and important and stuff?"

I snorted at the mere suggestion, but my mind raced. Taz never wanted to be a prince, much less king. He hated all the pomp and ceremony, the rules, the obligations. He wanted to be here, free, with me. I decided now was the time to be supportive, and we'd simply have to deal with his mother when we came across her.

"If you're happy, I'm happy," I said.

Taz's anxious expression settled and he held a hand out to me. I took it without a second thought and sat beside him. After a moment of hesitation, I pressed my cheek to his shoulder and swung my knees over his thighs.

He gave a little rumble of approval that sent happiness right to my heart, but I should have known the peace wouldn't last.

CHAPTER FIVE
No Rest for the Weary

"There she is, dirty stop-out." Beryl's voice filled my room.

I looked up to see her, Meryl, Cheryl, Hutch, Harvey, Ace and Milo all crowding together in the doorway, huge grins on their faces. The severity of it hit me, that I was home, that Taz was alive and not angry at me, literally sitting with me bundled on his lap and his arms showing no signs of ever letting me go.

I stared at all of them for countless seconds.

And burst into tears.

Through the instant blur, I could make out Ace and Milo giving each other worried looks, while Hutch and Harvey swivelled 180 degrees and made a rapid exit.

"Better out than in," Cheryl offered helpfully.

"Yeah," Beryl added. "And I'd do it quickly, because Petra's coming this way and she doesn't look happ- Hi, Petra!"

They tried to shield the door from her, bless them. A pointless task, but still.

"Do you want me to hide you under the covers?" Taz whispered, his smile shining with impishness.

I frantically wiped my eyes and tried to rein in my huffing, but Petra shoved past the Eastwick sisters and strode right up to me with her hands on her hips.

"Where the hell have you been? Not a single orb message, no check-in, just a barely there human message to Ace on a device that can't be trusted! The Queen has been asking for updates, Queenie is shouting at me because the Queen is shouting at her because *he* has apparently renounced the throne of Faerie." She jabbed a finger in Taz's direction. "He's also been shouting at me for the best part of a *week*. I'm tired of getting shouted at!"

Taz stiffened around me, a tense cage ready to throw me behind him and charge into battle. I actually had no idea who might win if he and Petra ever came to blows. I might ask Hutch and Harvey to call a bet to see who the favourite would be.

But that wouldn't save me now. Meekness was usually the only thing that worked with Petra, and it was rare when it did.

"I didn't mean to make so much trouble," I began. "I didn't realise the Queen would get involved, or Queenie, I was just-"

She huffed. "I don't care about any of that. Are you okay?"

"I am now."

She eyed me up and down. "Fine. Get a long shower or something, you stink."

She strode out of the room without another word and I eyed Taz's fist clenched on my knee as Meryl hurried after her. It was Cheryl that peered down the hallway and winked at me as she shouted after my irate mentor.

"Petra, are you *crying*?!"

The reply was not pleasant in the slightest, but it made me laugh until my sides ached. The doorway cleared like magic after that, but I stood up to do as I was told for once.

"Shower, then I'm going to sleep," I announced.

Taz stayed staring up at me. He didn't say a word as I linked my little finger around his and led the way to the communal bathroom because he was smelly too.

Although the bathroom was a unisex set-up, the boys tended to go round to the showers and stalls to the left, the girls to the right, that was just how it seemed to be.

I'd noticed it in my early days here, but that Ace and Milo and a couple of the boys would end up around our side, and a couple of the girls avoided the multi-stench of perfumes and floral deodorants by going to the boy's side, although I couldn't say in all honesty their sprays were any better. Either way it worked, and I loved it, as much as one can love a shared bathroom.

I didn't want to think about the last time I'd been in here, waking up after finding out about Taz's supposed death, but he was there beside me as we walked in.

We separated to go left and right, grabbing towels from the racks. The sound of the showers drowned out anything else, but I stayed under the hot water long after I heard his stop running. I had no doubt he'd be waiting by the sinks when I emerged, but the biggest peril my mind could cope with was having to put my dirty clothes back on, as my beleaguered brain hadn't thought to bring clean ones with me.

The moment I turned the water off, something landed on the top of my stall door. I stared at the familiar clothes, my *Demolition Ducks* t-shirt Taz had bought for me, my comfiest jeans and one of his hoodies.

"I'll let you be until you're done," Taz said. "Socks are in the pocket. Are you okay if I wait for you in your room?"

I smiled at the sheer thoughtfulness of it all. "Always okay."

I imagined him beaming as I got dressed, wrapped my hair in the towel and wandered back along the hall toward my room.

"Demi!"

I groaned under my breath.

They can't possibly need me for anything. I'm done. I'm so done.

I turned around to find Milo scampering toward me, his hair raked back off his forehead and his cheeks pink.

"There's been a development. I told them you'd done enough but Queenie shouted, a lot. She called him Oakthorn."

That brought my brain to a screaming halt. I couldn't remember Queenie ever calling him by his full royal name.

Milo saw the look on my face and nodded. "Exactly. Um, I'll take your towel back if you want."

I rubbed roughly at my hair, knowing the curls would be a total tangled mess once they dried, then handed Milo the towel.

As I rounded the doorway to my room, Taz took one glance at me and shook his head.

"Nope. Not happening, it's gone eleven o'clock, well after sociable hours. Get into bed."

I tried not to smile at that. "Queenie's throwing a fit and demanding our attention."

"Don't care. In."

After so much anxiety and anguish, the rising desire to play and have fun was almost impossible to quash.

"Is that an order?"

Taz eyed me, judging my reaction. "Yes."

"What if I take the pillow with me, does that count?"

He got off the bed, the turquoise in his eyes flashing green. I thought for a moment he might literally bundle me up and throw me under the covers, which I was surprisingly more than okay with. But instead he slid his hand into mine, laced our fingers tight and growled at me.

"You're impossible. You actually *want* to go now, don't you." It wasn't a question.

I nodded. "We don't have to agree to anything, just see what the latest is. I've missed so much."

He could have said something cutting like 'who's fault was that' or 'shouldn't have left me then', but he didn't. He simply huffed at me, shoved his feet into his trainers and let me tug him out of the room.

There would be time to seriously unpack all that had

happened, to discuss it between us, but that would take time. For now, I would simply swim in the sheer relief that he didn't hate me for all that had happened.

We didn't see a soul on our walk to the lift, or as we approached Queenie's office. I couldn't even remember what day it was now, or what time, but I was grateful for the silence. The last thing I needed was a ton of fairies and Fae gawking as we passed.

I'm not even a mentee anymore, I'm a qualified FDP now. I've barely even had time to process that yet, let alone the situation with the Apocalyptians, with Taz, Elvira and Emil and Kainen-

"If you need out, pretend to faint," Taz whispered as we approached the office doors. "I'll catch you."

I rolled my eyes at him but he just mimed licking my cheek in reply, millimetres away from actually doing it.

"Well, welcome back." Queenie eyed us up and down. "You seem mostly unscathed. I wish I could say the same for my hallway."

Taz opened his mouth, no doubt to say something foully dismissive, but I felt a quiet calm settle over me and squeezed his hand to stop him.

"You lied to me," I said, my voice stronger than I felt. "You and the Queen. You made me think he was dead so you could use me like bait to trap your prey. I get that. I understand it. I'm not happy about it."

Queenie sat back, assessing me. When she didn't have anything immediate to add, I carried on.

"This is my home. I'll defend it, and I always have done from the second I stepped foot into the arcade. But I'm not being used as a pawn without my consent. No more of that. No more tricks and manipulations."

She raised an eyebrow, but I hadn't finished.

"You seem to forget that we're employees here. I won't go on about starting a union like the trolls have got, unless it's necessary. But you have a responsibility for us. You might want to act like it sometimes. We're not pieces of some war game you high-born Fae can play and discard."

There, that should do it. She would either concede, kick me out or blow me to pieces.

"Would you have done it if we'd told you he was alive?" she asked, surprising me.

"Yes." Without hesitation.

"Would you have done it for Arcanium alone? Would you risk going back into the enemy nest for example?"

Barely a pause. "Yes."

"Then I'll respect your wishes and tell you straight. Arcanium needs you to do it again."

A cold chill trickled over me. I'd said I would just a second ago, but the thought of going back to the Court of Illusions, back anywhere near anything remotely related or linked to *him*…

I flinched as one of Taz's fiery wings surrounded me, almost blocking me from view.

"You are my favourite relative," he said, his voice stony cold. "But if you ask her to do this, if you put her in danger again, there will be no mercy."

I would have snorted normally at the tough boy act, and Queenie would have too. Rolled her eyes, told him to pipe down. Perhaps it was the fact that she didn't that frightened me, as much as the sheer power behind the threat. He wasn't word-tangling or throwing a tantrum. He was drawing every part of him behind his intention to protect me.

"Taz?" I squeezed his fingers. He looked down at me, his eyes flashing green. "We should at least listen. We took the pledge when we became FDPs. We can't throw that aside when we feel like it. There might be another way, like you were going to try before." I let my fingers slide along the ridge of his wing, the gentle brush that often worked in distracting him. "Also, you're kind of blocking my view."

His shudder was so small I think only I saw it. I released my touch on the downy fluff at the edge of his wing and he furled them back between his shoulder blades.

"How long have you known?" Queenie asked, her voice quiet, subdued.

Taz's eyes flared. "Long enough, but this isn't about that right now."

I wanted to ask him what they were talking about, but I didn't think I'd get an answer right then. That wasn't what we were here for either.

"What is the plan then?" I asked instead.

Queenie sighed. "The situation is worse than we feared."

When she paused, possibly for dramatic effect, Taz jumped in.

"Let me guess, they've escaped the vessel and possessed half the court to madness," he said. "We thought that might have happened already."

Queenie huffed. "Dare I ask how you got to that conclusion?"

"I found a book." I pulled a rueful face, guessing I'd have to be their go-between while they were both still drowning in their egos. "I decided to take a couple of days off. Actually, I don't think I've ever actually used any of my annual leave before. I went to my old mentor's house and was looking stuff up in his books, he's got really ancient ones- although, actually Milo stole most of them so Faerie knows if their rightful owner will get them back."

I heard Taz's almost inaudible sigh and hurried to the point.

"It said that if not all the essences are captured and the vessel sealed, then they can escape and overcome Fae or people. That was after Taz had found me and we came straight back."

I'd forgotten the situation the moment we returned, drenched in the sheer relief that I had Taz back at my side, but now the issue of the Apocalyptians loomed large.

Queenie rubbed her forehead with a forefinger and thumb.

"They have now apparently overcome the Queen herself. Two of the princesses. Several of the court. As they do so, their power increases."

"How do we know this?" Taz demanded.

I looked up at him then, seeing the potential of the king he could be one day.

Could have been. He abdicated, because the Queen used me. Just like Kainen used me.

Suddenly, his deep-seated anger seemed all the more justified.

"Marthe has managed to hide herself away in your conservatory," Queenie explained. "She skips in and out at brief intervals. She has been orbing me information, and I believe it's legitimate."

Taz frowned. "You saw the conservatory behind her? Nobody else nearby?"

Queenie pulled out a dark green orb from the confines of her skin-tight dress and I didn't want to linger on where the pockets might be. I also had to deal with not having an orb of my own, because I'd lost it at the Court of Illusions in an attempt to save Ace instead.

"Marthe," Queenie called out.

A second later, a pearly grey vision appeared. I recognised the old woman's face and felt Taz's sigh of relief beside me.

"Is everyone okay?" he asked without a greeting.

She nodded. "Alive, Master Oakthorn, but the Queen seems overcome with listlessness, she does nothing, speaks to no-one, cares not one bit as her court unravels around her."

Sloth, the perfect thing to hit a pro-active, battle-ready Queen with.

That thought was overruled by my sheer relief that the vessel was at the Queen's court, which meant I wouldn't have to return to Kainen's.

Taz started to pace but refused to let go of my hand. Not willing to be dragged along behind him, I held my ground so that he was shuffling back and forth over the few feet in front of me instead.

"Make sure anyone who needs sanctuary is taken into the conservatory," he told Marthe. "If they leave though, they won't be able to get back in again, make sure they're aware of that. Are most of the staff safe?"

Marthe nodded. "Yes, we have the emotional immunity barrier granted to us as part of our service to the Queen, so we are more level-headed than most. The essences pay us no mind, although they do order us about. But most of the War Council remained, and several have been overcome already."

Taz stopped pacing. "We can't do anything about that for now. Do your best to keep safe anyone who's still saveable. We'll try to figure out a way to fix this mess in the meantime. I may not be heir apparent anymore-"

"Oh, tosh." Marthe tutted, giving him a disapproving look. "Nobody's taken your abdication seriously, and with the Queen overcome the folk are looking to you to lead us."

I felt the subtle tensing in Taz's shoulders, his fingers tightening around mine.

"Well, they should take it seriously, but focus on getting

people to safety for now. We'll stay in touch."

Marthe nodded her head in a respectful bow, but I'd heard the derision in her tone when the abdication was mentioned. I had a feeling that somewhere in his past, she'd probably had a hand in raising him and saw him as much her own as I now did. Although, hopefully in a very different way.

Taz turned to Queenie next, eyes flashing.

"What's your plan for Demi, then?" he asked. "Get her to go in and be bait while someone nips around trying not to get overcome themselves?"

"We need to be careful," I added. "When Fury gave me the volatility, it went straight through my warding. We won't be able to defend ourselves."

Queenie stood, her hands pressed against the desk and her face grim.

"While the instinct would be to go in and fight, there are certain items that we need before we can make any kind of successful attack. There is tell of a material that is rumoured to be able to contain Apocalyptian essences."

I nodded. "Selessium, yeah. The vials are made from it."

Queenie blinked. "How do you know that?"

"Ace didn't tell you?"

Queenie sat down with a resigned grumble. "His not-so-highness-anymore over there had half of Arcanium out looking for you for two days, so I haven't seen Ace, no. Nobody has bothered to make a report either, I might add."

"Oh." I decided it was safest to leave it at that for the moment.

Queenie seemed to be reassembling the leash on her temper before she spoke again.

"I'll be brief. A team needs to go to the forgotten mountains and obtain Selessium. We have a few vials left, but not enough to encase a vessel.”

“And you want us to go?” Taz asked.

“I don’t know if you’re aware of this, but we have a severe shortage of FDPs at the moment. Those newly qualified with you recently aren’t trained or experienced. The rest are managing the charges that keep the money coming in. Do you think I’d willingly put you in danger?”

I wisely decided not to answer that as Taz scoffed loudly.

“I think you’d willingly put Demi in danger, yes. You and my mother already have done, countless times.”

Queenie pursed her lips and started tapping her nails on the desk. I scrunched my toes up at the abrasive clacking, trying to keep my mind level.

“I’d need to sleep properly first.” I ignored Taz groaning beside me. “I’d need time to gather information. I’d need to choose my own team.”

“More than fair.” A flicker of a smirk curled on Queenie’s lips as she picked something up from her desk and held it out. “I believe you need a replacement.”

I frowned, stepping forward until I could reach out and close my hand around the bright white orb on a shiny new keychain.

“I’m not going to get told off for losing the other one?”

She rolled her eyes at that. “Not on this occasion. Nobody could accuse you of simply being careless.”

I settled the orb against my palm, noticing the subtle sparkle in the white, like fresh snow in sunlight. It felt fresh and unfamiliar, but I would get used to it.

I pocketed the orb, threading the keyring onto my belt loop as Queenie sat in her chair, her expression growing serious.

“Now, your troll will be able to take you where you need to go, but the forever mountains are not safe by any means. There’s a reason they took the name ‘Forever’.”

"What's that supposed to mean?" Taz asked.

I was no doubt going to get blasted for agreeing to this the moment we stepped out of the office, but now that he was here, I'd do whatever I could to rid us of the enemy, if only to never have to fear losing him ever again.

"When traitors are banished, they must end up somewhere. It's not a prison as such, more of a barren landscape where the most deviant Fae and fairies are simply forced to survive. Demi will need to make sure she has a plan for every eventuality."

"*We* will need to make sure." Taz's shoulders hunched even higher when Queenie tried to speak. "I'm going with her. I abdicated, so I'm not of royal concern anymore. I'm going."

Queenie eyed me. "Is that your choice then? Take him with you into the lion's den?"

I bit my lip. Taz glared fire and fury at me as I hesitated.

If I leave him here, he'll be safe, but he asked me to trust him.

"If he thinks he can hack it, he's on the team," I decided. "Ace and Milo too. My usual team actually, if they'll go, including Hutch and Harvey this time."

Queenie snorted but managed to make it somewhat delicate.

"Your usual team? Would Kainen Hemlock be included in that?"

CHAPTER SIX
An Anchoring Explained

Taz caught hold of my wrist just before the shot of energy left my fingertips. I squashed it back down, although blowing up Queenie's ghastly desk was also tempting. Even the mere mention of Kainen's name pushed irrepressible fury crackling through me.

"Only if you want him dead," I growled.

Queenie's smile widened. "At least you've not lost your spark, that is something. Very well. Time is short so make your assignment preparations quick."

I heard the hint to get out of her office and didn't bother to answer, turning on my heel and stalking out. I would have slammed the door behind me, but Taz was the last one out.

"Okay, princess, time to calm down." He stared in alarm as I turned to face him. "Whoa, your eyes are glowing red."

I took a deep breath, willing the burning sensation to calm.

"Yeah, side effect of whatever volatility Fury landed me with. It should fade in a minute."

He held out a hand and I took it, drinking in the sheer relief of being able to and letting that cool my anger instead. As he led us toward the lift, the sudden drain of energy hit me and I sagged.

He frowned at me. "Right, sleep first. Planning later."

I shook my head, hiding a yawn behind the back of my hand.

"Food first, I can't remember the last time I ate."

"Actually, neither can I." Taz rubbed his eyes. "It must be the early hours now, but I reckon if we go to the canteen, the

Braunees will have something all but ready and waiting."

We stopped to wait for the lift and I had to ask. Even though I was apparently going straight back out on assignment as soon as I could get the team and a plan together, Queenie and Taz seemed to know something I didn't.

"What did she mean when she said 'how long have you known'?" I demanded. "Known about what?"

He bit his lip. He could answer, or he could try to avoid it. I don't think I minded either option right now, too hungry and weary to worry until I had to focus on the next assignment. With a sigh, Taz turned me to face him.

"I suppose keeping things from you isn't the best way to stay on your good side," he said, nerves sparking in his eyes.

"You don't have to tell me if you don't want to. Now I know it's really you I'm talking to, I trust you won't be out to get me."

He wrapped his arms around my waist with a ragged sigh, and I settled my head on his shoulder.

"Of course I'm not, I could never hurt you. That's actually part of it, what Queenie said. How much do you know about anchoring?"

I froze, my frown stuck against the soft fabric of his hoodie. He was holding me tight now, and I guessed he wanted to brazen this out without the awkwardness of us having to look at each other.

"I know it's like a bond, a union between two people."

He didn't answer, and I remembered the passage in the book I'd been reading at Xavio's.

"It can be broken," I recited, "but anchoring gives strength and weakness to the people involved. When the two learn to work in harmony, few can break them. There is no way to force a link, or conjure one, but it can be one-sided-"

Oh. I pulled back and he aimed a hesitant half-grimace half-smile at me. *Oh.*

I tried to think of something to say, something meaningful and profound.

"Oh."

His face fell. My heart started pounding.

"Are you saying-" I took a deep breath, needing it to be clear. "Is it just me?"

"Is what just you?" he asked, his brow furrowing.

"Is that it? Queenie asked how long you've known that I'm anchored to you, and you both looked really traumatised by the mere idea of it. Is that it? Old Tara said I was your anchor, and you agreed, but I know they can be severed. I'm not full Fae, and you're still part of the royal family, and I sort of died during the battle, so if I'm all anchored to you but you're not to me anymore- *Why are you laughing?*"

I pushed against his shoulder, baffled and somewhat insulted that I was beginning to panic and he was now creasing with laughter.

"Orbs alive, Dem, I don't care that you're not Fae, or royal, nobody does. Well, maybe some do, but nobody we know, and definitely nobody that matters."

It took him a moment to notice my seriously less-than-impressed expression. He tangled his fingers in my hair, inching closer.

"Anchoring is serious," he said. "When Queenie asked, I wasn't sure if you knew how deep it runs. I didn't want to risk telling you and have you freak out or think it was too much, too soon, too anything, especially now."

I frowned. "But why would she think it was even worth bringing up? Is it like, you can smell it on someone or there's a big flashing sign above their head?"

I looked up above me.

Do I have a big flashing sign over my head? Can he tell? What if what happened with Kainen was what severed it?

The lift finally arrived but neither of us moved an inch.

"Queenie recognised my behaviour," he murmured. "She saw that I'd die to defend you above anything else. When I came back here, she told me about the hallway, about what you did to my mother's favourite spot. Then Hutch told me about the tattoo."

I could barely find breath, he was so close and saying things that might mean exactly what I craved to hear. His face turned mischievous.

"Then I saw you wearing my t-shirt at the funeral over that dress, which I'd like to see you in properly one day, or maybe in just the t-shirt is better."

My cheeks heated and I growled at him. "Stop mucking about."

He kissed me, a gentle brush against my lips.

"I realised then that the anchoring went both ways, for both of us. I was furious at you for disappearing, but I knew."

Happiness spilled through me so fast that my connection woke up and sent a flare of energy through me.

Both ways, for both of us.

My arms glowed white-blue as I wrapped them tight around his neck but Taz barely noticed, immune to my energy gift thanks to his mother's plotting last year. His mother, who we would still have to face at some point.

"How long have you known?" I echoed Queenie's question.

He bit his lip, avoiding my gaze. "About my side? When I came back from the Queen's court after those couple of months away."

When he saw Kainen and I sparring, before the last battle here or me going to the Court of Illusions.

"That's when you realised you liked me?"

I didn't care about when, not really. I just wanted to keep hearing him say it, to fix it in my head so it could never get away from me.

"Um, no." His cheeks turned pink. "That's when I realised the anchoring had set, at least for me. I think I liked you the moment you got back from your first assignment, before we even knew Leo existed. You were so happy and shiny about achieving it, and I realised then that I'd do whatever it took to make you smile, to protect you. It was really inconvenient actually."

I blinked up at him, but he was still avoiding looking directly at me. I settled my fingers under his chin and lifted his face up.

"You remember when I brought Leo back, and we went to the library and you wiped that smudge off my head?" I asked. He nodded. "I think that's when I realised that I had more-than-just-friends feelings, which is basically the same thing. I just figured it was a me thing and I pushed it way down, pretended it wasn't there."

He grinned then, his face lighting up. "Can I tell you a secret? There was no smudge. I just wanted to see how you'd react."

"You lied?" I frowned.

The lift pinged, warning us it was about to leave without us. Taz slid the grill aside and followed me in.

"Actually, I was going to call you Smudge as a nickname, because your first assignment you came back absolutely caked in mud. But by then Sparky had stuck instead. Nicknames don't even count as word-tangling really."

I didn't even see what button he tapped, didn't care, too giddy with the realisation that he felt the same as I did, as deeply as I did. Then I remembered and started grinning.

"I found your letters, the ones you wrote when you were at

your mother's court."

Taz's smile froze. "Oh. Crud. That's embarrassing. I thought I'd hidden them."

"No, it was cute! Wrong time to find them maybe, but I'm glad I did. It settled some things in my head after, you know."

"Fine." He pouted. "But don't get used to it or anything.

I kissed his cheek and swept the moodiness away from his face, knowing that was only one of the many affectionate gestures since he'd written them.

"So, now what?" I asked with a loud yawn. "Soon we go back into yet another one of your family's wars, but I don't want to think about that tonight."

He slid his fingers over the back of my hand, shivers following in their wake.

"You go get ready for bed and I'll go get the food."

He said it so simply, as though 'going to bed' was something we did every day. I mean, it was, but the boundaries were somehow so blurred now that I had no idea what normal was anymore.

The lift stopped at the residents' hall floor and we found Ace pulling the grill open before I could insist I go to the canteen as well.

"I figured you'd need food," he said. "So there are sandwiches, crisps, drinks and sweets on Demi's bed. Every artificial chemical and E-number a growing fairy needs. I put them in a big box and taped it up, but I reckon Leo's maybe got through half of it by now. He's also eaten about three cricket salads in the space of twenty minutes, so there might be another projectile regurgitation situation just as a warning."

I grinned, and almost told him I loved him in a matey type way before realisation crashed in.

The first time I'd said 'I love you' to Taz hadn't been him at all. Kainen was the one who'd heard it, soaked it up and then treated me like a toy he wanted to manipulate.

Taz noticed the change in my face, and no doubt felt the tension of my hand. He inched closer and pulled me out of the lift.

"Thanks, I have to say sorry while I'm at it." He spoke to Ace as we walked along like nothing was wrong, giving me space to recover, to sort my head out. "I think I said I'd kill you at one point, but I didn't mean- well, you know."

Ace chortled to himself. "Yeah, you did, but I won't take it personally. Other people came off way worse. You threatened to turn Beryl's hair into snakes. Harvey's been calling her Medusa ever since and they've broken up twice over it."

I let the soothing balm of my friends' dramas wash over me. Kainen might have stolen things from me, twisted memories and tricked me. Even if he'd been forced by Elvira and Fury to protect the rest of his court from their vengeance, it was still done by his hand. But I had a second chance now to try again, to do better.

"I'm going on assignment again in a couple of days," I announced.

Ace swore.

"Exactly," Taz grumbled.

Ace folded his arms across his chest. "Where are we going this time then? Please be the Bahamas, *please*."

"Afraid not." I shook my head. "The forever mountains, unmanned prison realm for all the traitors of Faerie. I'm not forcing anyone to go if they don't want to though."

"Ah, we're all bonkers, we'll be there. If Milo objects, I'll just tell him they have a collection of antique stolen folios or something, it'll be fine."

That made me smile. "Thanks, Ace. Library session first

thing in the morning then to set out a plan, but first, food and sleep.”

Ace said goodnight and went off down the hall toward his room, and I let Taz tug me toward mine. We found the box of food untouched and Leo fast asleep on his logs. Even when Taz peeled away the layers of hastily placed sticky tape, Leo only flicked open one eye, huffed and disappeared into his quiet box. Taz and I sat on the bed side by side, scoffing the food like ravenous monsters.

“Right, I’m just going to ask.” Taz faced me the moment the food was finished. “I don’t want to leave you at the moment, mainly because I’m scared you’ll vanish like last time, but also because I’m a bit sensitive about going to sleep and not waking up again right now.”

I bit my lip and pressed my hand over his. He twisted his fingers and entangled them with mine.

“Can I stay?” he asked, his voice barely audible.

“Stay here? What like overnight?”

He nodded and I saw the tiniest hint of shame in the way he wouldn’t meet my eyes.

Often we’d doze off side by side if we were up late, but he always went back to his room after a couple of hours when he inevitably woke up. We’d also shared my room a few times right after the last battle, but back then he’d slept on a mattress on the floor, only climbing up when I was having a nightmare or needed reassurance.

“I might not give you much rest,” I admitted. “I’ve had my share of nightmares the last few nights, since… but yes, if you want.”

He smiled then, sheepishly meeting my gaze. “I’ll be on my best behaviour, I promise.”

“Then I’ll definitely know something’s iffy.”

He stuck his tongue out at me and in those few moments we were normal us again.

He disappeared to the bathroom with a hesitant look back, and the random, inane domesticity of it made me smile as I cleared the food wrappers into the bin.

The bin I'd puked into after finding out he'd died.

I shook the thoughts away and nudged it under the desk with my foot. He was here, alive and safe.

But how long for if I drag him to the forever mountains with me?

Even I couldn't accuse myself of dragging him against his will, but the thought of anything happened to him filled me with dread.

I'll have to be careful. But one step at a time.

I clambered into bed, reassuring myself that I would be wiser this time, more careful with my assignments and those I loved.

I could feel sleep calling for me the moment my head hit the pillow, but I forced myself to stay awake until Taz came back.

He slid in beside me, turned off the bedside lamp and hesitated in the dark.

"Hugs okay?"

I nodded, even though he couldn't see me. "Hugs more than fine."

As he wrapped his arm around me, and both of us all but passed out, I made myself a promise.

One way or another, we're going to be okay.

CHAPTER SEVEN
Off to See Uncle

I woke the next morning with a few seconds of untamed ignorance before everything came roaring back. I'd been too exhausted for nightmares, but waking up sent fear screaming through me.

Taz is still dead.

The Apocalyptians are still roaming.

I'm still at Xavio's house, or Kainen's still mucking with my head.

I sat up in a frantic flailing of limbs, staring wildly at the blue walls of my bedroom and the abundance of arms tangled in the covers.

"What's wrong?"

Taz shot upright, wiping sleep from his eyes while trying to look alert at the same time. I blinked at him, the panic taking too long to ebb away.

He's here. He's safe, alive. This is real. I have to believe this is real.

I stared at the tattoos on our wrists, marking them out in my mind in case I'd ever have to use them for an identity check.

Taz squeezed my hand and I tried to recover. Even as I caught my breath back, he didn't press me, didn't ask if I needed space. He folded his arms around me featherlight, letting me decide if I wanted to pull away or sink against him.

I pressed my face against his chest. "I thought you were gone again."

"Still here." He rubbed my back and kissed my hair. "I'm

always here."

I looked up at him, amazed that in all my worrying, I'd never truly accepted that it was the truth. We were anchored to each other, solid together, all but unbreakable. The sleep seemed to have stitched back together several parts of my mental state, and although the anxiety still thrummed through me, I could recognise it rather than react to it.

"You really are, aren't you?"

He nodded. "For as long as you'll have me. I don't have a grand birth-right as such anymore, no great future career as king or anything, but-"

"I love you."

The words slipped out without any intervention from me.

I blinked, feeling the familiar all-natural burn begin in my cheeks that had nothing to do with gifts or anything fairy.

Taz blinked back, looking as surprised as I felt.

"Good."

I froze. "Good?! That's all you can say?"

I hit his arm as he started laughing.

"I've told you I love you like a thousand times." He was struggling to breathe now, he was laughing so hard, but I let him pull me into a tight hug. "You just say 'you too', so I figured, okay, it'll take time. Now you blurt it out just like that and you're all shocked and mad and blinky. Orbs alive, I've missed you so much."

I sank into him, aware that if I cried any more tears, Arcanium would end up flooded. I wiped my eyes on his t-shirt and pulled back.

"I'm starving," I admitted.

Taz let go of me and swung himself off the bed, holding out a hand.

"Big breakfast then. But remember that today, we get a very

rare opportunity. No trial to train for. No classes. Just you, me, the library. And probably about eight other people who are going to insist on talking to you all day, but I'll scare them off."

I could well imagine that. He disappeared to his own room to change, and I threw on jeans and the first hoodie my fingers landed on. One of his, naturally. Before I could do more than pull on a pair of socks and shove my feet into my boots, he reappeared.

"Milo told Ace to tell Cheryl to tell Beryl to tell me that Petra's looking for you," he whispered. "You translocate down to the library quick, and I'll pretend I'm also looking for you."

I snickered at the sheer delight on his face at the prospect of doing something sneaky, but we both needed to be childish for a while and I revelled in it.

I closed my eyes, building the visual of the library around me, with the main desk under my outstretched fingertips and the sight of the office door behind that. I pressed my fingers against the cool, smooth surface and opened my eyes with a grin.

"Oh!" Milo looked up and jumped. "You scared me. Petra's looking for you."

I grinned. "I know. Taz told me, but we're hiding now apparently so I guess breakfast is off."

Milo smiled at that and looked around as if someone might overhear us. I couldn't see anyone milling about, but then the library was often sparsely populated now that everyone had their own orb-readers. Milo was even going through the hideous process of scanning all the physical books into whatever part of the Ogle managed those things.

"If you want to sneak something in, I'll allow it this once," he whispered. "But don't let anyone see you."

I gawped at him. Nobody, and I mean *nobody*, probably not even the Queen, was allowed to bring food or drink into his library.

He seemed to be doubting his decision as his mouth quirked in anxious thought.

"But not near the actual books," he added. "And only dry stuff. Nothing smelly, like hot food. It might be best if you sit on the floor, and get a blanket to cover your lap."

I nodded, still amazed. Before I could thank him, or reassure him to stop his hands twisting around each other, Taz appeared beside me with a large bag that smelled suspiciously hot-food-related.

"Milo, I know the rule, but just this once would it be alright to eat in here?" Taz asked, his face a picture of innocent pleading. "We won't go anywhere near the books, we'll eat on the floor and won't tell a soul, I promise."

He had to have overheard that last bit.

Milo eyed the bag, which seemed to now be leaking something baked-bean coloured, and threw up his hands.

"Why do I bother offering if you're just going to do it anyway?"

He stormed off toward the office and Taz gave me a guilty look that didn't quite cover his smile.

"Come on." I grabbed his free hand. "We'll find a place to sit on the floor. You did promise to that. And try not to let that leak get anywhere. Did you at least bring food that doesn't need to be licked off the bottom of the bag?"

Taz dropped my hand and wound his arm around my waist instead, dragging me toward one of the staircases leading to the higher levels.

"Cruel, wicked princess," he murmured. "Count yourself lucky I won't make you eat the bag."

I decided, given the lively mood he was in, I wouldn't test him on that offer.

We managed to avoid everyone for the best part of the morning, holed away at the top of the library. My mind kept revolving guiltily back to the state of Taz's mother's court and the Apocalyptians taking it over, but we needed to plan before we rushed in to try taking them on.

Once he was sure we hadn't made a speck of mess, Milo conceded to bringing us relevant books about the forever mountains, Selessium and the Apocalyptians in general.

I had one of the library's many comfy armchairs, a small table beside me, and Taz fidgeting at my feet. He'd started off in a chair, then paced back and forth flicking through pages without reading them properly, and eventually flopped down with his back against my knees.

"Anything yet?" he asked for the hundredth time.

"Nothing that will help, although we know roughly what the enemy's plan is."

He sighed. "We've not had much time to talk about any of that. Is there anything you feel up to telling me? Not anything you're not ready for, but about the enemy plans or anything they might have said? Don't if it's too painful."

I couldn't help but smile at how worried he sounded, how hesitant. He twisted so he could see me, and his face softened when he saw me smiling.

"Elvira is still the same," I said. "vowing vengeance on us lot and she *really* doesn't like me, but we knew that already. The Apocalyptians are planning to merge with Elvira as a host body, which will consolidate their power, but last I saw was them arguing over her not telling them she was a shifter-"

"She's a shifter?"

I nodded. "And I assume your mum and your aunt knew, considering she was their childhood friend gone bad. Or your mum's at least."

"Typical." Taz's eyes flashed with ire. "Now my mother has been overcome by them, and no doubt the enemy will be knocking at the door sooner rather than later, especially if they find out the other essences have escaped the vessel thing."

"Yeah, so we'd better get on with it. I'm not having any luck so far though, nothing about the forever mountains being a place to find Selessium or what we need to be prepared for. We may have to go in as we are and work on the defensive."

He tilted his head back, looking up at me. "You sound so official."

I stuck my tongue out at him as Milo came sidling up with Ace behind him.

I caught the hesitant look on Milo's flushed face, the grim look on Ace's.

My heart started to pound, my chest tightening in preparation. I let my hand drift along my thigh, resting my fingertips against Taz's head to reassure myself he was still there.

"I might know someone who can help," Milo said. "It won't be easy though, and he's not the kind of person to give anything for free, or out of kindness."

I frowned. "Who?"

"My uncle, the one who wanted to get rid of me."

I had half expected him to say it was someone he'd seen while working at Gallow's Oak before he came to Arcanium, but I knew how much his uncle's cruel treatment had affected him.

"You don't have to," I insisted. "We can find another way, any other way. We can go in and out, nobody ever said anything about a charge, or having to stay at the forever mountains. We can realm-skip in for five minutes, then out and back in again if it's not safe."

Milo clenched one hand into fist, Ace clasping his other hand tight.

"I need to face him," he said. "I need to tell him that I'm happy and he can't hurt me anymore. I mean, he might not be able to give us anything helpful, but he's always been a Forgotten supporter when he has the choice and he's got his nose in many different social dealings. One of his friends I think used to tell him about the forever mountains when I served them at card games."

I understood that. "It's your choice then. If you think he can help, we'll give it a try. But if you change your mind-"

"I won't."

"Okay, but if you do, that's fine, even if it's last minute."

He nodded, his shoulders sagging.

"Where is he?" Taz asked.

Milo shook Ace's hand off and started tidying up our books, placing them back into the cart as if he needed to keep himself busy with routine tasks.

"Alcartan."

Taz's nose wrinkled. "Right."

"Something you want to share with the class?" I tapped the top of his head.

"Alcartan is one of the further parts of Faerie. It's all but outside the Queen's control now, full of Fae who don't want to incur the courts' wrath by being labelled a traitor, but still want to run on the wrong side of the laws."

"There's more." Milo grimaced. "My uncle is the Governor there."

I'd been imagining Milo's uncle as a penniless lowlife somehow, but the news he was someone who sounded important surprised me, even though a lowlife being higher up the political Fae chain rather than further down it was almost a done-to-death stereotype in Faerie.

"Someone we can manage?" Taz sat up straight.

Milo shrugged. "He'll take trades willingly if they suit him, but he'll always look for a bigger opportunity, or wait and play a longer game. If he recognises who you are, he'll know he can hold out until you're desperate enough to offer him a better deal. I wouldn't put it past him to trick you into staying somehow and then send a ransom to the Queen for your return."

I dropped my book onto the table, earning me a wince from Milo.

"Okay, no. Not happening," I insisted. Taz grinned up at me, but I was completely serious. "We'll find another way. Either that, or a few of us go in glamoured while someone else ransacks his place for information. We may not find anything that way though."

"I can compel him," Ace offered. "But we'll only get a few questions before he realises so they'll have to count."

"Or we do it so gently, play to vanity. Milo, does he have any?"

"He likes gambling. If you were to challenge him to a game of cards, he might be so wrapped up in cheating to win the game that he doesn't notice."

I sat back, my mind whirring.

"Would he believe you if you just went in and asked him? Say you want to meet, and ask him where to find Selessium. Make it sound like your place here depends on it and you're desperate, like he's your last chance. Bring us with you and we'll talk about a card game between ourselves, see if he bites. We can pretend to be arrogant, entitled Fae with no smarts, or in Taz's case, just turn up and do the usual."

"Hey!" Taz reached back and pinched my knee.

Milo managed a nervous smile. "I'll have to contact him first, request an audience. He might still say no."

"Come on then," Ace said as he rubbed Milo's shoulder. "We'll go and see what appointment he deigns to give us."

I bit my lip. "No need to drag everyone into the melee for now. We'll go just the four of us."

Milo nodded and I watched him and Ace disappear toward the stairs, Ace's arm around Milo's shoulders. I let the sigh building up inside me tumble out, and again Taz twisted to look up at me, his chin now between my knees.

"Talk to me," he said, his voice soft. "Tell me what you're thinking."

I frowned down at him. "You'll have to go in with a glamour. By the sounds of it, Milo's uncle will see you as a target."

"And you." Taz's lips twitched. "They've tried to use you to get to me before. Don't underestimate anyone."

I didn't plan to, and he knew it, but the rivulet of caring in his tone warmed me anyway.

"We'll go in with protection wardings up," I decided. "We'll stay together. Milo and Ace for Milo's realm-skipping ability, and me with your magic princely red shoes."

Taz raised his eyebrows. "Red shoes?"

"Ruby slippers? Wizard of Oz? Oh come on, I would have thought that one was pure Fae down to the bone."

He shrugged. "Not a clue what you're talking about, but I have never owned red shoes in my life, despite many objections from the fashion parade at mother's court. I can realm-skip us back here though, so that'll have to do. Do you have a plan for getting him to talk?"

I nodded. "Milo will do the talking to start with, and no doubt his uncle will ask for a trade for information or a favour. I'll figure out some kind of joke or taunt aimed at you about losing at cards while they talk, see if he takes the bait."

Taz twisted around and got to his feet, coming to settle on the arm of my chair. I squeaked as he dropped down beside me, wiggling until we were squished side by side.

"You were saying?" He grinned at my flushed cheeks.

I gave him a disapproving look before continuing, with absolutely no power behind it at all.

"If he doesn't take the bait, we'll have to offer to play him for the information instead. While he's distracted with cards, I'll casually ask questions and Ace will compel him to answer."

Taz put his arm around my shoulders and lifted his free hand, pressing his fingertips to the top of his thumb palm up and flicking his hand open. One moment, his hand was empty and the next he was holding a pristine pack of cards.

I stared at him in amazement.

"Simple summoning enchantment," he said with a shrug. "I had to practice something while we were apart. Now, oh wicked one, if we're going to word-tangle about games, you should learn how to play."

I arranged my face into a suitable look of trepidation. I couldn't lie to him, but I could find other ways to convince him that I had no idea about the game.

"Very well, oh great card master. How does it work?"

CHAPTER EIGHT
A Brush With Milo's Past and Taz Gets a New Disguise

Taz was still sulking a few hours later as we gathered on the despatch platform to realm-skip.

I'd insisted we arrive via Trevor's rickshaw for the effect, wanting to keep Taz's ability to skip us home and Milo's own skills as hidden as possible. It was likely Milo's uncle knew about his abilities, but not Taz's.

"Taz, come on, you have to glamour before we go," I reminded him.

Okay, maybe I could have let him win one game, but it's not my fault I got Petra as a mentor and she thinks cards are a huge part of Faerie politics.

He gave me a pouty look. A moment later, he grew a few inches in height, his shoulders broadening. His curls straightened into dark locks around a sharper, more rugged jawline. This wasn't the boyish Roger disguise he'd used at Gallows Oak last year. No, this was a fully grown young man.

"You should change your eye colour too, just in case," Milo suggested. He blinked at me innocently, before adding, "how about a nice deep violet colour?"

I decided then that I wouldn't be attending any more informal book clubs with him any time soon.

"Your wings are kind of a giveaway as well," Ace suggested, his smile far too vague to be blameless. "Maybe go for a different type of animal, like a bat?"

I glared at Milo before he could make any further additions

of his own as Taz's wings rippled and inky black trickled over the feathers, encasing the fiery orange.

"It'll be harder to keep the glamour if I go beyond colour," Taz insisted, turning to me with his arms and wings splayed wide. "Will I do?"

I gulped and nodded.

If I weren't so taken with him as he was normally, I'd be crushing hard right now.

"No possessive displays either, you two," Ace said. "They may not guess Taz is with us, but we can't take the risk."

We'd decided that while Taz should be glamoured to hide his value as Prince-now-no-longer-in-line-for-the-throne-despite-nobody-taking-his-abdication-seriously of Faerie, I would go in as myself and hope that was enough of a draw for Milo's uncle to take interest in us.

I might be considered princess consort still, but I doubted anyone would take that seriously, especially not those who were hoping our enemies would win the war anyway.

I smiled as my realm-skipper, Trevor, hurried up with his rickshaw in tow.

"Hi, Trevor."

He gave me a smile but it was somewhat less than his usual beaming grin.

Is he upset that I've been relying on Milo or Taz lately instead of asking for him to take me places?

I opened my mouth to babble some inane explanation about the loss of my orb, but then noticed the more likely reason for his harassed expression as the head of a small troll-child with alarmingly wild sprigs of hair appeared around the edge of the rickshaw.

"I promise this never normally happens." Trevor said, sounding even more apologetically like me than I'd been planning to. "Glynnis was sick and Moira's on her way up but she got called to the Quarantine floor so I'll be with you as soon as she's here to pick up Moss."

I'd heard several mentions of Trevor's daughter, Moss, and met her once. She was both a five-year-old tearaway always getting into trouble and obsessed with Jelly Babies. Apparently, according to someone who would remain nameless (Taz), she was very similar to me.

"That's fine, honestly," I insisted.

Trevor didn't look convinced, then he noticed his daughter swinging from the overhanging roof of his rickshaw.

"Moss! Down from there now."

She grinned, ignoring him. I exchanged a look with the others, except Taz who'd dropped his glamour and was already beside the rickshaw grabbing her by her feet.

"We'll have to throw her over the edge I'm afraid," he said gravely.

She squealed and wriggled, the noise ricocheting across the platform and bouncing off the domed ceiling above us. As Taz dangled her over the edge of the walkway above the atrium far below, she stopped struggling.

We all knew that there was a protection in place to catch anyone that fell, but apparently she didn't.

"Going to be a long drop." Ace joined in. "I heard you can sing all the words to *Fae Fae Fantastic* before you reach the bottom."

"Nooo… Taz is mean," she wailed.

I couldn't help laughing. I'd forgotten that Taz sometimes helped out with the kids who Glynnis looked after while their parents were working on Arcanium business. Many of them lived here, worked here and some even grew up here.

Moss clearly knew him well, but maybe not enough to trust

he wouldn't drop her off the edge of the platform.

Taz removed Moss from not-so-certain peril and set her down. I tensed as she ran toward me next and hid behind my legs.

"Taz is mean," she whispered loudly.

I nodded. "He is. But he's ticklish behind the backs of his knees."

Taz gasped and pretended to run. Once I started laughing, I couldn't stop, but seeing the apparently-no-longer-Prince of Faerie being chased by a five-year-old troll with mad hair is enough to do it.

None of us noticed someone else approaching from the lift.

"Oh now I leave for half an hour."

I managed to pull myself together as Trevor's wife appeared, her ears wrapped with a bandana and her face failing to hide how amused she was.

"Come on, Moss," she insisted. "Dad's got to work and you and I have to go see your aunti-"

"Nooo… not auntie!"

Once again, I was being used as a shield by a five-year-old about to tantrum, but Moira apparently wasn't going to let anyone get in the way of family visiting time, not even the princess consort or whatever I was supposed to be now.

I gave Moss a sympathetic look as her mother dragged her kicking toward the lift, and decided not to comment on the potential reason why Trevor always seemed so happy to be at work.

Trevor rubbed a hand over his face.

"Sorry about that. Normal service now resumed."

I grinned. "That's fine. Gave Taz a chance to get a bit of exercise."

I squeaked as Taz threw an arm around my shoulders and

pretended to throttle me, but then he resumed his glamoured appearance and I remembered what we were up here to do.

And why we're here to do it. So kids like Moss don't have to grow up being treated badly or used by Fae-folk.

I clambered into the rickshaw, my heart warming as Taz's hand brushed my waist. Sitting next to him looking so different felt weird, but I focused on the assignment ahead.

"Okay, Trevor." I took a deep breath. "We need to go to the Governor's house in Alcarten. Nice and easy on the landing, we want to look graceful, like we have power anywhere we go."

Trevor grinned over his shoulder and launched toward the sparkling wall of Quartz. I had the briefest glimpse of the evening growing dark through the glass dome above the platform, then closed my eyes against the wisp of nether that brushed my face. Taz's arm tightened around me as the rickshaw landed, then slithered free.

I opened my eyes and stared as we came to an effortless halt.

Dusky blue mountains filled the horizon, snow-capped but otherwise barren of vegetation. The bare brown earth and grey rock towered around us, a place almost devoid of life. The only sign of civilisation was a house built of cold grey stone in front of us, with a suspiciously lush garden full of greenery and what looked like pink and white roses.

A shiver rumbled through the rickshaw, starting with Milo as his fear radiated throughout the group. I stepped out onto hard rock, aware of Taz in his glamour right behind me.

The whole place looked rotten. Some scrub trees were still trying to grow, low-lying and gnarled over by harsh winds, but they had a weird smell and the bark looked soggy and decaying. Everything except the house's garden which seemed to be flourishing .

"My uncle has everything brought in by a carrier," Milo

mumbled.

I checked him over. "It's okay if you don't want to do this."

"No." he shook his head. "I don't want to, but I have to. If I don't, I'll regret it. I have to face them to put it behind me."

Ace's soft smile glimmered with pride as I threaded my arm through Milo's.

"Stay in twos at all times," I said. "Even if we swap, one with Ace and one with, um, Roger."

Taz flicked me a grin then, his sulking over the cards apparently forgotten. In his glamour he looked like darkness and hushed whispers.

Okay, no more fanciful books for me for a while.

I steeled myself and half-led, half-followed Milo toward the metal railings topped with spikes that surrounded the house. Milo seemed to be focusing mostly on regulating his breathing as the front doors swung open.

Two young men strode out, perhaps only a few years older than us. I bristled as they noticed Milo and similar expressions of gleeful malice crept across their faces. One blonde-haired and taller, one brown-haired and slender.

"Welcome," the blonde one said, eying me. "Father was most concerned to hear from you, cousin. He thought you'd finally understood your place and disappeared for good."

With the wind whistling cold around us, it was easy to suck in a sharp breath without being heard. I forced the prickle around my eyes back down. There would be time perhaps before we left to teach these two idiots a lesson in kindness.

"I had to ask Uncle something." Milo's voice wavered.

The taller boy tsked and surveyed me again. I looked back at him, silently daring him to try me.

"You're being rude," he said, presumably to Milo although he was still looking at me. "You haven't introduced us to your companions."

I bristled. "As the hosts who've come to greet us, you haven't introduced yourselves either."

"Forgive me." A smile spread across his face. "I'm Carron, and this is my brother Derrin. No need to ask who you are, even here in our little idyll, we can recognise the Queen's champion and the prince's pet."

I half-expected some kind of reaction from Taz, but couldn't hear one and he was somewhere behind me with Ace. I managed to smile, finding that fairy wickedness as I tilted my head to one side.

"Then there's little need for us to be bothering with you two is there, now that introductions are done. We're here to see the Governor of Alcartan. Either lead us in or get out of the way."

I caught the lightning quick snarl on Derrin's face, but Carron hid his reaction much better, bowing his head.

"Certainly. Follow us then."

I clung to Milo as we moved into the house, aware he was doing the same to me. His cousins moved on ahead but we kept our pace slow, taking in the potential exits just in case. A quick glance over my shoulder proved we had Taz and Ace right behind us.

"You know the Faerie tales about the orphan who had the odd kind friend growing up, or servants who doted on him?" Milo whispered. I nodded. "Yeah, that wasn't me. They all delighted in making my life hell, every last one of them. When my Uncle hires, he looks for cruelty as one of the pre-requisites. Says it makes for smarter staff."

I thought about how Marthe had always been kind to Taz, doting on him by all accounts as he grew up. I thought about how at least Mum was kind to me, loved me even if my sisters didn't. Again I looked back, and Taz caught my eye with a grimace. I could tell he was thinking the same.

"So, these are your cousins," I murmured. "Do they have gifts we should be aware of?"

Milo shook his head.

"My Uncle won't allow them to be gifted, not yet. He took me in as a potential heir when my parents died, but then he married their mother and chose them instead."

The brothers had reached a pair of double doors at the end of the hall, dark wood inlaid with veins of gold.

"It's you, you're being ridiculous, get out of the way," Carron snarled at Derrin.

We came to a stop a few feet behind them, and I saw then what the problem was. Every time Derrin reached for one of the handles to open the door, the handle disappeared. The moment he removed his hand, it reappeared. Carron tried but received the same mystifying effect. He tested the other door with no better luck.

Taz appeared at my side, Ace on Milo's other side as I slid my arm free. Taz gave me a devilish smirk.

"*What?*" He mouthed, suddenly the picture of innocence, as if he wasn't using his transmutation power to turn the handles to air and back again.

The door flew open before I could return the look, and I nestled my arm firmly against Milo's as his uncle surveyed us all.

"Milo, you brought guests, how surprising." He raised one eyebrow. "Welcome, I am Governor Alcarten. Please, come inside."

He was a tall man, slender and impeccably dressed. His deep voice sounded calm and level, but I heard the tiny bite underneath. He didn't know why Milo was calling this meeting, other than for 'information', but clearly the mere idea of Milo having people to accompany him had come as a shock.

The Governor stayed by the door as we trooped past, but I saw his gaze drift over me. He no doubt recognised who I was, and I pushed my nerves aside and focused on assessing the gilded grandeur of his office.

He quickly summoned more seating around his huge desk, and we settled into formation with Taz on one end and Ace on the other, Milo and I in the middle.

Governor Alcarten flicked an impatient glare at the door, and I heard the disgruntled huff of Milo's cousins as they left the room and shut the doors behind them.

"Now, I know Milo of course, and you, my dear, need no introduction." The wide wolfishness of the Governor's smile made my skin crawl. "I take it there's little point in getting to know the rest of your group? Given their stature, they're clearly here for protection."

His gaze flicked between Milo and me. I inclined my head, trying to keep my smile confident and my shoulders relaxed.

"As you say." I went for the standard word-tangling fallback. "We're here for information. I've got things to do so I'd rather not dance around the polite politics, but this is between you and your nephew."

I gave my best performance of a restless, reckless person. Given that I'd been a part of the recent battles with the Forgotten, and the only visual most of Faerie had of me was a less than graceful diatribe about elitism through *The Faerie Net*, it was probably the easiest mask I could wear.

Milo sat up straighter.

"We need information, but there will no doubt be a cost, so let's get that out of the way first."

Governor Alcarten clicked his tongue with a mock frown that did nothing to hide his amusement.

"So formal, nephew. Not a single question about the family, how we've been doing."

Milo was still shaking, but he met his uncle's gaze.

"That goes both ways."

I wanted to applaud and hug him for being so brave, but I remained in my seat, leaning back against it, lounging for effect.

"Fair enough." The Governor's host mask slid away. "Request your information, and I'll name my price."

Milo flicked a glance at me. I nodded. That simple look of permission no doubt marked us for what we were, working as part of the Queen's court, but it wasn't an allegiance I wanted to hide anyway. It might push the price of our debt up, but we knew that would be the case.

"We need to find any information about Selessium and the forever mountains," Milo said. "The whereabouts of how to obtain Selessium specifically."

His uncle regarded him for a moment, assessing his next move.

"That is a wide-ranging topic about a dangerous place and a very in-demand material," he said. "Perhaps it would be prudent of me to gain some insurance as part of the bargain. If the Queen's champion would concede to being my guest for a while, to remain here, I should feel safe enough to divulge what I know."

I expected Taz to explode at that, or even Ace after what happened with Kainen. But I think all four of us were astonished when Milo got to his feet, his fists shaking and his shoulders bunching wide.

"No. No people, no manipulation. You won't take and treat her as you did me. Name a payable price. You're a shortcut, not an answer."

I grinned then, my insides tumbling with undisguised pride

and delight. I slid my arm through Milo's, tugging him to sit down, and pressed my cheek to his shoulder as I hugged tight.

"Anyone would think you cared." I beamed at him, then launched to my feet. "As it is, Governor, I'm not for sale today I'm afraid. If that's your only price, we're done. Oooh, is this an original copy of *Beasts and Baronies*?"

I strode to his bookcase. It obviously wasn't an original, because according to Milo the original was safe in the Arcanium library's vault, but I wanted the Governor to believe I recognised his worth and would cave when he priced his trades high.

"It isn't, sadly. Very well, Milo. I will think of a different price, but it will be a high one. So far, the only use you have brought me is the trade of you to Gallow's Oak as the payment for my keeping the Forgotten's secrets."

He dares say that in front of the Queen's champion. Would he say it if he knew who Taz really is? Probably.

"Are you a gambling man?" I asked.

I turned to face the room and flinched when I saw Taz right beside me, still caught off guard by his changed appearance.

"I have been known to grace the card tables on occasion," the Governor said. "Not always with the best of luck."

I folded my arms, seeing the hopeful gleam in his eyes. We'd found his weakness, which meant he would beg, borrow, steal and above all, cheat like hell to win.

"How about we play you for it, to make it more interesting then?" I offered. "Rather than think of a trade which is always boring when everyone refuses to say what they really want. Ask your price and we'll play you for it."

The Governor sat back in his chair pretending to think. After too short a moment, he nodded.

"Very well. I would demand an introduction to the Queen

herself. Alcarten is far off the map and outside her control, but I would like to ensure myself some measure of safety if the other side falls."

I wondered if Ace had compelled that information out of him, but couldn't see any doubt or confusion on the Governor's face.

No. He's got no fear of playing both sides. He's a chancer, happy to be well-known as unreliable. That way when both sides need to appear virtuous, he's indispensable to do their dirty work on the sly.

I noticed the slightest dip of Taz's chin, a wordless confirmation that he'd secure it for us if we lost.

"Alright." I faced the Governor. "If you win at this card game we're about to play, then we will get you an introduction to the Queen. If we win, you tell us all about Selessium, the forever mountains and anything you know about what the enemy plan to do, today."

The Governor smiled. "Very well. Please, take a seat."

I smiled back. "Oh, it won't be me playing. The collective 'we' gets a bit confusing, but we as a team can nominate any player we choose. Standard Fae rules." I glanced at Taz. "Play the nice man at cards. Sorry, Governor, he doesn't talk much but he's learning a lot about games."

Taz had his back to the room still, and I saw the subtle flicker of his eyes turning turquoise for a moment, a devilish flash of himself. I guessed I'd be paying later for making him do this, but I had to keep my focus on asking distracting questions as he sat opposite the Governor. Milo stood and came to me, leaving Ace beside Taz, in twos at all times.

"I don't suppose you have any *Carrie's Castle* books in this library of yours?" I asked.

It was as good a random inane thing to begin with as any.

The Governor scoffed.

"Fiction? I hardly think so."

Taz dealt the first hand and I sought for a way to bring the conversation around to more important things as they began to play.

"It is a good collection though. Perhaps we should keep you playing at cards and get the information from your books instead."

"There are many things that only I know, my dear."

A-ha.

"Like what?"

I trusted Ace to know when to use his power and what exactly to compel. He'd told me once that compelling was like giving instructions, you had to make it clear and precise.

"That both sides are interested in Selessium at the moment, what with the Apocalyptians determined to reclaim their full power."

I erred on the side of caution. "I think most people with a brain know that."

I tensed as Taz lost a hand, but I couldn't see any sign of trepidation on his face. Either he had ultimate poker face, or he was trying to lure the Governor into getting cocky.

"Well, those that are already seeking it might want it that way," the Governor added.

"You mean the Forgotten," I pressed. "And the woman who would be the next Queen?"

The Governor nodded, his attention flicking between Taz's face and his cards.

"Her advisor has already been here with similar questions. Unlike you lot, who still play by the rules of gallantry, they don't ask. They take. I had little choice but to give them everything they needed."

"Oh yeah? Very kind of you. Like what?"

He lost a hand and his mouth thinned, his eyes beginning to dart.

"The location of the Selessium foundry, which is hidden inside the forever mountains. The entrance, which only the league of the Nether Brethren know. The price to be paid for Selessium."

My mind raced. We needed those answers from him, then we'd have everything.

Taz won another hand. If he won the fourth, he'd won the game. I forced my voice to remain unconcerned, conversational.

"What price is that?"

The Governor frowned, my question an irksome fly batting around his attention to his cards. He was hunching over ever so slightly, but I saw the card slip lightning quick out of his sleeve, and one from his hand replace it. No doubt he would lure Taz into thinking he could win, then cheat the next three rounds to best him.

Bastard.

"A sacrifice, something lasting," he muttered. "It could be dignity, it could be life, it could be as simple as an apple from your pocket. They weigh the person requesting it, I'm not entirely sure how."

He was frowning deeper now, his attention starting to fray from the game. Now that he knew he was going to win, his concentration was shifting back to the nature of my questions. We had to make this last one count and I caught Ace's eye.

"Are you cheating at this card game, Governor?"

He froze as the answer leapt from his mouth.

"Yes."

"How?"

Sweat burst onto his brow. "I have cards up my sleeve and a

gift that can move small objects."

He shook his head in confusion but I ploughed on.

"Then we win by default as you cheated," I insisted. "You must tell us the information."

The Governor, perhaps still clinging to the desperate need to be the one in control, rose to his feet like a glowering ferret.

"All Fae cheat, you stupid girl. I also said I would give you information about 'the enemy'. I didn't clarify whose. Now that you have made an enemy of me, I can tell you everything I know about you."

I laughed. "Don't bother, I was there and it's hardly a gripping story."

"What about your dear friend Milo then?" he asked, desperate to shake me.

I froze. "What about him?"

Milo blinked at me, but he looked as unsure as I was.

"He has an unusual gift. One the Forgotten wanted to keep in check, to keep safe until it was needed. He can realm-skip at will, anywhere in Faerie. He has no limitation to his ability. Except here."

I stared back at him. I knew about Milo's gift, but nobody had mentioned it not working here.

Sensing he finally had the upper hand, the Governor grinned, his features flashing sharp and terrifying.

"Oh, yes," he continued. "I had wards put on this place to ensure he couldn't ever escape if he returned. After your little trick at Gallows Oak, I was tasked with returning him if he ever stepped foot in this house ever again. Now, not only will I be able to hand the Queen's champion to the Forgotten, but also the missing realm-skipper."

Milo can't realm-skip. The danger of it slammed into me. *We have to get out of here.*

Taz was out of his chair, Ace too. If we got into some kind of fight, if the Governor called guards and had us separated…

I stormed toward the desk, ire flashing in my eyes. I could feel the burning and guessed they'd gone red again, but I didn't care. I only held my anger in check, kept my energy gift pinned, because I would have to touch the others in a few moments.

The Governor still thought he had the upper hand as Milo and I reached Taz and Ace.

"Oh, yes," he crowed. "The future Queen will be very happy to see you again, my dear champion. Once she has found the remaining Apocalyptians still at large, she will find a way to join with them, infiltrate the current Queen's court and become the most powerful ruler Faerie has ever seen."

He blinked as realisation dawned. Ace had his hand around Taz's wrist as if to hold him back and Milo grabbed Taz's other arm.

"You… You *dared* compel me?" The Governor's shock gave me just enough time to wrap my arms around Taz's neck from behind. "You filthy, low-born, dirty-blooded…"

"Show him who you are," I murmured in Taz's ear. "Then take us home."

I grinned up at the Governor, struck speechless as Taz dropped his glamour. The dark hair wriggled back to honey-brown curls, the shoulders cinching in and the freckles exploding across his nose. I gave him a loud kiss on the cheek, just for effect, the second before the Governor's office door crashed open and we were swallowed by the nether.

CHAPTER NINE
Trust is Rarely Re-Given

"That was close," Ace muttered the moment we opened our eyes.

Taz had brought us back to the top level of the library, as if he knew that Milo was shaken and would need his safe place around him.

I was still roiling with pent-up energy, so I let go of Taz and started pacing instead.

"We'll leave you be," Taz said quietly to Milo.

In my adrenalin rush, I'd not considered how this altercation with his family must have affected him. With a rueful grimace, I patted his arm.

"I'm sorry you had to go through that. He's an absolute scum-bucket, if that's any consolation."

Milo managed a small smile. "I didn't *have* to go through it, I offered. I'd do it again if only to see the look on his face. But I think I need to take some time to calm down. I'm going to ask Petra to look after the library this afternoon."

I froze. "Oh orbs, Petra! She's been looking for me since this morning. She's going to be *furious*."

Taz started laughing. Milo and Ace gave me knowing smiles before disappearing down the stairs together. I groaned, pressing my hands to my forehead, only to find Taz pulling them back down, his fingers gentle around my fingers.

"I found her before I got breakfast this morning," he said. "Told her to give you a day or two. She just wanted to see how you were, so I said you were fine and you'd catch up with her tomorrow."

I let out the ragged, relieved sigh and pressed my hands to his shoulders, sagging against him.

"Thank you."

He chuckled. "It's getting late again. I reckon you need to eat and sleep. Somehow, we always seem to end up having to skip that part."

"Except I should report in," I said with a woeful grimace. "I don't even know if I'm meant to be reporting to Petra or Queenie anymore."

Taz huffed and slung his arm around my waist, guiding me toward the stairs.

"None of this is normal procedure. If you're adamant about doing a report, I vote we go to Queenie and give her the update. She'll be in a foul mood and we'll be in the canteen for dinner before you've so much as drawn a breath."

I liked the sound of the quick route to the canteen.

We fell into companionable silence as we crossed the deserted library toward the lift. Taz pressed the button for Queenie's floor and I rested my head on his shoulder.

"He was pretty mad," he said.

I could feel his grin radiating through the small confines of the lift as we shot upwards.

"You played a good card game." I shot back.

"You know, I still get nervous watching you. These days you're so much more confident than you were when we met."

I groaned. "Don't get all deep and meaningful on me now."

"Hey." He prodded my side, making me wriggle away. "It's a compliment. You're strong, but I want you to know you don't have to be all the time. You can let me take some of the stress."

I lifted my head, looking up at him. "Is that the anchored part of you talking?"

"Nope, all of me. What I'm trying to say is that you don't have to only give me the card games."

I smiled at that as the lift slowed to a stop.

"When we first got thrown into this mad crusade against the Forgotten, it was you giving me the card games. It was you telling me not to drink the cocoa at Gallow's Oak, and saving me from Reflecto-sisters, and stopping my lizard from getting banished to quarantine. I'm finally returning the favour."

Taz opened the grill and froze. "Hold that thought then."

I stared past him to find Queenie's office doors open and several familiar people standing inside.

"This can't be good," I muttered.

I could just make out Hutch and Harvey nearest the door, and a couple of bright colours beyond which suggested the Eastwick sisters were there too. This was the team I'd asked for, so why were they in Queenie's office without me?

"Walk quiet," I said. "If she's planning some kind of ambush again, I want to know."

Taz nodded and I felt the subtle brush of his wing at the edge of my shoulder.

We crept toward the door on silent feet but nobody inside was focused on the hall. When we reached the doorway, Taz grabbed my hand and stormed in.

"This looks cosy."

Hutch and Harvey jumped, as did Cheryl and Beryl. Meryl contained her shock a bit better, until Ace accidentally caught her arm with his elbow and made her jump. Milo shot us a worried look.

I could have handled that.

I could have even handled Queenie standing behind her desk, hands on the top with a frown now fixed on me, but it wasn't her I was looking at.

Standing on the opposite side of the office to my friends was Kainen Hemlock.

He bit his lip, looking up at me with chastened guilt in his dark eyes from the opposite side of the room.

I'd expected to feel rage when I saw him again, or that lethal calm that came shortly before I exploded with fury. My connection splurged as I took a step back, but it wasn't to attack.

The protection warding sprang around me like a reinforced bubble, the instinct to shutter myself away forcing even Taz back. He blinked at me, wide-eyed, but didn't make any move to approach as I stared past him.

The last time I'd seen Kainen, I was ready to kill him.

I sought out Taz, catching his gaze with desperation. He turned his right arm palm up and gently slid the cuff of his sleeve back so I could see the white-blue orb tattooed there.

My chest was heaving with shock, my head spinning. I should have eaten more, shouldn't have let Queenie throw me straight back into an assignment.

I should be stronger than this.

"Well, this is dramatic," Queenie said, her tone bored as if I wasn't about to collapse in her office. "I understand you went off on your own errand this evening so I'd like a report. I've also assembled your team for you as requested."

I thought Taz would shout at her, but his eyes were wholly on me.

Another example of how this anchoring could weaken us instead of making us stronger. If Kainen attacked him now, if anyone did, he'd be defenceless.

"Dem." Taz held out his hand, palm facing forwards.

He mimed pushing against something and I saw it then. I'd not warded myself, I'd warded all of us. Everyone except for Queenie and Kainen.

I focused on letting the threads drop, unwinding them and letting the process calm my mind and my racing pulse. The others had linked hands too, most likely on entering the office. They didn't trust Kainen either, or Queenie apparently.

As my mind slowed, the realisation seeped in that Kainen was here for a reason. Until I heard Queenie out we weren't leaving this office.

The moment the warding was down, Taz stood beside me. I gave him a hesitant look of apology but he grabbed my hand and kissed my wrist briefly before turning to Queenie.

"He's not coming with us," he said.

Queenie rolled her eyes. "Kainen has debts he can call in with various inmates that have been banished to the forever mountains. That should get you to your goal faster."

"No." Taz shook his head.

Queenie turned to Kainen and pointed. "Show them."

I had to look up at him, not able to focus directly on his face, but enough that I saw him lift his arm as Taz had done moments before. I froze.

A white disc in the shape of a star sat on the inside of his wrist. I'd seen those discs before, on Sagar and Eldrich, two men who were guards sworn to the Queen's court.

"There you are," Queenie said. "Kainen has pledged himself and sworn official fealty to the Queen. He is in her service."

That meant he couldn't make any moves against the Queen or her court without horrible things happening to him.

Or her family. Does that mean he can't manipulate me, or Taz? Would that extend to us? I can't take that risk.

"The Queen has agreed that I should keep my double routine," Kainen said, his voice subdued. "But Elvira and Emil aren't using my court as a base any longer, so I only get information from Emil. You saw me on the day of the... well, you saw me."

I nodded. I had seen him speaking to Emil. I'd accused him of being a traitor. In my heart and my head, he still was. But perhaps it was only me he was intent on damaging.

Either way, the star on his wrist said that he couldn't move against the Queen or her court, or her family. By extension, that meant he couldn't betray Taz either. But this was my assignment, and he could still betray me.

Taz squeezed my fingers, reclaiming my attention.

"Come talk to me."

I nodded, letting him lead me out of the office without a single thought for the others. He closed the doors behind us and sighed.

"I hate him so much," he muttered. "I want to do curse him where he stands. But if he is sworn to the Queen and able to help the mission, and you decide he should come with us, then I'll understand."

I blinked at him. "Er… what?"

The smallest flicker of a smile. "We're anchored, Sparky, and I know you love me. I trust that you feel nothing for him. If you don't want him to come with us, we can say no. Queenie will argue, but it's your assignment. You decide. If you do, if you think he can help us, I'll understand. I won't even threaten him. Much. So, it's your decision."

"This isn't a card game I can make you play?" I asked, hoping despite knowing the answer.

Taz chuckled. "Nope, afraid not. I just want you to know if you have to make a hard decision, not only will I support you, but I'll protect you. From him, from all of it."

I rubbed my face with both hands, trying to settle my mind enough to think. I'd been ready to kill Kainen at the Queen's court, but shortly before everything had gone wrong, he'd given me time to run from the Apocalyptians. He'd tried to save me, something I'd forgotten in my raging grief.

Does he deserve another chance to prove he's not a monster? He always will be to me, he's burned those bridges, but what about to the rest of the world. Do I really want to make his redemption my burden?

"Is there any way of muting his gifts?" I asked.

Because of course, that was what really worried me. I wasn't some lovesick puppy pining after him, or holding remnants of a secret crush. I was afraid of how easily he'd been able to trick and break me. I was petrified of my own failures.

Taz shook his head. "No, but others could be gifted with immunity to them, like my mother did when she gave me conditional imperviousness to your energy gift."

That could work.

"If I do this, if he agrees to all of us being made impervious to his gifts, I still don't want to have to so much as speak to him. Not even look at him."

Taz raised his brow. "You think I'd let him close enough to try speaking to you? I may be supporting you if that's what you choose to do, but that doesn't mean I'm not going to destroy him if he steps even one toe out of line, or goes anywhere near you."

I had to smile at that. "You said you wouldn't threaten him."

"No point dealing with threats. If he tries anything, I'll stop him."

I could well believe that. Exhausted, I realised my choice was already made.

"You can be the one to confirm that to everyone then," I grumbled.

Taz pulled me close as we walked back into the office. Silence reigned, although Queenie had taken to reading a magazine as she waited. She barely even looked up when I stopped beside the others. I looked at Taz but he mimed pinning his lips together, leaving me to announce the decision even as his fingers squeezed tight around my hand.

"I have conditions," I announced.

Kainen lifted his head, but I addressed Queenie instead.

"If he comes with us to the forever mountains, he has to agree to everyone being impervious to his gifts. No manipulations, no mind tricks, no illusions. I want that guaranteed."

I tensed as Kainen took a step forward, drew a breath to speak.

"Demi, I-"

"I threatened you once before." Ace's voice rumbled through the room, startling all of us. "That still stands. If she wants you to speak, she'll tell you."

I was close enough to lay a hand on his arm. He looked down at me with a grimace, as if to apologise. I found a small smile, enough to let him know I appreciated his big brother routine.

Kainen took a step back. "Imperviousness to me is fine."

I eyed everyone else assembled.

"If anyone doesn't want to be, or doesn't want to come on the assignment, it's fine."

Hutch actually spluttered. "Refuse my first assignment? Absolutely not!"

"I go wherever my darling Beryl goes," Harvey piped up

He winced as Beryl's hand caught him square in the gut. She shared a look with her sisters, then grinned at me.

"We're in."

Milo smiled at me. "We never say no."

That appeared to be that.

I turned to Taz, and found a small touch of amusement lingering behind the wary scowl he kept shooting Kainen's way.

"Don't look at me, princess," he said. "I might be royalty,

but my sisters and I were never given the permission to gift others by birth-right, only those sworn to the court are."

I refrained from grumbling that the card games seemed to be wholly one-sided since leaving Alcarten. The Queen had welcomed me as part of her court, but not asked me to swear loyalty and fealty to it. By all accounts so far, I was an oddity in that respect. But it did mean I could gift people.

I even risked looking at Queenie and got a scathingly raised eyebrow for my trouble.

"I know you weren't about to ask me," she said drily. "But even if you were, I may be court Fae but I am sworn to remain impartial to Arcanium members."

Of course you are, how convenient.

With my insides twisting, I worked out the safest wording in my head and leaned up on tiptoe to brush my lips over Taz's forehead, speaking the words in my mind.

"I gift you with imperviousness to Kainen Hemlock's gifts, so he can't bewitch, manipulate, control, compel or cast visions on you."

I reached back, dying to test it just in case. Taz lifted his head, his eyes flashing green at Kainen as his hand tightened around my hip.

"Compel me, get me to do something," he barked.

Kainen sighed. "Take two steps back."

Taz remained where he was. Kainen took a breath and blew out. I flinched, throwing up a warding around myself as the glittering black dust clouded around Taz's face.

"There's a bull behind you," Kainen said.

Taz twisted. "No, there isn't."

The dust dissipated with a click of Kainen's fingers.

"Looks like it's worked to me," he said.

I ignored the hint of glumness in his voice, more unnerved

by the idea of having to bestow the same gift on the others by kissing them. Everyone dipped their heads one by one, until only Harvey was left at the end.

He leaned close to my ear, ignoring me tensing, and whispered loud enough for everyone to hear.

"You can't somehow gift me Beryl's undying love and loyalty, can you?"

I snorted, amused to see Beryl go bright red. It seemed Harvey was literally the only thing that could ruffle her that badly.

"I can't," I admitted, not sure if I actually could or not but knowing it wouldn't be right. "Something to do with free will and all that. I can gift you with the ability to serenade her if you like, but she might kill me."

I ignored Beryl staring daggers at me, gave him his imperviousness and turned to Queenie.

"Satisfied?" I asked, my tone cutting.

She gave me a similar look in reply over the top of her magazine.

"Delirious. Keep me updated with your plans."

I wanted to say something equally dismissive, but I was tired and hungry and fed up with having to deal with people.

"I'll send word around when we have a plan," I told the others. "For now, I'm starving and beyond done."

Taz grabbed my hand and dragged me out of the office, all but sprinting down to the lift without waiting for anyone else. He bundled me into it, ignoring the disgruntled grumbling of the others trailing behind us, and slammed the grill shut. The moment the lift was on its way downwards, he turned me to face him, catching my hands in his.

"Your bravery astounds me sometimes," he said with a glimmer of amusement.

"Don't mock me," I grumbled.

"I'm not. I just find it bewitching. How Beryl didn't strangle you, I have no idea."

I snorted. "Oh, that. He's the only one who can get to her, so I figure she would have put him out of his misery if she really wasn't interested."

"Yeah, and his singing is awful. I wouldn't inflict that on anyone. So, tomorrow we have to plan."

I nodded. "But not tonight."

"*Demolition Ducks* on the orb with midnight snacks? I'll go down and get the snacks."

"Perfect." I grinned at him. "Sometimes, and I say this sparingly, you're actually not half bad as a boyfriend."

CHAPTER TEN
A Less Than Cheery Reunion

I paced up and down the top floor of the library the next afternoon, my brain firing as Taz shot suggestions at me from his slumped position in one of the armchairs.

"Let's go over it one more time," I said, ignoring his loud groan. "We know the Forgotten are likely already at the Selessium foundry, or close, thanks to Governor Alcarten. To find it, we need the location from some Netheren Brethren, and be prepared to make sacrifices."

Taz scoffed. "Nether Brethren. They're the ones who manage the nether we realm-skip through, part of the Nether court."

"Do you have any familial contacts that might help?"

"Nobody that would want to help us, asking them would just slow us down. But I'll ask Queenie to put out a call to our FDPs to see if any of them can call in a favour or similar."

I folded my arms as I stormed back and forth. This assignment had to go perfectly, had to be planned with meticulous detail. I needed to be sure we weren't walking into any traps or dangers we couldn't handle, especially if I was taking everyone else with me.

"Once we have the location of the foundry, we'll need to go and barter for the Selessium," I muttered. "We have no idea what they'll ask us to sacrifice if it truly is based on weighing a person's merits. Then, how heavy is Selessium? How much do we need to bring back?"

Milo lifted his head from behind a mammoth pile of ancient

textbooks. He was slowing us down by insisting none of us 'cloven-hoof-handed idiots' sullied the delicate pages, but I couldn't huff at him when he was the only one coming up with helpful, albeit small, bits of information.

"I'm making notes," he said, as if the massive roll of paper next to him wasn't obvious. "That huge vase we saw at the Queen's court will contain them, but we'll need enough Selessium to trap each essence, so fourteen vials."

I bit my lip, remembering the size of the vials at the Court of Illusions.

That at least sounds carriable.

"I could try asking Marthe to see if there's anything useful in the Queen's private library," Taz suggested.

I winced as Milo made a high-pitched noise and started tapping his pen on the table.

"*Private library*," he grumbled under his breath.

I gave Taz a 'really?' look and he grimaced an apology.

"We can't take any chances on being able to steal Elvira's vials this time either," I said. "Or trust that the ones my mother used at my grand awakening haven't been smashed or lost."

I had given Taz an overview of what had happened at the Court of Illusions last night during our *Demolition Ducks* marathon, and although Ace had told him most of it, being able to unload the experience had given me some small amount of peace.

Taz nodded. "Fourteen it is then. Maybe a few extra, to be safe. But we have to find the way in first."

Footsteps echoed on the stairs, and moments later Ace came up with Kainen of all people behind him. I eyed Ace's expression, trying to judge if I needed to protect myself. While I had gifted the others safety from Kainen's manipulations, there was nobody around to gift me the same luxury.

"I've been doing some social research," Ace said.

He paused long enough to smile at Milo's derisive huff at the mere suggestion that research could be done without books. I half-expected Taz to appear beside me, but one look over my shoulder and I saw he was still in his seat, his shoulders tense and his gaze fixed on Kainen with predatory warning.

He's giving me space, letting me make the moves.

"All avenues led to the same answer," Ace said. "One of Kainen's contacts in the forever mountains is an outcast Nether Brother, and likely the only way we'll be able to get the foundry's location. The Nether court wouldn't give up the information freely, not to us."

I trusted Ace to have extracted proof. His gift at compelling and word-tangling, as well as his affinity at dealing with people, meant he would know exactly how to tell if Kainen was trying to dodge the truth. There was the possibility that things had been omitted of course. Important, potentially dangerous things. But it was the only lead we had. If the remaining essences found their way into the Queen's court, if all fourteen were joined, then we'd failed.

We were all but out of time, with trusting Kainen as our only option. For the first time since Taz's supposed funeral, I looked Kainen in the eyes.

"Explain."

He shuffled sideways until he reached a bookcase to lean back against, keeping himself separate from us. Perhaps it was a childish point to make, but I crossed the floor to Taz's chair and sank onto it next to him. His arm wound around my shoulder, and I glanced at his wrist to make sure the tattoo was still there before facing Kainen again.

"I won't bore you with how I gained the debt," he began. "One of the Nether Brethren was visiting my father's court and

I saved him from making a grave error, but I refused to claim the debt. Then he was caught arranging illegal realm-skipping for Forgotten sympathisers, clearing them out of the Queen's domain, but the debt still stands."

I wondered then if the man he mentioned had realm-skipping abilities like Milo, or if all Nether Brethren had it as part of their courtly powers. Milo might know but I didn't interrupt to ask.

"So, off to the forever mountains he went." Kainen sighed. "I checked with the Queen's court last night, and he is still alive, living on the outskirts at the base of the mountain. If we go and find him, I'll call in the debt and make him tell us where the location is, and how to get inside."

"Is it dangerous?" Taz asked.

Kainen shrugged. "In terms of walking through outcast Fae, as dangerous as anywhere. But, as long as they don't see you as a target, they should leave you alone."

"Will they have any kind of weaponry?" Ace asked. "Are they still allowed their gifts?"

Taz shifted beside me, his hand brushing over my back.

"I know all gifts are rescinded," he said. "Part of my mother's determination to spite every single traitor and any minor indiscretion against our family or her court."

Kainen frowned. "Weapons will likely be anything they've managed to make out of the surroundings. I believe they live in makeshift accommodation with no amenities. It's an ironic justice I guess, that if they don't want to live by the Queen's rule, they can live without the benevolence of her comfort."

I froze but if Taz disagreed he didn't let on. He seemed adamant in his efforts not to get over-protective, which I appreciated.

Ace sighed and rubbed his mouth, looking between Kainen and I.

"I think we need to get some things out in the open, if we're going somewhere that isn't safe," he said. "We need to talk honestly about what happened at the Court of Illusions."

I froze. Taz's hand stiffened against my shoulder blades, but he didn't step in to answer for me like I thought he would.

"*We* don't need to talk," I said, folding my arms. "But maybe he does."

Kainen lifted his head, meeting my gaze. I ignored the uneasiness as those dark grey depths searched my face and waited for him to answer.

"It was a condition of my clemency after the battle," he said. "To swear allegiance. There are parts I can't discuss on the Queen's orders, but the whole time you were at my court, I was trying to keep you safe."

I couldn't look at him for any length of time without remembering, so I stared at the floor instead. Taz grumbled softly beside me when his mother was mentioned, but didn't interrupt.

Kainen raked his hands through his hair with a sigh.

"I was out of my depth. The Queen insisted I keep the Forgotten on-side and host their guests. She didn't tell me any more than that. When I hired Reyan's protection, she said I should insist on you."

I could imagine that. The Queen, no doubt worried about how close Taz and I were getting, saw a perfect opportunity to both separate us and use us at the same time for her own ends, even to the point of faking her own son's death to draw the Apocalyptians out.

"I couldn't exactly refuse." Kainen pulled a face. "Then when Elvira found out you were there, she was furious at first but soon started scheming. I told you my father had made vows to the Forgotten that the court couldn't get free of, so when she told me what to do, I couldn't disobey her either."

None of this makes up for what he did to me.

Taz's hand started rubbing comforting circles over my shoulders, as if he knew.

"I did try to give you the chance to get out," Kainen said. "I left the library by the back exit to show you there was another way. Then before I know it, you've captured two Apocalyptians, drawn the rest to you, manipulated me into the hardest piece of Fae magic I've ever had to do to lift the orb-block for a mere few moments, and tried to take on Elvira."

Taz snorted then. When I turned my head, he was staring back at me with a small smile on his lips.

"You never do anything in moderation, do you?" he asked.

I almost smiled back, almost, but I knew Kainen needed to finish his side of the story. I'd never trust him again, never feel safe around him, but if we needed him as part of the wider plan, I might have to at least acknowledge him. I faced him again, managing to look at his face without feeling queasy.

"Then they started torturing you." He shook his head, mouth twisted. "Fury seemed to like you, and she wanted me to make most of your torture an illusion. I tried to sprinkle in signs without it being obvious, little things to say it wasn't real, but I couldn't be too obvious about it."

I had seen those, although I didn't know that he was doing it on purpose. Even so, my instincts fought the pity threatening to well up.

"But Elvira had told me not to let you escape," he continued. "So I couldn't even smuggle you out without consequences for the whole court. I did try to give you something to hang onto though."

I frowned. "You did?"

"Of course. I told you I'd made sure Diana was okay didn't

I? I don't know if you were aware enough by that point to remember. Perhaps not."

He fell silent as I bit my lip.

Did he say that? I vaguely remembered him saying something about Diana, and hating him for it. *Why on earth would he think that'd comfort me?*

"So?"

He grimaced. "I thought telling you that would reassure you that Arcanium were aware of what was going on, that I'd been able to get a message out and they'd be coming. You only had to hold on until they did."

"It's not the greatest reassurance though is it?" I mumbled. "She hates me."

Taz sighed. "It was her that came to tell us. Even if she was bound by that 'never able to hurt you' thing I tricked her into during the last battle, she was the one who told Queenie that the Apocalyptians were gathering and you were being tortured."

Kainen sighed. "I couldn't take away the pain when Fury tormented you either, but I tried to make it as pain-free as I could get away with."

I knew he couldn't lie to me and even the anguish in his tone sounded genuine. He cast his gaze down at his boots, his expression resigned.

"I know I'm not going to be anyone's friend, but after the fight, my court is in tatters. Elvira and the others have fled and broken ties with us, which is a start, but-"

"You were speaking to Emil that day." I said, my voice hard.

He nodded. "They've left my court because it's not considered safe anymore. I don't know where they've gone, but Emil sends me the odd instruction. I then secretly relay them to the Queen, or her guards at least."

I eyed the white star on his wrist, but there was no sign of betrayal, no hint of it turning red. Taz sat up straighter, his mouth set in a hard line.

"Well this is all very touching," he said. "But you'll never get close enough to her to do anything again, good or bad, so your sudden 'good guy' act is irrelevant. What's the plan, Dem?"

I gave him a weary look, but at least he wasn't throwing some kind of possessive tantrum. Perhaps he knew as well as I did that we needed Kainen for the next part of our assignment, and prolonging it by talking was pointless.

"With the number of us involved…" I hesitated, thinking. "Trevor will take the five of us in to a safe space nearby wherever this person is. Kainen will claim the debt and keep it quick. Then we come back here to reassess."

Taz's arm tightened around my shoulders. "Now?"

I nodded. "Unless anyone has anywhere else to be."

Everyone shook their heads. I guess, even if they did have somewhere else to be, saving the fate of Faerie trumped whatever it was.

I slid my hand into Taz's as we walked down the stairs to the main floor of the library. He curled his fingers around mine and squeezed, reassuring. Even when we got into the lift and shot upwards to the despatch platform, he guided me to stand in front of him, with Milo and Ace forming a wall to block Kainen behind them in the confined space.

I stepped out onto the despatch walkway and saw Trevor already waiting for us.

"I had an inkling," he grinned. "We can wait for the wide-seater, or you can fit three in the back or front."

"I'll sit up front with Taz and Demi," Ace offered immediately.

I eyed Taz then, hesitant to have to ask again. Even in the

forever mountains, he would be a walking target as he was.

He gave me a devilish grin as his features rippled and his disguise from yesterday reappeared, straight black hair hanging over his forehead and bright violet eyes.

As he slid into the rickshaw beside me, his lips brushed my ear before the others could join us.

"Anyone would think you wanted me to make this permanent the way you keep staring," he murmured. "Something you want to tell me?"

I blinked back at him, feigning innocence. "Ask Milo."

That wiped the silly smirk off his face fast, the confusion enough to make me smile. He always complained about having to sit through Milo and I talking on and on about books and book boyfriends, so he wouldn't have any idea what I meant.

"Okay Trevor, we need to go to the forever mountains to find someone," I said. "Need to land a discreet but reachable distance, the man's name is..." I glanced over my shoulder, realising I had no idea who we were even going to meet.

"Marten Hemlock," Kainen said.

I froze. "You never mentioned he was a relation of yours."

"You never asked."

Fair point, but still.

With trepidation thundering through me, I faced the front.

"Right then, somewhere discreet as close to this Marten Hemlock as you can get us."

Trevor nodded. "Hold tight!"

I'd forgotten to give him the addition that I wanted a smooth landing and clenched my eyes shut as Trevor launched at the despatch wall, but I needn't have worried. The air brushed my face and moments later we glided to an effortless halt.

I opened my eyes and my heart sank at the sight.

"It looks just like Alcarten," Milo beat me to it.

The forever mountains were shrouded in night-time darkness, lit only by the flicker of fires nearby. We were on a slope behind a cluster of towering rocks, but I could see a makeshift camp further down below providing the firelight. All around us, the land was desolate, barren without a sign of vegetation in sight.

The others clambered out of the rickshaw, but I caught Trevor's eye first.

"We may need a quick getaway if this goes wrong."

He nodded. "No problem, call and I'll be there."

I joined the others and watched Trevor vanish, taking that split second to steel my intentions. The others were impervious to Kainen, even if he did try to double-cross us. As Taz clasped my hand, I let that be my safety line. Even if Kainen tried to twist my mind, the others would know.

Taz's lips twitched. "I have the realm's strongest warding up, don't worry. You do what you need to do, and ask what you need to. I'll keep you safe."

I smiled at him, grateful and reassured. Of course he would have been protecting us from the off.

Something I probably should have done. I shook my negative thoughts off. *I have to be strong now, organised.*

Kainen led the way down the slope toward the camp. Thick fabric had been woven from what looked like a mixture of hide and old clothing, enough to make tents. Some were larger than others, but all had the same awful stench radiating around them.

"No plumbing, no heating, no sewage run-off." Taz shook his head. "This is how my mother punishes people for their crimes against her. Some will be here because of mere sleights against the family."

I frowned. "Can she call people back though? Is she physically able or is it bound up in Faerie law?"

"Oh, she can summon anyone she wants and pardon them anytime, but to my knowledge she never has unless it's useful to her somehow. Never let it be said that Faerie royalty isn't vengeful."

I shuddered. "Would you keep things this way, if you were forced to be king I mean?"

Taz's eyes flashed electric blue in the firelit dark, his mouth twisting with distaste.

"The process of banishment? Yes. This barren squalor? No."

I eyed Kainen as he strode ahead of us. He'd been part of the Forgotten, but the Queen had offered him a chance to beg forgiveness, to repent and join her cause. She'd offered Kainen that choice and he'd taken it. Given the sight around us, I could see why.

Faces peered out of tent openings at us and other people stared openly as we walked through the camp. I didn't dare ask if Kainen knew where he was going, but his pace never faltered.

When he stopped a minute or so later beside one of the tents and tapped his hand on the filthy canvas, I prepared myself to take control. Ace and Milo were close enough to realm-skip out together, as were Taz and I. But Kainen stood on his own as a gaunt young man emerged from the tent.

The man only looked in his mid-twenties, with dark hair and a similar build to Kainen. But where Kainen's hair and clothes were washed, this man had no sense of cleanliness about him at all, his shoulders slumped and his clothes ragged with holes.

He eyed us, a thorough once-over, before letting his narrowed gaze settle on Kainen.

He's already working out what use we might be to him.

"Marten, I've come to claim my debt," Kainen said. "You promised to owe me 'anything', which was foolish. Luckily for you, I've been on an emotional growth journey, so the price to be paid shouldn't cost you too much."

Taz snorted at the mention of emotional growth, but nobody paid him any attention.

"What do you want then?" Marten asked.

Kainen folded his arms. "Take a walk with us first of all, to somewhere with less prying eyes and ears."

Marten huffed as if mortally offended. He reached into the tent and re-emerged with a coat that was more air than fabric. I bit my lip, wondering how these Fae survived winters. Did the Queen keep the conditions this hostile by choice, as a punishment? Or had she merely forgotten this place, an irksome fly batting around in her memory that she swatted away as a duty and nothing more.

What about fairies? If they're banished here, I'd hate to think what these outcast Fae would do to those with part-human blood.

We followed Marten and Kainen back the way we'd come through the camp, the others looming around tents to watch, their eyes hungry for something, anything to break the monotony of their banishment. Keeping my glances lightning quick, I could see some with injuries and others so cowed that they didn't even dare to look.

The moment we were away from the tents, far enough not to be heard but still in view of anyone who might try to approach, Kainen faced his relative.

"I'll be quick, let you get back to whatever delights you were enjoying," Kainen said.

I winced. *Petty, even for him.*

Marten only shrugged as Kainen's expression hardened.

"Tell us where the entrance to the Selessium foundry is. We know it's here, but where is the entrance?"

Marten's eyes widened a small amount. He eyed all of us,

but Kainen gathered darkness around him and clicked his fingers with a sharp *snap*.

"The entrance is at the very top of the mountain," Marten said. "Between two blue stones."

Kainen nodded. "Are there any specific ways of getting in, wards, enchantments?"

"No, no wards or enchantments."

Marten was doing his best to avoid giving us literally anything other than what Kainen asked him. As Fae he couldn't lie, but no doubt he was determined to make this as difficult for us as he possibly could.

I glanced at Ace, who nodded.

"Is there anything that would stop us getting in?" Kainen pressed.

"There are three guards on the gate. To enter, you choose between a riddle, a gift fight or a physical fight. If you win, you're allowed to enter."

He'd probably intended to say something unhelpful like 'there are many things to stop you getting in', but a quick look at Ace suggested there were compulsions now at work. I could almost see the threads of the conversation weaving, leaving errant strands untouched.

"Will winning once allow a whole group to go in," I asked. "Or is it one guard for one person's entry?"

Marten turned his head in my direction. Eyed me up and down.

"Fairy scum."

He winced a moment later, his head bowing as his eyes flicked up to Kainen. His lips receded into a sickening grin.

"Protective, are you? Of a fairy, oh dear. The family would be horrified."

He winced again, ducking as though an invisible force was

pressing his head and shoulders toward the ground. I had no idea what Kainen was doing to him, but apparently it was something.

Taz stiffened beside me but didn't make any attempt to intervene. My energy gift woke, but although I kept my connection ready, I pushed the energy back down.

I could show what I can do in the only language Marten probably understands, but I'm not going to be the one to cause him pain.

"Answer her truthfully," Kainen spat.

Marten grimaced. "One win for an entry, for a group or a person it doesn't matter. But whoever defeats the guard must be the one to be weighed for the Selessium. That alone decides how much they will let you trade for."

Silence descended as I sought frantically for anything we might have missed.

"How do we get to the entrance, exactly?" I asked.

Again, Marten gave me a filthy look.

"You walk up." He flinched. "Ouch! Okay, fine. That ravine path over there leads to the entrance. It's the only route, and if you take any other, or try to find a shortcut or way in by air or by realm-skipping, the entrance conceals itself. Many have gone mad or died of starvation trying to find the way in."

I frowned. "Straight up that path? Are there deflections or ways the path tries to mislead us?"

"No." Marten's sickening grin returned. "But there might well be monsters."

CHAPTER ELEVEN
The One Where Taz Gets Possessive and May Have Been Reading Too Many Romances

Monsters. Terrific.

I forced my face to remain neutral, knowing that Marten's gaze was hanging on me for some sign that he'd gotten to me. He had, but I wouldn't give him the satisfaction of knowing it.

"Very well." I shrugged. "Then we have the answers we need. Back the way we came."

I didn't want to risk anyone trying to jump in the rickshaw with us, or seeing Milo and Taz able to realm-skip us. Taz might be safe with his glamour, but it would make Milo too much of a target if anyone else happened to pass through here looking for information.

"That's it?" Marten's eyes flickered. "You don't want to know what else I can tell you?"

Kainen folded his arms. "You can't tell me anything after rotting in here, surely?"

"But what about the people who came here just two days ago, looking for exactly the same thing as you? Old friends of ours, no less."

Kainen cast a lightning quick look at me, and Marten started a breathless laughing.

"Oh, even taking orders from the animals now, that's-"

He crumpled to his knees without warning, clutching his head. I had no idea what horrors were lurking inside there, but I could guess by Kainen's narrowed eyes that he was wielding them.

"I'm not bothered about his not-so-sunny moralities," I barked at him. "If he knows something useful to us about the Forgotten, get the information and let's go."

Kainen seemed to be ignoring me or beyond hearing, his face pinched and swirling dark with vicious malice. Taz's hand slithered from mine, his wing brushing my shoulder a moment later.

"Is this the plan?" I raised my voice. "Make another show of everything and stall us until your real friends get here?"

Kainen froze. His eyes widened slightly as Marten slumped to the ground. When he met my gaze, the sheer pain in the dark depths hit me like a brick to the face. He looked down at Marten again, his jaw clenched.

"Answer her, or I'll leave remnants of that Yuletide memory in your head forever."

Marten shuddered, not bothering to lift his head from the ground.

"The future Queen and her advisor found me two days ago. They asked for the same information as you and ventured up the path yesterday. She was going on about a final six, and something about missing anger, or something."

Fury. Fury's gone missing.

I clenched my fists, willing the swelling volatility gift she'd given me back down before my eyes began to burn red again. Even the mention of her name, what she'd done to Taz, what she'd almost taken from me…

Taz's arm landed around my waist, clutching me tight.

"And we're done," he growled. "Kainen, finish your little reunion."

"Gladly."

Kainen turned on his heel and strode off toward the rocks we'd landed behind without a backwards glance. Marten didn't dare even look up as we followed, leaving him on the ground.

"You okay?" Taz asked, his voice gruff.

I nodded. "Fine, why, aren't you?"

I expected some kind of mocking comment or a laugh, but he didn't say a word. The moment we got behind the rock, his arm left my shoulders.

Bemused, I grabbed my orb.

"Trevor, we're ready to return to hub now."

The air shivered and Trevor materialised in front of us with his rickshaw.

"Barely any time at all," he said with a grin.

I couldn't tell if he was trying to wade past our sour and worried faces, or if he just didn't care enough to tone his cheerfulness down. Either way, compared to him Taz was scowling so deep he looked like the devil incarnate.

As we realm-skipped back to Arcanium's despatch platform, I let my mind dwell on what Marten had told us.

If Elvira is already up there, she's probably got a plan in mind. Either she's coerced or convinced them to empty their Selessium supplies into her care, or she's still attempting it.

I climbed out of the rickshaw and said an absent-minded thank you to Trevor as the others made mumbled excuses to escape. They fled so fast that I was left behind with Taz to take the next lift. As we stepped inside, he removed his glamour and became himself again, the scowl remaining on his face as I sank into my worries.

Would someone like Elvira weigh worthy of any Selessium? I wondered. *And would Fae guardians of such a treasure consider traditional Fae values worthier than kindness and morality?*

Taz jabbed a button but I didn't notice which one as the lift shot downwards.

How can I ask anyone else to bear the weighing or having to fight the guards? Which guard do I choose? Riddles aren't exactly my speciality, but fighting with gifts or in combat against an actual Fae guard will be beyond tough.

I scoffed at myself as the lift came to a stop on the residents' floor.

Queen's champion indeed.

Only when Taz wrenched the grill open with enough force to almost lift it clean off its hinges did I take any notice of him. He stormed toward my room without waiting for me, and I couldn't exactly do anything other than follow him considering I'd hoped for a few hours rest and thinking time in bed.

I closed my bedroom door behind me, pressed my back against it and folded my arms.

"Okay, what's wrong with you?"

Taz turned to face me, eyes ablaze with frustration.

"What do you mean what's wrong with me? I'm trying, orbs alive, I'm trying to be supportive and "chill" and all that, then he looks at you like he's *in love* with you."

He stormed toward me, hands slamming against the door either side of my head. Perhaps it should have unnerved me, this sudden fiery rage, but it was Taz. Even if I tore out his fingers one by one, he'd never retaliate, wouldn't ever hurt me. He was the one thing I could be sure of.

"So?"

He glared down at me. "I don't like it."

I stared back up at him, refusing to give a single inch.

"So?"

"Dem, come on. It's difficult for me to be near him without punching him. I'm trying to be the bigger person, to rein in whatever possessive madness this is, but it's frustrating and hard- and don't you *dare* say 'so' again."

I couldn't stop myself smiling then, amused warmth rippling through me. I traced my fingertip over the curve of his top lip. I remembered how unsettled I'd felt the night I first kissed him then saw him whispering with Diana. Even though it had been innocent, on his side at least, the mere sight of it had hurt me. I could only imagine what Taz was feeling now.

"I've got your artwork on me, remember?" I told him. "I'm not interested in him, never have been."

Taz shook his head, his expression still twisted.

"It's not you I'm worried about. None of this sudden change of heart he's having is because he's actually changed. He's doing it for you. Don't you understand, it's always been about you. If he could manipulate you back beside him, he wouldn't hesitate."

I hadn't allowed myself to consider that, not until now.

The pain in his eyes was because I taunted him, because it was me doubting him. No doubt Taz is right, but is it okay to let Kainen continue helping us if he's not doing it for the right reasons?

No doubt that was why Queenie had forced him on us, because she figured the only trigger for Kainen's recent good behaviour was apparently me and we needed his contacts and owed debts. She'd have no qualms using him, but did that make it okay if he was technically using us for his own gain too, even if that gain was supposed to be me?

Taz sighed, catching my attention as his anger ebbed. His hands were still pinned to the door either side of my head, but I didn't move, letting him work it all out.

"He looks at you, and I want to gouge his eyes out," he admitted. "He speaks to you and I want to cut out his tongue. I wish he never existed."

I couldn't hide my smile. "And yet you're the one that keeps

talking about him. Are you hiding a secret crush in there somew-
"

Taz growled and kissed me before I could finish the sentence. I slid my hands around the back of his neck, happily sinking against him. He groaned as his arms slipped down and folded behind my back, but a tiny warning bell tinkled inside my head.

If I don't stop now, I won't stop.

I had to plan the next step of the assignment, had to figure out our best chances. I made a mental note to detangle myself from him after one more minute but he beat me to it, pulling away with a disgruntled huff.

"Sorry, I know I'm being an idiot," he muttered.

I pecked a kiss on the tip of his nose. "Yeah, but you're my idiot."

That swept any remnant of moodiness right off his face so fast it startled me.

"Alright, wicked one." He grinned. "We'll accept I'm doing my best for the moment and leave it be. What now then?"

I pressed my tongue between my teeth, knowing the first thing that was likely to come leaping out of my mouth right now was "more of that".

"We know what we have to do next. Go to the foundry, I pick a guard and get weighed and-"

"Whoa, hold on." Taz pushed against the door and held up his hands between us. "Why are you automatically going to put yourself up?"

I stared back at him. "Because it's my assignment."

He folded his arms, the scowl back on his face.

"So that automatically means you get to do everything? What if someone else was better suited to going up against the guards huh? Or being weighed?"

I blinked, swayed by his vehemence. "I don't want anyone suffering just because I get given something to do."

Taz gripped both sides of his head, fingers snarling in his hair.

"People are volunteering to join you. Let them help. Choose based on the end result, how best to achieve the assignment, not just doing it all yourself. A good FDP puts their ego aside."

"You think this is about my *ego*?" I gasped.

He eyed me then, hesitation scrawled across his face. He dropped his hands to his sides and took a breath.

"No, I don't, but you're so determined to do everything on your own. It stopped being your assignment when you put a team together."

I wanted to ask how he knew so much, considering he'd never had an assignment of his own, but it seemed too cruel a taunt. He surprised me as a smirk flickered at the corner of his mouth.

"Go on," he said. "What were you thinking, right then?"

I shrugged, tilting my head away, but he pressed a knuckle under my chin and lifted it until my eyes met his.

"What were you going to say then, before you stopped yourself?" he asked.

"You've never had an assignment, so how would you know."

The words came out as a whisper and I stared into his turquoise eyes, expecting a flash of hurt, or for him to shutter himself to me completely.

Taz smiled wider.

"Good. Those are the kind of questions you *should* be asking. You try to do everything yourself to keep people safe, but also because you don't feel like you can bear the responsibility of relying on them, or owing them. You're too scared to trust anyone."

My insides spiralled downwards, sinking like a cannon ball.

Is that true? I couldn't trust my sisters, or people at school. People at fairy class were always distant. Even since I've been here, I've had Diana at my back and Fae like Kainen trying to trick me. I couldn't even trust Taz when I thought he'd used me with his mother.

"Before everything that happened, you were all sparky and defensive," he continued. "You put me in my place, Ace too. You refused to back down when I was a pain to you. I don't want you to lose that. I don't want to see you distance yourself, fade away, take everything on your shoulders just to shut us all up safe in here like it's a pretty glass box."

I blinked at him, amazed. "I would never-"

"Not yet maybe." He brushed my hair back with gentle fingertips. "But you're going to. You'll start thinking you can't tell us things because it would upset us, or it's too dangerous, or you should go and do stuff by yourself. Then, you'll start thinking you're better off alone and push us away."

"Is this about before, when I went to Xavio's?" I asked, my voice a harsh whisper.

Taz nodded. "That, and I can see you thinking things through instead of talking it out with us like you used to. You used to babble everything, and now I can see you withdrawing about serious stuff. I will concede to putting up with the Dimwit of Darkness, and I'll back off when you tell me you need to manage stuff on your own. I know you're strong. But trust goes both ways."

I hate it when he's right. I sagged, my chin weighty against his hand. *We'd spend hours talking things through before everything that happened at Kainen's court, and we'd decide these things together. Hell, apart from Taz, everyone else is a year older than I am already.*

"The others will expect me to be in charge," I mumbled.

Taz smiled and I saw the weight tumble from his shoulders too, relief that I wasn't using this as an excuse to push him away again.

"And you will," he said. "But you'll lead by trusting us and including us on all of it, not just the bits you need done. You didn't even include the sisters or Hutch and Harvey in anything you've done today, but they're meant to be part of the team." He sighed, fingers wrapping in stray curls near my face. "I don't like having to say stuff like this. I'm not good at it."

I frowned. "You're better than you think you are."

"I don't want to hurt you by saying stuff, but I'm not going to wrap you in a bubble either. I'm worried you're not facing what's happened, just trying to bulldoze away from it."

Again, hate it when he's right.

I let my head fall back against the door with a soft thud.

"I am facing it in my own way. But you're right, I've been internalising stuff I should be sharing and it's not fair on everyone else in the team."

He smiled. "They'll live."

"Okay, if you promise to try and not panic about *other people*, I'll practice trusting again and blabbing everything I'm thinking. Deal?"

"Nope." He shook his head with a lazy grin. "If we're going to this foundry tomorrow, then tonight you need to promise me one more thing."

I raised my eyebrows at that.

"Promise? That sounds serious."

He chuckled. "It is. You have to promise me that you'll relax tonight. Properly throw off all the crud we've dealt with lately and enjoy yourself. There's meant to be a revel tonight, with a skip-way to a location outside of Arcanium. We should go."

The guilt plagued me even though I pasted on a smile for his benefit.

I pushed Taz away without even giving him a chance to explain, even after I thought he was dead. What kind of girlfriend does that?

"Yeah, sounds good."

I eyed my wardrobe, guessing I would need something other than jeans and a hoodie or cardigan for a proper revel. Before I could stress about my lack of revel clothing, Taz turned my head back to face him with a knowing look.

"You're thinking again."

I pulled a face. "You'd rather I skipped around with nothing between my ears at all?"

"No, but you can talk to me instead. There's still stuff bugging you and I'd rather know what it is. Go on, practice."

I took a deep breath. *He asked for it.*

"I'm worried about everything you said, and how it's true, and how I didn't even give you a chance to explain before flitting off to Xavio's, and that you said you forgave me but you're still bringing it up."

His expression gave nothing away. "Fair enough. What else?"

I stared at him for a long moment, wondering how much I could get through before the revel began. Knowing this might be make or break, I let the rest spew out.

"I'm petrified something's going to happen to you again. I'm worried that I'm making all the wrong decisions. I'm worried this stupid volatility thing will hurt someone if I lose control of myself, or if I get really angry. I'm the only one Kainen can still manipulate, while the rest of you are immune now."

I took a huge breath, but his face told me nothing about what he was thinking.

"We've never even talked properly about what happened back then," I continued, my voice cracking. "We have about the enemy and what happened to me, but not about what I did or what he did to me, and how real it all was, and how I still feel awful that it happened, because I should have been smarter, better somehow. *I should have been able to tell.*"

The tears exploded out of my eyes like a waterfall, my skin beginning to tingle with a mix of chills and the heat of my connection waking inside me. Taz set his hands on my shoulders, thumbs stroking my soaked cheeks.

"You need to be able to let all this out, Dem. It's not good to bottle it up. But I want you to tell me all this stuff because you trust me enough to tell me, not because I make you."

I sniffed. "So if I think you're being an arse, you want me to tell you?"

"Yes! Shout at me, shove me if you have to, but don't keep sinking into yourself. I can't bear it."

I stared up at the slightly blurry vision of him, his eyes blue with concern and his mouth pinned on one side as he watched me.

He wants to share all of it, not just the decisions or the practical stuff. The horrible things that are destroying me, he wants to share them, like I would do for him in a heartbeat.

"I get it now."

He peered at my face. "Promise?"

"Promise, my mind is an open book to you."

"Only if you want it to be." He let out a tumbling sigh. "I want you to *want* to tell me stuff, because you're not afraid of how it'll go down, or how I'll react. But if you don't want to divulge stuff, that's a different matter. You don't have to tell me anything if you don't want to."

I wiped my face quickly with my sleeve and managed a

weary smile.

"Okay, but a girl has to retain some mystery."

His smile all but lit up the room. "Oh, trust me, the girl side of things will always be completely baffling to me. Like, why does Petra put that pencil stuff on her eyebrows? What's the point? What does it actually *do*?"

I snorted as he kissed my forehead and mumbled about changing for the revel. As I watched him disappear through the doorway, leaving my bedroom door open behind him, I steeled myself.

I can do this.

CHAPTER TWELVE
A Brief Revel amid the War

Someone, I had no idea who, had taken the liberty of retrieving my dresses that I'd worn at the Court of Illusions. I let my fingers drift down the rich purple cotton of the strapless one, my insides chilling.

I'd worn it on the first night there, before Kainen had been pretending to be Taz. I didn't dare look at the more risqué see-through one I'd worn on that night. If someone had bothered rescuing that one, they might have even sewn up the gash over the stomach portion, but I didn't want to see it.

Both had golden acorns and oak leaves stitched on. Purple and gold, the Queen's court colours. Except I had no idea if any of that was true.

This is what Kainen's trickery has cost me, whether he was forced into it or not.

That was how Petra found me a few minutes later.

"We're all dressing up in full fare tonight," she said, startling me. "I can lend you something if you need an outfit, but perhaps you should wear one of those again. Make a statement and scare away the ghosts."

I bit my lip. "Isn't that like social death or something to wear the same thing twice?"

"Absolutely not. They're only dresses and they cost me a fortune." She held up a hand, pre-empting the opening of my mouth. "Don't start offering to pay me for them either. Most of the girls here only have one or two dresses for this kind of thing."

I pulled the first dress out as she left again. It was elaborate but the skirts were forgiving with a slit up one side, good for dancing without being weighed down or hemmed in. The top half was somewhat revealing, but after all the horrors the idea of scaring away the mental ghosts did have a certain poignant strength to it.

I shimmied into the dress and tugged at my hair, trying to get the dark mess into some kind of order. By the time I'd wiped some basic make-up over my face and slid my feet into the purple ballet-style slippers, the dress didn't feel so daunting any longer.

With my door open, I could hear the comforting sounds of others getting ready. People ran into each other's rooms to swap items or shouted jokes to each other. I would have put money on the chorus of wolf-whistling coming from one of the Hutchinson brothers.

By the time Taz appeared, I was standing in my doorway soaking in the atmosphere.

Dressed in finery of his own, he looked exactly like I imagined a prince of Faerie should. Dark purple trousers complimented a matching waistcoat threaded with golden acorns, his white linen shirt open at the neck and his worn black boots looking like they'd been expertly shined. I wanted to ask him if he'd sent them off to Marthe, but the thought of the Queen's court would only mar the occasion. It seemed unfair that we were revelling while others were suffering, but I had promised him this one night stress-free.

Then Taz stopped a few feet away. Blinked. His throat bobbed and paranoia crept through me.

I'd never had the conversation with him that I remembered, about how these were his court colours. It had all been part of Kainen's trickery so he might see my wearing them as a statement.

"It's the only one I had," I explained. "After… you know. Petra said…"

He shook his head as if to cast off a thought, his eyes flicking up and down once more.

"Do you know what these colours mean?" he asked.

"I was told they were court colours." I conveniently left out the specifics, hoping he'd fill them.

He nodded. "Yeah, they're mine. I know Petra wanted to make a statement while you were there, but don't feel you have to do the same now."

"You'd rather I didn't?"

He grimaced. "No, that's not what I meant at all. I don't want you to feel pressured or anything though. The whole social protocol thing is a pain, and you shouldn't feel obligated-"

"It's a dress, not an engagement ring or a handfasting ribbon, calm down."

I folded my arms and glowered back at him. Even as his lips twitched, I was fighting a smile of my own. Arguing about dresses was the exact frivolous nonsense both of us needed.

Taz extended his elbow and I slid my hand underneath it, pressing my cheek to his shoulder briefly as we started down the hall.

We passed the sound of Beryl Eastwick yelling, either at Harvey or her sisters, I couldn't tell. Something came flying out of what I thought was Petra's room as Taz hurried me onwards.

"Where's this mysterious skip-way then?" I asked as we waited for the lift.

"In the canteen, believe it or not."

Taz pulled the grill aside as the lift arrived, guiding me inside. The moment it was shut and the lift shot downwards, he tweaked a stray curl of hair away from my ear.

"I didn't tell you how amazing you look, because I was too busy paying attention to it."

I flushed at that. "It's just a dress."

"It's not the dress, but you're clearly overwhelmed by the sheer power of my ability to compliment you, so I shall desist."

His grinning face and sparkling turquoise eyes never looked more Fae than they did in that moment as his freckles darkened in the half-light of the lift. I shoved my hand against his shoulder, smiling when he caught it in his fingers.

"Idiot. You're very Fae when you want to be, aren't you."

"Don't insult me like that!" He gasped, even as his face softened. "It's everything to see you smile properly again."

I would have found something witty to say in reply, eventually, but the lift stopped and we stepped into the canteen.

It looked much the same, the Braunees at work behind the buffet counter and the rows of wooden tables with benches in the usual rows, except for a wooden archway painted white and decorated with green boughs and branches, all tied with golden ribbon.

Taz held out an arm toward the archway, his lips curving up as he aimed for a low bow.

"My lady."

I merely rolled my eyes and dragged him forward by the hand. Despite the brief brush of air across my face as we crossed through the skip-way, I didn't bother to close my eyes against it, too absorbed in what lay on the other side.

It was like a scene from *Midsummer Night's Dream*, a forest under a dusky purple sky, the sensation of warmth and golden firelight curling around us. Down a short slope cut between the trees was a glen with enough space for dancing on the grass and tables set out for food and drink.

A fragrant evening scent filled the air, jasmine possibly, but then Taz and I were merging with the crowd already assembled.

Wild strings and the beat of drums filled the air, the sound of flutes dancing over the melody with lively precision.

"You've been to a formal dance at the Queen's court and a party at Arcanium," Taz said with a smile. "But this is a true Faerie revel, where we can dance until dawn and go get lost in the woods if we desire."

I grinned. "Maybe you'd get lost."

"That sounds like a challenge."

"Maybe. Is this a special festival of some kind then?"

He nodded. "The wheel of the year is tilting. Humans call it Midsummer, but we see it as the marking of an older time where the Oak King would give way to the Holly King."

I remembered that from Xavio's incessant training. The Oak King rose and ruled the summer half of the year, the time of light, and the Holly King ruled the darkness of winter.

"So, the fact your family has links to oak things is relevant?" I asked. "Like your court colours always have acorns on?"

Taz nodded. "You could say my sisters and I are the last link in the family chain of the oak lineage, but there's not been any ruler crowned with holly for longer than anyone can remember. These days, Faerie is everything elemental and my mother is just a regent."

"I wouldn't say it like that to her maybe."

"I did wonder if the enemy were trying to become the holly line," he admitted. "But when I asked my mother said if that lineage has died out, which apparently it has, only the nether can crown a new line."

I frowned. "Which I'm guessing would have happened by now if it was going to."

"Or the nether is waiting for the right person," he teased. "I reckon I would look great in green and red."

"Oh sure, now that you've abdicated your princedom the nether is going to snap you up to make your own royal dynasty."

He laughed and bowed low again, his hand held out as if he could chase away every worry and upcoming situation facing us with one night of mischief.

"You never know, but for tonight we're just us. Dance with me?"

I nodded, taking his hand. I doubted I could refuse him anything.

We danced together for a while, spinning like sycamores with our hands linked as we whirled in and out of other dancers.

We leapt about as a group with the others, although we stopped for a while to get a drink and watch the showdown that was Beryl and Harvey fighting over the correct terminology of their relationship status.

Ace was sulking because Milo had brought a book with him after promising not to.

The night wore on but the crowd continued as if we could chase away the dawn forever. Aching all over from dancing so much, Taz and I found a quiet tree to sit against, him with his back against the trunk and me with my back against his chest. I let my head drop against his shoulder, exhausted.

"You're comfy," I mumbled, my eyes closing.

Taz's laughter filled my head. "I've been called worse. Sleep, my wicked princess, and we'll meet our new dawn together."

More Faerie nonsense. I grinned.

I must have spoken the words out loud in my half-slumbering state, as his voice echoed right back to me.

Only the best for you.

The words danced in my head, slaying any approaching nightmares, until I woke with a start to gentle morning light.

The comforting anchor around my waist tightened and I remembered where I was. My cheeks burned as I peered through the trees, noticing the glen was now deserted.

"Taz, wake up."

I tried to sit forward but he had his arms firm around me so I couldn't do much more than wriggle a bit.

"It's okay," he said, his voice lazy with sleep. "They'll know where we are."

"They'll assume… you know."

He snorted right in my ear. "It's not like we did anything unsavoury, Sparky. Come on then. You hungry?"

I nodded, easing my creaky joints forward as he let me go. A blanket made completely from actual leaves lay across my lap, and I smiled at the thought of Taz magicking up a blanket for us. I started folding it until I saw him frowning.

"Where did that come from?" he asked.

I shrugged. "I don't know. I thought you'd summoned it or something."

He shook his head, so I left the blanket folded at the base of the tree for its owner to reclaim it. We walked through the trees hand in hand, silent but for the sound of birds tweeting.

As I glanced back at the glen, I noticed the blanket had vanished.

Good thing we didn't do anything unsavoury, I realised. *No doubt Old Tara is keeping an eye on us anywhere nature has roots.*

I didn't mention this to Taz, knowing he was still huffy about finding out that one of his parents was essentially Faerie itself. That and I was too busy soaking in the quiet to ruin it with words that didn't change anything.

Even the canteen was deserted as we stepped through the skip-way.

Taz frowned. "The Braunees aren't even on the go yet. Crud. Back to bed then for a while."

I flushed at that but there was nobody around to hear him. I half-expected someone to jump out and start raging at us to ask where we'd been or what we'd been doing, but nobody did.

As we took the lift up to the residents' floor, Taz sighed.

"No doubt we'll be back in the mayhem soon enough," he said. "Until then, we're going to do whatever we want."

"And what is it you want to do?" I raised my eyebrows at him.

He raised his in reply. "Honestly? Food. Then nap. Then more food."

"Human world might be open," I suggested. "But that involves effort."

"Yeah! The café will be open. Let's do that."

I smiled to see him so gleeful about something so simple. He often forgot the human world was just a lift ride away, even though he was obsessed with human sweets since I introduced him to a few different kinds.

"I need to change then first. But you're not going to try and pay for everything with piles of 5ps again though, are you?" I teased.

"Come on, I only did that once!"

We opened the lift's grill and stepped out, only to find Ace waiting for us. Given the serious look on his face, we weren't going to make the café after all.

CHAPTER THIRTEEN
A Game Plan is Made

Ace gave me a well-known grimace which said everything I needed to hear.

"News, Queenie or time to go?" I asked.

"News from Queenie, so time to go," he said. "The court is barely holding, so Queenie has summoned all the FDPs and allies she can, but if we're going to get the Selessium it needs to be now."

I took a deep breath and tipped my head back, finding Taz's shoulder ready behind me.

"Right, fetch everyone to the library. We need about twenty minutes to assess and sort out safety plans, then once we're ready we'll realm-skip in."

Ace hurried past us into the lift we'd just exited, and I stood to watch it go, soaking up the last quiet moments.

"No nap, or café," Taz said with a sigh. "Come on, quick change, update Petra and off we go."

I followed him to the end of the hall, turning left to my room while he went right to his. Wishing I had time to shower, I yanked on fresh clothes and hung the dress back in my clothing unit. Leo poked his head out of his quiet box, perhaps sensing the emergence of my satchel as I slung it over my head.

I bit my lip. *If I take him, it'll be dangerous.*

Leo gave me a dismissive look and flicked his tail. Before I could make up my mind, he was on the floor and trying to climb up my jeans.

That's answered that then.

I helped him into the satchel, still amazed to see his body shrink to fit inside.

"No heroics or anything though, okay?" I muttered.

I threw in a bunch of salad to keep him occupied, attached my orb to my jeans and opened my bedroom door to find Taz waiting right outside.

"Ready, princess?" he asked. "Got your orb?"

I nodded and locked my door behind me. "Orb, Leo, a packet of Jelly Babies just in case you get hangry-"

"I do not get hangry!"

Even as he was protesting, he caught my hand with a smile and led me back toward the lift. These moments were so precious, even ahead of potential danger. I leaned against his shoulder as we stepped into the waiting lift, and he closed the grill while I pressed the button for the library.

"Here we go again." I sighed. "I reckon once we get to the top of the forever mountains, if we get to the top, we see if the guards will elaborate before we choose who to put forward. I'm not ruling myself out, but if it's a riddle Milo might be best. Also, do you reckon they weigh you based on your merits or your Fae qualities? I probably wouldn't be the best choice if we're going based on Fae."

Taz's eyes lit up, his lips curving.

"There you are, welcome back." He tucked me against his side as the lift shot upwards. "Milo will likely know already, but if he doesn't then we'll ask when we get there."

"If we get there."

He tweaked my nose, grinning wider as I growled at him.

"*When.* Have faith, princess."

I pulled the grill open and we walked across the deserted library to find Milo waiting at the main desk for us. I eyed the oval orb-reader in his hands, feigning horror.

"An orb-reader Milo? Surely not!"

He scowled at me. "Ace refused to carry two rucksacks, and I had to bring all the data somehow."

I let that slide, knowing Ace would be suffering his grave error for hours to come.

"Do we know anything about the actual entry trial, the guards or what we're weighed for yet?" I asked.

Milo nodded, his irritation fading instantly. "We do actually. The entrance is at the top of the mountain between two blue stones. The guard tests are purely for entry and there are three guards to choose from, so if you choose combat for example it's to disarm only. Once a person has tried they can't try again, but someone else can."

"That'll give us a few shots at least," I said, relieved.

"Also, the weighing is apparently based on your dedication to Faerie. You're all FDPs, so I imagine any of you will be weighted quite highly."

I grimaced. "Sounds almost too easy to be accurate. What of the supposed monsters on the route up?"

Milo shook his head, peering past us as the others piled out of the lift.

"No luck there on information about any monsters, but there's safety in numbers."

I wondered if he was saying that more to reassure me or himself. Taz squeezed my waist as everyone came to a stop in front of us, Kainen standing slightly apart from the others.

"Right, what's the plan?" Beryl asked.

I let their expectant faces wash over me. I could do this. I'd done it before, and I had Taz beside me.

"We're going to get something called Selessium, it's a rare material that we need to trap Apocalyptians." I hesitated.

I have no idea how much they even know about everything.

"Long story short for those that aren't aware," I continued. "Apocalyptians are very powerful essences. Imagine if you were overpowered by Sloth and you couldn't get yourself out of bed, kind of thing."

"That's Harvey on a normal day then," Hutch quipped.

Laughter rippled around the group and I found a kernel of courage in it.

"He can go first then. So, these essences need trapping. You were all at the Queen's court when they attacked and six escaped. Before we can capture them and seal the lot, we need to get something to trap them with. That's where the Selessium comes in."

I started pacing, moving away from Taz's arm although I could sense his eyes tracking me back and forth, no doubt monitoring Kainen's attention on me as well.

"To get the Selessium, we need to walk up a long path through the forever mountains. It probably won't be safe. We need to stay in assigned groups at all times. Beryl, I'm giving Trevor to you for this journey. If we need to escape, Taz, Milo, Ace and I can likely sort ourselves out, but you're in charge of calling Trevor and getting everyone else out to safety, okay?"

She blinked, a momentary second of surprise that I was nominating her. But she covered it well by giving Harvey a death-glare, as if daring him to say something funny before she nodded at me.

"Stick in groups of three or four," I continued. "But ideally we move as one big group. Nobody's to be left stranded. There's no telling how long it'll take to walk, and apparently due to Fae trickery we have to start at the bottom or we won't find it at all."

"Climb hostile mountain, check," Harvey said.

I duly moved on. "Assuming we reach the top of the mountain and find the entrance between two blue stones, we'll come up against three guards. To gain entrance to the foundry where Selessium is mined, we need to pick one of the guards to beat."

"Either at a riddle, gift trickery or straight combat," Milo added.

"How serious are we talking?" Cheryl asked.

"Milo's reassured me it'll be to disarm only, but we need to be careful until we know what their abilities are. Once we're inside, whoever bested the guard will be weighed on their devotion to Faerie. That apparently defines how much Selessium we get."

"Your dedication to Faerie," Milo corrected.

I frowned. "What's the difference?"

"Devotion doesn't necessarily mean you've done something about it. Dedication would imply effort."

"That'll be Demi then," Meryl piped up. "Nobody's given more to Faerie than she has."

I eyed Taz, who sat uncharacteristically silent. He smiled at me but continued saying nothing. I wondered when the right time to give him an earful would be, considering if he wanted me to talk to him about everything, he could bloody well do the same and pitch in a bit.

"We'll see what happens when we get there," I finished. "There are no guarantees but I doubt we'll be able to spare time to ping in and out as we like. So if anyone wants to back out, now would be the time."

Everyone shook their heads. I'd been carefully not looking at Kainen, but I forced myself to flick the quickest of looks at him. He met my gaze and then looked pointedly at Taz instead.

"I don't suppose there's any way of going in sneaky-like?" Hutch asked.

I shook my head. "Not that we know of."

Meryl raised her arms above her head with a groan.

"When do we leave?" she asked.

"The time is strange in the forever mountains," Milo piped up. "Permanent night-time at the base of the mountain, middle of the day at the top."

I nodded. "At least we can use that for navigation then, although the instruction is 'go straight'."

I held in the urge to sigh. It was likely to be a long assignment with no idea how long we'd be climbing the mountain for. I had no idea if it would get increasingly steeper like a normal mountain, or if any of us were fit enough to climb actual rocks. But there wasn't much more we could do by debating it.

Before I could suggest we get moving, Kainen cleared his throat.

"I know none of you want me along and I get that. I won't get in the way and I won't make any trouble, but if you'll allow it, Demi, I can give you a wayfinder."

I frowned, reluctant to admit my ignorance in front of everyone.

"Wayfinders are rare," Taz grunted. "How did you come by one?"

Kainen shrugged. "My father was a collector of sorts. Demi can have it, and then you'll know there's no trickery on my part. It'll answer only to her or whoever she gives it to once it's changed owners."

Taz opened his mouth, presumably to argue, but I gave him a look and he closed it again.

"What's the cost?" I asked, facing Kainen with my arms folded.

Again, that flash of pain in his eyes.

"No cost, just a gift. I think after everything it's the least I owe you."

I could only imagine what Taz would say to that. I could almost hear his mind thundering with thoughts of how this was some ploy to get me back on side, to manipulate me into feeling something for the pitiful creature Kainen was now painting himself as.

"It would take too long to bring here, surely?" I countered.

Kainen clicked his fingers, summoning the glittering black smoke. I flinched and cast a protection warding. He noticed the flinch, although he wouldn't be able to see my warding unless I included him inside it, and his eyes narrowed.

"I need the wayfinder on my office desk," he said into the smoke, his tone sharp and commanding.

Moments later a hand appeared holding a small, many-pointed metal star balanced on top of a spindle. Kainen took it, but I had a wholly different thought in mind now as he vanished the black smoke.

"Can you use that ability to realm-skip?" I asked.

He shook his head. "No, but I can summon members of my court if needed. It's draining though unless I'm inside the court boundaries so I would probably only be able to manage one or two people."

I bit my lip. "If we needed someone to spy for us, be a lookout in the shadows, you could bring someone extra to us?"

"You're thinking of Reyan?" he asked. "I can if you need me to."

"Not right now, but good to know if the need arises."

I wouldn't bring any potential debt or service from him onto my head unless it was absolutely necessary. He held out the spindled silver star to me.

"It's yours."

I didn't step forward to take it, an idea forming as I glanced around the assembled group instead.

"Right, last thing before we leave," I announced. "I need to know who'll be willing to face the guards and possibly go through the weighing. We've all fought in our own ways. There was also mention of needing to make a sacrifice, so we have to bear that in mind while not knowing what it might be."

All hands went up, Milo's slightly after everyone else's. I understood his fear of facing the weighing and knew how deep the scars on his fragile self-esteem ran. He covered it with irritability and his books, but I knew he saw himself as next to useless. I faced the group, my mind made up.

"We need to think about defending ourselves as much as getting inside the place. Whoever takes the wayfinder may need to guide everyone back out, and they can't do that if they're also running the guard weighing gauntlet. Milo, are you okay to take that on?"

He blinked up at me. "The weighing?"

His hefty shoulders started shaking and my heart went out to him.

"No, the wayfinding. Make sure everyone gets up and down the mountain safe, no matter who ends up going in."

He gave me a look of pure relief and nodded. "Of course."

I bit down the smile as he hurried across to take the wayfinder from Kainen.

"Right, let's go cause some mayhem."

Everyone set off toward the lift, but I stayed still a second or two until Taz was walking beside me.

"Well, I did all the talking," I retorted. "I didn't hold anything back."

He smiled. "Nicely done, princess, and I didn't punch anyone."

"Look at us, being all grown-up and stuff."

The others took the lift in two groups, but they couldn't

exactly realm-skip without us, so I lingered a moment longer before we got into the lift.

"Whatever happens, we do it together, okay?" I said.

Taz hustled me into the lift, shut the grill and pressed the button for despatch. The moment we were on our way upwards, he hugged me tight.

"Together. Remember, anchoring makes us stronger so you don't do any of this alone. You're stuck with me to the bitter end."

I pulled back. "Good to know. Is there also like a word for getting rid of you to the bitter end?"

The words danced out of my mouth without any intervention from my brain. In the pause that followed, my heart almost died a death at how callous that sounded after I thought I'd lost him.

Thoughtless, insensitive IDIOT.

Then Taz started laughing. Loudly, the rumbles bouncing off the brickwork outside the cage of the lift.

"Ah, my wicked princess, I knew I'd get you back to your charming self somehow."

He leaned close to my ear as the lift came to a stop and he slid the grill open.

The suggested word he whispered to me sent a wholly natural fire over my face, leaving me stunned into mortified silence.

Taz fled out of the lift and along the walkway to join the others before I could find any suitable response or fitting retaliation. As I followed him, I vowed then and there we would survive this next ordeal, if only so I could make him regret what he'd just said.

<h1 style="text-align:center"><u>CHAPTER FOURTEEN</u>
<u>A Brush With Some Old Friends and Demi</u>
<u>Nearly Loses Her Cool</u></h1>

Trevor used the wide-carrier to skip us to the base of the forever mountains which were shrouded in gloomy darkness. Only the fires burning in the camp below gave us any light to see the ravine path by.

As Trevor disappeared, everyone huddled close.

"Okay, we stay in groups and close together," I whispered. "Milo, you ready to lead the way?"

He nodded. "I've researched wayfinders before so I know how to work it."

"Then keep your eyes and ears sharp, and off we go."

I merged my warding with Taz's, keeping it close around us as we followed Milo and Ace toward the rocky slope that led upwards.

Even though everyone was stepping light, the muffled shuffle and crunch of boots drove my anxiety up to unbearable heights. Each knocked pebble could be a monster lurking in the shadows, or the enemy lying in wait to ambush us.

"We haven't hit a single turn or curve yet," Taz muttered.

I'd noticed that, but hoped the others hadn't.

"Part of the trickery and misdirection of keeping the foundry hidden no doubt."

Up ahead, Milo seemed to be twisting his body ever so slightly left or right, but the path remained dead straight ahead.

"What was that?" Beryl hissed.

Milo came to a halt, the rest of us bunching up behind him. I

149

couldn't see anything in the dark, but self-preservation surfaced.

"Form a circle, backs inward," I said. "Hands and wardings together."

Everyone obeyed, taking the hand of the person next to them and merging their protection.

Silence fell.

Are we overreacting? We can't keep moving like this either way. Maybe it was a mistake to bring so many-

A snarl tore the air around us, followed by several identical rumblings from all directions.

I risked letting go of Milo's hand and lifted my arm, pulling my connection taut inside me and letting my energy gift flare. It flickered on the surface of my hand, giving just enough white-blue glow to light the area around us.

"Oh, that is not good," Taz said. "What the hell are they even doing here?"

I counted eight scaly creatures, lizards on four legs crouched low to the ground but as far from Leo as a reptile could get.

"Oricadae," Milo whispered. "That is definitely not good."

I gasped as my satchel wriggled. Before I could free my hand from Taz's grip or quash my gift, the flap flew open. Leo exploded out of the satchel, his body expanding as he hit the ground.

With a feral hiss, he wheeled around and darted past us, now large and hefty enough to shake the rockfaces either side of us.

"Leo, be careful!" I shouted.

He either ignored me or didn't hear, opening his mouth wide to let out a bellowing roar as two of the Oricadae charged him from either side. I tore my hand from Taz's, determined to go and help Leo, but there were still six beasts approaching our group to hem us against the rock.

I sent a shot of energy at the nearest one's scaly leg, wincing as it whined in agony.

"We can't just kill them off," I insisted.

Several of the group shot incredulous looks at me.

"What do we do instead then?" Beryl asked. "Sing them a lullaby?"

"Can't you do your voice thing again?" Cheryl added. "Like you did that first time we were up against these?"

I frowned. "I could, but it probably wouldn't summon anything useful here."

I turned my back to the advancing Oricadae and took a deep breath. Pushing the sound out as strong and loud as I could, I made an imitation of a mongoose giggling noise.

"Do it again! They froze."

I closed my eyes and sent the noise out a second time, doing my best to split the various notes so that it sounded like the giggling was coming from all directions.

"It's not working," Ace shouted.

I rotated back round to find the Oricadae had all but penned us in, Leo still using his tail and his size to keep the two attacking him at bay.

My chest squeezed tight as one caught his shoulder with their claws.

What's the use of being gifted if we can't even defend ourselves without hurting them?

None of us had thought to bring any weapons either, although we'd all been training with blades and self-defence.

I *hadn't thought.*

"Would they see through a glamour?" I asked.

"Most likely." Taz caught my eye.

I think we both had the same idea at the same time. I shook my head, even as he grinned at me.

"Taz, don't even think-"

Before I could finish my sentence, Taz disappeared. In his place, was a short furry animal. I'd forgotten about his transference gift, that he could change into an animal.

I stared as the mongoose winked at me. Then a real chattering noise filled the air.

Even the Oricadae attacking Leo halted, and he took the opportunity to slam one into the rock with a lash of his tail.

I turned my head away so the animals couldn't see and filled the air with a reply to Taz's noise. The chattering echoed through the ravine like a hundred mongoose were racing closer. I could barely breathe, but I kept pushing the sound out, one eye on Taz as he darted toward the beasts.

"What the hell is going on?" Hutch shouted.

Milo gasped. "That's so clever! Oricadae are made from old magic and snake bones. No doubt the whole mongoose vs. snake thing is drawing their instincts."

I ignored that, my chest crunching like a grape underfoot as Taz streaked away back down the ravine path with the Oricadae thundering after him.

"No!" I screamed after him. "He doesn't have a wayfinder, he'll get lost!"

I struggled to go after him, even though I had no strength against Ace and Milo both holding me back. My anger spiked but neither of them let go despite the seething sounds they were both making.

I lifted my hand higher, fighting against Ace's hold on my upper arm as I tried to use my gift to see where Taz had gone. For all the meagre rays of light my gift could give me, he could have been crushed by the charging pack for all I knew.

"Dem, come on." Ace slid into big brother mode. "Taz gave us a shot at getting this done, and he's not stupid. He won't have left you unless he had a plan."

I bit my lip, the throbbing pain giving me a constant to focus on. I knew Ace was right, but my insides were making me sick with worry.

He'd want me to trust him.

I took a ragged breath as Leo ambled up to me. His side was scratched, but as he shrank down to normal Leo size, the wounds shrank too. I picked him up with careful hands and opened the satchel flap for him to wriggle back inside.

"Okay. We go on. But after we do this, I'm going to look for him."

Ace nodded. "*We* are going to look for him. Come on. Quicker we get this done, quicker we find him."

I pushed my feet forward, one after the other.

Ace has to be right. Taz will have a plan. He might get lost, but he's smart. He'll change himself into a fly or something small enough hide in the rocks.

We walked on and I tried to keep myself calm. The others were still looking to me to manage the assignment and my emotions flaring up wouldn't do us any good.

I almost missed the sound of flapping above us, but Ace and Milo twisted either side of me and the group formed a circle looking up. Hands gripped mine and our wardings knitted around us as something dark flew over us and landed some metres ahead.

"Oh thank Faerie," I muttered, charging forward.

Taz furled his wings, a broad smile on his face. He slid an arm around my shoulders, lips brushing my ear.

"Good to see you trusted me enough to go on without me," he said.

I frowned. "I almost didn't. How did you get away?"

"I turned myself into a fly and hid behind a rock until they'd gone past. I could still see you up ahead but I stayed as a fly for a bit in case."

Great minds think alike. Or does anchoring extend to minds as well as hearts?

I couldn't help grinning as the others reached us, but I tried to look at least a little bit like I was in control of myself.

"On we go."

We moved as before, Ace and Milo taking the lead with the rest of us in clusters behind. I couldn't hear any sounds of returning beasties but couldn't stop thinking about them either.

"If Oricadae are a banned species in Faerie, why are they here?" I murmured.

Taz's expression darkened. "Because clearly the rules of Faerie don't apply to the Queen. I had no idea she was using them here. It's still part of her domain, her prison for her enemies."

"Maybe the Oricadae are here because they're being punished too?"

"I doubt it. The power of this place lies in people fearing its mere existence and a lot of animals won't understand that kind of punishment. Also, most Fae aren't able to get here like we can so nobody would know she's using banned species for her own ends. Most people can't realm-skip wherever they want like we do."

I tried to imagine it, a whole host of Fae living where they were born, or travelling through Faerie using designated skip-ways like humans might use a train.

"So this is literally a dumping ground for anything that doesn't get killed off?"

Taz nodded. "By the looks of it. I feel awful because I never even considered what happened after people were cast out. They just disappeared to the forever mountains and I figured it was like a Fae equivalent of those prison shows humans watch, with someone managing it. How naïve of me to assume my mother had any humanity."

I snorted. "She's a Fae Queen, so humanity isn't exactly in her job description."

We continued on in silence for a long time after that, until dim grey light began to tinge the tops of the cliffs towering either side of us. By the time it grew into full daylight, the air growing warm although the sky stayed white above, my legs were aching and I'd given up wiping my sweating brow.

We might be doing this for days. I need to consider if we send someone back for more supplies, but then splitting up would be dangerous with the Oricadae still roaming.

"Look!" Milo pointed up ahead.

I breathed a huge sigh of relief to see two tall blue stones flanking a dark gap in the rock ahead. I recognised that blue, deep and veined with flecks of silver and gold like sunlight on water.

I couldn't see any sign of life at first, but as we approached three guards appeared to block the way. I'd expected something that looked more like a fantasy realm for some reason, at least the guards being cloaked or veiled. Instead, they were exactly like us, wearing either jeans or chinos, one in a sweatshirt, another wearing a hoodie while the third, slightly shorter than the other two, wore a plain black t-shirt.

"What brings you here?" The shorter one asked.

The others looked to me. I cleared my throat.

"We need to get some Selessium."

All three guards eyed the group, assessing us, but it was the shorter one who spoke again.

"To pass through the entrance, you need to earn the right to enter."

As he hesitated, I ploughed straight in.

"We've done our research, so we know we have to defeat one of you in either a riddle, a gift fight or a straight combat fight, is that right?"

The guard blinked at me as the pause between us lengthened.

"Yes. Choose one of us and we will begin."

I frowned. "But which of you is which?"

The guard exchanged a knowing smile with his companions, and splayed his hands out wide to me.

"That is up to you to decide. Pick one of us and you will see which test you are to earn."

I tried to see if there was anything that might give away who might do which task, a sign of battle-worn hands, or a sense of confidence that tended to come with being strongly gifted among Fae. I couldn't dredge a single hint from the stance of their bodies or their expressions.

"I'll go for it if you want, Demi," Harvey offered. "I'm not sure how much I'll weigh, but I'll give it a go."

This could work to our advantage. Even if Hutch doesn't get through, we'll know what skill at least one of the guards has.

"If one of us fails, do we get to try again?" I asked.

The guard nodded. "Those who fail cannot, but those who have yet to try can step forward to face us. Once one of you has succeeded, all may enter, but only the successor may be weighed."

I wrapped my fingers around the back of my neck and turned to Harvey.

"Good luck."

He grinned and strode up to the shortest guard. It took all my effort not to suggest to him that if this was purely to impress Beryl, it was unlikely to work given the disapproval on her face.

"What's the test then?" he asked.

The other two guards stepped back as Harvey faced his

opponent.

"A riddle."

Harvey groaned loudly and despite the situation, I had to snuffle a laugh behind my hand.

"Go on then." He gave me a wry grimace over his shoulder. "Apologies in advance everyone."

The guard rubbed his chin and eyed Harvey up and down, a small smile flickering over his face.

"When does today come before yesterday?" he asked.

Harvey stood silence for a long moment, his face scrunching.

"I can't ask for help I'm guessing," he confirmed. The guard shook his head. "And I'm guessing I can't take all day about it."

The guard shrugged. "We have all day, but it appears that you may not."

Harvey gave me a rueful grimace but I was already puzzling over the clues and keywords of the riddle. Beside me, I could almost see Milo's brain on fire as he blistered through the potential answers.

When does today come before yesterday?

I raced through the possibilities. Not in any kind of linear calendar. Perhaps in memory, or forethought, or worrying about the future.

But riddles were usually practical. I ruled out some kind of booking schedule or diary, and I couldn't remember any famous motivational speeches about putting today before yesterday or the present before the past.

Taz rolled his eyes as I started tapping my thumb over my fingers. Beside me, Milo was mouthing words with an agonised expression on his face.

Practical, practical, practical. The word danced in my head.

Words. Order. Order of words. Alphabet. T before Y.

I gasped as Milo's head shot up. He looked at me and I

nodded, unable to avoid a smile breaking over my face at the sheer relief on his.

I bit my lip, aware that Harvey didn't seem to be any closer to the answer as he muttered under his breath.

If he doesn't get this, I can volunteer to go up against the same guard next.

My legs ached from walking half the night, and I could feel my stomach threatening to revolt from hunger and the meagre offering of a cereal bar and apple, but I tried to keep a patient expression on my face as Harvey looked back in anguish.

"I'm sorry," he groaned. "It's hopeless. My brain just doesn't do well with these sorts of things. I was hoping for combat to tell the truth."

I smiled as he stepped away from the guard, his head hung low.

"No matter, even Milo couldn't have worked that one out easily," I offered.

I'd said it to be kind, but I wasn't far off. As Harvey passed me, I noticed Beryl give him a less violent than usual poke in the arm.

"If we get another riddle, will it be the same one?" I asked.

The guard shook his head.

"No, do you want the answer?"

I waved a hand at Milo who was fidgeting from foot to foot, almost exploding with the desire to answer it.

"It's the dictionary!"

The guard nodded. "Right, but no entry I'm afraid."

"I'll go next then if nobody else wants a go," I said, looking at Taz.

He grinned at me and caught the guard's eye.

"Can two compete together?" he asked.

I hadn't thought of that.

The guard shrugged. "If you feel it's necessary."

Taz curled his fingers around mine with a mischievous look.

Together? I could almost hear his voice in my head, as if he was beaming a telepathic message right into my mind.

I nodded a reply. *Together.*

"We'll give the riddle a go then," I said.

The guard faced us. "You choose to go up against me?"

Something didn't feel right, perhaps the amusement dancing in his deep blue eyes, or the devious quirk of his mouth.

"Er, yeah."

He smiled wide. "Very well. Gift combat it is."

CHAPTER FIFTEEN
Wassailing is a One Time Thing

"Wait." Taz held up a hand. "You can't just change your skill, can you?"

The guard laughed. "Of course we can. Perhaps something you should have ascertained before approaching us. Unless you wish to concede without trial?"

I shook my head. We'd come this far, and between us Taz and I had a fair few gifts we could wield.

"We'll try our luck," I said, aware I was making the man sound like a fairground attraction.

He didn't seem to mind, rolling up his sleeves.

"Very well. Trial by gift combat takes many forms. Either first to best the other's protection, or first to disarm or incapacitate. But today, I think I will go for gift combat with natural gifts only."

I bit my lip. "Sorry, I have no idea what you're talking about."

"It's fairly simple. No Faerie gifts, only natural talent. If you tell jokes, you need to make me laugh. If you dance or sing, you need to leave me in awe. Wow me."

I sagged. Looked at Taz, who shrugged.

"Do you have any talents?" I asked glumly.

"Nope." He eyed the guard. "Does sending a person absolutely raving mad count? She's good at that."

The guard laughed but didn't answer. We'd come this far, escaped a whole pack of Oricadae, only to be hampered by who we were. I couldn't think of a single story to tell, or a single thing I could do without some use of my gifts.

I could tell him about my childhood with my sisters, see if it makes him cry, but I doubt it.

I gulped, my throat still sore from the mongoose noises and screaming after Taz. I froze.

Maybe...

"What about abilities you were born with?" I asked. "Do they still count as gifts?"

The guard tilted his head to one side. "If you were born with a skill, it is yours, not a gift given."

"Okay." I bit my lip, glancing at Taz. "Can you sing?"

He wanted to do this together, his hand still an iron grip around mine. I could do imitations, but if he wanted to be weighed with me, he'd have to add something.

"I don't scare people out of the bathroom or anything," he said with a frown.

I took a deep breath, knowing this was either going to be a triumph or a total disaster.

"Okay, try to keep up then, because I know you'll know this one."

I launched into the *Demolition Ducks* theme tune without waiting for him, splitting my voice to add in as many sound effects as I could remember.

I almost choked with laughter when I had to make what Taz usually called the 'boinging flipper noises' from the end part, but I managed a passable attempt.

Taz's voice echoing strong and in perfect tune alongside mine was a huge surprise. I'd never thought to ask him if he could sing, although I tended to hum to myself when my mind was elsewhere and often heard him joining in with songs he knew.

When we finished, I'd all but forgotten the guards and the

Selessium, trying hard to look at Taz without bursting into laughter. He pulled me into a one-armed hug, holding me close to him.

"That's a one-time thing," he grumbled with a huge grin. "Don't think you're going to get me going wassailing at the next solstice or anything."

I chuckled and stuck my tongue out at him, pretending I hadn't been thinking of things exactly like that in our near future to annoy him.

"Well, that was… something," the guard said. "Entrance is yours, although I'm not sure what Gladys is going to say about the weight of you two."

A trickle of foreboding chilled my skin, but I refused to pay attention to it. We'd succeeded the first two hurdles and had one more to face. We could do this.

"Thank you." I nodded to the guard and then his companions as we passed.

I took a deep breath as we approached the dark gap in the rock. It was tall, but fairly narrow, so much so that Taz had to walk slightly behind me and keep his hand on my shoulder as we entered.

I blinked as my eyes adjusted to the dim gloom inside, light filtering from holes in the rock and a large firepit in the centre of a large chamber. As we all shuffled inside, a tiny woman with jolly features strode toward us, the air of no-nonsense purpose fluttering around her.

"Well, fresh meat, good." She smiled wide at us. "Who am I weighing."

I lifted my hand even as Taz snatched it in his so I was raising both.

"Us two," he answered for me.

The woman flicked a glance over us, then a slower scan up

and down. After a moment, she clicked with her mouth and frowned, folding her arms.

Uh-oh.

"Barely seems fair," she muttered. "The last person I weighed was so dredged down in hatred that she almost had to owe me by the end, very little which doesn't make for a good sacrifice at all."

I raised my eyebrows. "That'll be Elvira then. Do we sit on one side or is there more to it?"

I trailed off as I got a proper look at the enormous golden scales glinting in the far corner of the room, the huge plates hanging from hefty chains.

When I refocused, Gladys was still giving us the disapproving look.

"I can assess the weight of your dedication," she said. "But you two together, eesh, you're heavy."

I frowned. "Er… thanks?"

She gave us one more glance with a furrowed brow and a quirked lip.

"We will source you Selessium," she said. "We can give you as much as you and your group can carry, but there is still the sacrifice to be made, which needs to be equal to the weight of your dedication. What will you give me?"

I stared at her for a few moments. *How can I possibly answer that correctly?*

"What kind of things do you consider equal to our weight?" I asked. "We can't judge given that we don't know what you consider our weight to be."

The woman only smiled wider.

Fae trickery. I frowned.

Taz had told me I needed to tell everyone everything, so it would be his fault if this lady ended up throwing me out on my ear for what I was about to do next.

"If you're judging the weight of our dedication to Faerie, then we're not talking physical weight, or even a sizeable amount. We could sacrifice a gift, or something meaningful to us to show our ongoing dedication, but the *Selessium* is for Faerie, not for us. I could argue that you should weigh Faerie instead."

I bit my lip, mind teasing out all the potential tangles before I raced on.

"The real question is what is the Selessium worth, and the answer would depend on how badly we need it, or how badly *you* need to be rid of it. Which makes this whole thing a bargain, or a trade, not a sacrifice."

The woman cocked her head, amusement dancing in her eyes. That had to count for something positive so I kept going.

"Selessium is valuable sure, but if you're not able to name your price then all I can offer you is something I've brought with me, and it's not much."

I turned out my pockets, making sure not to unearth my orb in the process. The only thing I had other than a tissue, was a small plastic keychain that Taz had won for me in the arcade a month ago. It had a plastic yellow duck dressed as Darth Vader, and I was actually quite attached to it.

I held it out.

"This is all I've got. Unless you want a pair of socks?" I patted my satchel.

I could hear Taz mumbling to himself, no doubt thinking that I'd finally broken and gone completely bonkers.

Gladys started laughing. I tensed as she ambled toward me, but she merely swiped the keychain from my palm.

She opened her mouth, perhaps to tell me to be serious or get out, in which case I wanted my plastic duck back, but a loud voice drew everyone's attention.

A loud voice I recognised.

Anger flared through me, the swell of Fury's volatility burning behind my eyes in an instant.

"Three bottles!" It was Elvira's voice, shrill and incandescent with rage. "It's not enough. Nowhere close. You need to go and be weighed. We need more than this."

She came into view before I could react, Emil trotting along beside her.

I threw up a protection with Taz alongside me doing the same, our group crowding together until we stood firm under a communal warding.

I hadn't seen Elvira since Fury tortured me. Not since the Court of Illusions, when she had wanted me dead.

"Traitor!" Taz let out a feral roar, his gaze fixed on Emil.

He hadn't seen them properly since the last battle at Arcanium, but Fury's element could feel the hatred rolling off him and leapt to meet it.

"Oh no." Elvira noticed us and shook her head, raising her hand. "I should have expected you lot. Emil, attack them!"

I snorted, because of course she wouldn't do her own dirty work, even though she had her own power. But we'd beaten her before. We would do it again.

Emil glanced over us, assessing. He'd fought Taz last time and come off badly, and I'd inflicted my own punishments as best I could since. But against all of us, our group that had moved to stand together under one combined protection warding, he had no chance and he knew it.

"You will not bring your petty Faerie squabbles into the sanctity of my weighing room."

Gladys' voice boomed through the chamber, rolling off the walls with ominous intent. Elvira narrowed her eyes, her gaze momentarily distracted from us as we faced Emil down.

"When I am Queen, I will pull your little 'weighing room' to the ground," she hissed.

Gladys drew herself up tall, which maybe added an inch onto her short frame. But one look at the disgust in her eyes, the calm, relaxed shoulders, and I knew who I would have put my money on.

"You are not Queen yet, are you?" she taunted. "So until then, take your bottles and leave, or have your minion wait his turn."

Elvira's lips twitched, comebacks swarming like flies.

Gladys didn't as much as flinch a single muscle in preparation for an attack and we stood ready. It was an unfair fight even after our hours of walking, but Elvira didn't seem to notice that she was outnumbered, her arrogance ready to take all of us on regardless.

She raised her hand, her gaze flicking to me. I summoned my energy gift to my fingertips ready to attack. Taz and I had practiced countless times, him with his transmutation to defend, me with my energy to attack. We worked as one unit and I had no fear for the others as they slid themselves into grouped formations as easily as water pours down a windowpane.

I sent a shockwave out as a warning, singeing against their protection, but before I could attack again a loud roar filled the air.

I turned back and forth searching to see what Elvira might have conjured.

"Oh, hell," Taz muttered. "Are those hers or wild ones?"

Six Oricadae filled the archways around us, stalking into place to block us in.

"Keep wardings up, focus on defence," I hollered to the others. Then, because I was me, "but try not to hurt them if you can help it!"

I ignored the disbelieving glares being shot my way as Beryl shot past with Meryl clinging onto her hand and pulled part of the wall free with her gift. The debris shot through a row of shelves which toppled to create a barrier between us and the beasts.

"Get the bottles!" Elvira's scream tore my ears. "Now!"

"Oh no you don't," Taz muttered.

He flicked out a hand and one of the enormous plates of the scale dribbled to liquid brass. It washed down toward its target, splashing over the floor, but Emil leapt out of the way.

If he'd managed to secure himself another *metirin* iron crossbow, then we were in serious trouble.

A part of the broken shelving unit zoomed past my head, Taz anchoring an arm around my middle to pull me back in time.

Elvira lifted a hand, her eyes awash with ire. She swiped her arm sideways and another part of the shelf lifted off the floor.

"Levitation gift," Taz said with a grunt.

He solidified the scale bowl into a misshapen run of metal, using it to further create blockages to the Oricadae. I sent a shot of energy out at Elvira as a large shelf battered against mine and Taz's warding. I winced at the impact, my gaze sliding over someone else's fight.

Nearby and alone, Kainen stood wreathed in shadowed smoke, sending it out to confuse the Oricadae and drive them away from the Eastwick sisters.

"Do something!" Elvira glared him. "You need to be breaking them, not misdirecting them."

He shook his head. "No, I'm sworn to the Queen's court and it overrules the debt my court owes you."

I watched him, my hesitation almost landing us a lethal crack of Emil's gift against our warding. I sent my energy out to meet him with a snarl of retaliation, managing to catch a whip of pain around his ankle so that he dropped to his knees.

Kainen had one hand out now, smoke tendrils flying from his fingers to obscure the Oricadae from seeing their targets.

I noticed Emil crawling away toward a gap in one of the archways, but Elvira sent a loose chain of the scale lashing toward us.

Taz turned it to liquid and I electrified it, sending the charged splatters against her warding instead. She staggered back, arms flailing. In that moment, I wish I'd had time to learn whatever Fae magic Xavio had used before that had turned her briefly into a chicken.

"I've got them!" Emil's shout filled the air.

I knew without looking he meant the vials and sent my energy crackling toward him. In that moment, I didn't care if the vials cracked, only that he didn't get away with any.

Elvira hovered, torn between continuing her vendetta against us and fleeing with the vials.

I eyed Emil's hands and noticed two. Two vials. Unless he had some in his pockets, which might not make any difference given the way Harvey and Hutch were sending a volley fire of random tennis balls at him, they wouldn't get far with two.

He knows they can't win here.

I aimed another shot of energy at him but he was putting all his effort into defending himself and keeping the vials safe now.

In moments, Elvira was across the hall and beside him. They stumbled backward through one of the broken archways, the others surging after them to give chase.

I started forward but a loud voice full of darkness filled the air, dominating the room and possibly the entire mountain.

"You will go no further," Gladys intoned, her eyes roiling purple.

Taz tugged me back away from her as the same purple smoke cloaked her body.

Even as Emil and Elvira turned to run, Gladys raised her arms.

"No mercy," she boomed.

Oricadae twisted in mid-air. The beasts that were still stalking toward our group wriggled in one flip to face Emil and Elvira, who were now dashing out of sight.

Harvey swept Beryl into his arms and leapt to one side as the Oricadae gave chase and almost charged right through her, but for once she didn't even have the presence of mind to berate him about it.

The others clustered together and Taz led me over to them, the warding firming around us as we faced the aftermath.

Given the smoking remnants of the destroyed weighing room, I guessed we weren't going to get away from this unscathed. Even if Elvira started it.

I took another look. The room was ruined. The scales were broken, half of one side melted and re-solidified by Taz.

"The Oricadae are bound to protect the scales," Gladys said, sweeping the remnants of purple away from her body. "They obey me when all is lost."

She didn't seem angry at us which was something, and I knew it wasn't exactly our fault. But as I eyed the scales and the carnage, I couldn't help feeling guilty.

"I'm sorry. Your scales are broken, and we needed the vials to beat her. We *really* need to beat her."

Gladys scoffing and rolling her eyes wasn't exactly the response I expected.

"The scales are a necessary part of the charm," she said. "But they're mostly for decoration."

I stared back at her as she started to smirk.

"Well, we are stuck up a mountain with only ourselves for company. We have to have our fun while we can, don't we? Now, I believe you gave me a keychain and offered me your socks?"

Taz gave me a nudge with his elbow before wrapping a possessive arm around my waist as I ferreted in my satchel for my spare pair of socks.

"I'll ignore the fact these sacrifices are from one of you instead of both of you," Gladys said. "So, for the sacrifice you're making in the name of Faerie, I'll accept your offer." She chortled at the shocked look on our faces. "It's never the sacrifice I ask you to make that stands, it's the one you deem worthy yourself. Not often people understand that, Champion."

I froze at the title but she continued chuckling as she slid the keychain into her cloak.

"The ready Selessium is formed into vials here. Go through that archway there, and you may take as many as you can carry. You'll see the exit on your way through. The Oricadae won't trouble you on the way back down, dears, not after all your hilarious efforts. I'll make sure of it."

"I- thank you!"

The realisation that we'd actually succeeded trickled over me. Gladys laughed.

"It's a long way down though, so do stop at the gift shop on your way out. We've tried advertising on the orb-waves but for some reason, not many people are keen to visit."

I wasn't sure what to say to that, but Taz was grabbing my hand and hauling me after the others before I could think of anything.

"When we get home," he muttered through clenched teeth. "I'm either going to hug you or strangle you."

With the sudden onslaught of elation swooping through me

as I realised we'd done what we came to do, I blew him a kiss.

"How about 'thank you for being so awesome'?" I suggested. "Also, I'd prefer a huge sandwich to the strangulation, with a cherry bubble juice, but I'll take the hug."

He grumbled something under his breath as we hurried through the archway into a long room lined with shelves full of Selessium vials.

We joined the others in grabbing as many vials as we could carry. I estimated we had at least thirty-five as we headed toward the gift shop, if not more.

Hutch and Harvey insisted on buying us all a cherry bubble juice to celebrate, which led to a spirited argument about gender equality between them and the Eastwicks, but Ace quietly paid for everything and we helped him sweep everyone outside. All the while, I couldn't quite stop myself from smiling.

But the night air nipped my cheeks, which didn't seem right considering it had been morning when we entered.

"We probably can't call Trevor here," I said. "So we go back down the mountain. Eyes sharp and we'll need to move fast. Gladys said the Oricadae wouldn't trouble us, but you never know who or what might be lying in wait."

I wouldn't put it past Elvira to do exactly that and try to steal our vials. I shuddered at the thought and eyed the clinking rucksacks the others wore.

"Once we're back home, we can dump the vials with Queenie," Taz added. "Then we're going to sleep for at least an hour before anything more happens."

Harvey let out a raucous cheer but quickly turned it into a hiss when everyone glared at him.

"I can give us some darkness cover if we end up in daylight again," Kainen offered. "It might be enough that we can slip past any enemies undetected, but it won't mask scent or sound, so step light."

We clustered into our groups and set off, Kainen keeping up front with Ace and Milo, Taz and I following a short few paces behind and the others at the back.

I flinched and winced every time I heard the clinking somewhere behind or ahead of me, but I focused on keeping watch while Taz warded us. The moment the firelit shadows of the base encampment tents were visible, I sagged with relief.

"I've never been so glad to see a prison camp in my life," I whispered, then lifted my voice enough to hiss behind. "Beryl, call Trevor."

I heard her whispering his name as Taz leaned closer.

"Whatever happens when we get back, no agreeing to anything until morning," he murmured. "We need sleep."

"And food," I added as my stomach growled its agreement.

Trevor appeared but without the wide-carrier I was expecting. His eyes found mine in the veiled darkness and he grimaced an apology.

"I figured best to come back immediately and do two runs rather than wait around for the big one to be free," he said.

I nodded. "Sensible. Get in everyone, and we'll load the bottles in with you."

Beryl, Cheryl and Meryl got into the back row, with Hutch and Harvey in the front. I handed my bottles to Meryl and the others did the same.

I opened my mouth to tell Trevor to come back for us, but voices floated up from the encampment and they sounded scarily close.

"Go and wait until I call," I hissed to Trevor.

He nodded and I barely saw the rickshaw leave in the dark.

"Behind the rocks," I told the others.

Taz had my hand in his and we moved as quietly as we could.

I had to trust that Ace and Milo were behind us. And Kainen.

As the voices drew closer, I clenched my free hand into a fist. I recognised them and it took all my effort not to send my gift flying straight out to meet them.

Calm it, idiot. If we're sensible, we might be able to overhear something.

Even so, as Elvira and Emil came within earshot, I counted heads just to be sure. Taz, Ace, Milo and Kainen were all crouched behind the rocks with me.

"It's hardly even a contest, my queen." Taz's hand crushed mine as we heard Emil's voice.

A not-so-ladylike snort filled the air. "True. I have been using these mountains as a base, gaining allies and favours for our new world. I have frequented more than one court in recent days, making connections, and we have our base in Egloriem still. While the Queen sits brewing in her palace, I am seen among the people, dealing with them."

I heard the sneer in her tone and took a slow, deep breath to quell the burning anger rising inside me.

"She has a point," Taz muttered.

I glared at him, but wasn't sure he could even see it in the darkness. At the end of our row I could make out by the gloomy firelight that Kainen looked extremely worried.

So he doesn't want to be found by them now. Is he afraid they'll attack him or his court now he's admitted he swore fealty to the Queen?

Or, the more frightening thought struck me, that he'd been given instructions by the Queen and her council all along. I of all people knew how easily the Queen used those around her as pawns to win her war.

He did give us time to run when the Apocalyptians burst into the Court of Illusions, but what if he really is just choosing whichever side suits his own interests? Who would he choose here?

I looked down at my left wrist, marking out the orb tattoo. Kainen could still easily manipulate my mind if he chose to but as long as I had Taz's hand in mine, as long as I trusted him, I would be okay.

"Our plan is almost in place now at least," Emil said. "The six have been caught, all except for Fury, and Sloth has done well to overcome the Queen's court by all accounts. They will be less than useless when we attack tomorrow."

I froze. *Tomorrow? It must be almost midnight by now already.*

I flinched as someone kicked up a stone beside me. I couldn't tell who it was, but the noise bounced out of our hidden gap and across the entrance to the ravine path.

"What was that?" Elvira's voice sharpened. "I heard something."

Emil twisted around, surveying the area. I nudged Milo beside me and nodded to Ace, then Kainen. Milo slid around Ace so that he was hunched between them, ready to realm-skip.

I clutched Taz's hand in mine, knowing he would pull us back to Arcanium before any danger hit. But I wasn't about to let this opportunity go either.

As I nodded, Milo disappeared with Ace and Kainen in tow.

I straightened up, aware of Taz warding us and standing tall beside me, no glamour, wings outstretched. The firelight from the camp caught his fiery feathers, illuminating us.

Elvira's face stretched into a snarl, but it was nothing to the pure, ferocity of the growl that ripped from Taz's throat as Emil summoned his crossbow. I held Elvira's gaze, feeling the waves of hatred flowing off her and sending the same hostile vibes right back.

I smiled and summoned my best sing-song voice.

"I know something you don't know."

Even as Emil levelled the crossbow at us, the ripple of swirling grey nether wrapped around us, and a moment later we were in my bedroom.

"That was rash," Taz grumbled.

He pulled me against him and kissed my forehead, my cheeks, my lips, even my chin as he let out a sigh of relief.

"We need to go and see Queenie," I reminded him after a long, *long* moment of waiting.

"Only sleep and food, you promised," he grumbled, not letting go.

I pulled back and grabbed his hand. "Technically didn't promise. How about this, I'll go see Queenie and you go get the food."

He shook his head.

"Nope, we go together or not at all."

I couldn't exactly argue with that, so I led the way to the lift only to find the others cascading out of it.

"We dropped the bottles off with Queenie," Beryl said, her expression disagreeable. "She wasn't exactly delighted to see us but she said to send you on down."

I wasn't even surprised by that point.

We found Queenie pacing the floor of her office, her scowl not lightening in the slightest as we walked through the open doorway without knocking.

"You've had the vials," I said by way of greeting. "And we overheard Elvira talking to Emil, saying they're attacking the Queen's court tomorrow."

Queenie's eyes widened. I don't think I could ever remember a time I'd seen her surprised before. It didn't make me feel any better seeing it then.

"It'll be tough," she sighed. "But we've got the FDPs marshalled and ready. If they attack tomorrow then so do we."

Taz raised his brow. "Do we have an actual plan?"

"Numbers and confusion are the only defence we have against them now," Queenie said. "We need to be everywhere at once, luring them until they're caught. They're not stupid by any sense but they are driven by their urges."

I forced the memory of Lust and her frequent mentions of urges from my head. I didn't want to see any of them again. Anyone except Fury. We still had a score to settle.

"Then we'll just have to be ready for them somehow," I added glumly.

Queenie flicked a disparaging glance over us then. "Go get some rest while you can. We'll need everyone to go in fresh, including you two. Especially you two."

Taz shook his head. "How do we get in?"

Queenie sank back into her chair, the bored expression drifting across her face, telling us that she was essentially done being social. That sentiment at least I could understand. But it gave me an idea.

I looked at Taz. "Nobody can get into your conservatory without your consent, right? So we realm-skip in there and slip out unnoticed bit by bit. If the place is total mayhem, we may even be able to send someone in unnoticed to scope out the situation, and I think I know who."

Queenie clapped her hands and I jumped. Taz huffed at her, as if my reaction to the noise was her fault.

"Good thinking."

I faced her down. "Thanks. With that in mind, and everything else your family have put us through, you can be the one to organise it. Tell Kainen to summon Reyan from his court, if you'd be so kind. She travels with us tomorrow."

Queenie raised one eyebrow, the rest of her dangerously still. I waited for sarcasm, maybe some shouting or a few non-veiled threats.

"Very well." She nodded. "Go rest both of you. Tomorrow we will have a plan to follow."

Taz looked like he might say something else, tense beside me, but I turned and he followed me without argument. The moment we got into the hall, I started to feel the exhaustion seeping back in.

"I have to say," he said conversationally as we ambled into the lift. "You just had my aunt, of all people, running your errands. Do I need to start bowing or bringing you gifts to appease you?"

I stuck my tongue out at him and pressed the button for the canteen.

"You're ridiculous," I replied, trying not to laugh. "Would you rather I went and asked Kainen to summon Reyan personally?"

He wrinkled his nose at the thought. "No, I would have gone. And maybe managed not to punch him a lot. Your way is better though because now I get to have you all to myself."

I grinned as the lift stopped and I pulled the grill open.

"Well, you might have to share me with half the food in Faerie, but apart from that, I'm all yours."

CHAPTER SIXTEEN
The Fight Beckons

I woke up the next morning with Taz's hand on top of my head. I wriggled downwards to free myself, but he grumbled without opening his eyes and wrapped his arm around my waist instead.

Like it's the most natural thing in the world.

I couldn't help but smile, twisting to try and get comfortable.

"You're very noisy when you're awake," he grumbled.

"I haven't said a word!"

He opened his eyes, staring at me. "You fidget."

"Oh yeah? Well, you snore."

"I do *not*."

"You do, like a walrus."

He winced. "Ouch. Couldn't have at least gone for something powerful like a lion?"

I chuckled at that and stayed still. What with this being completely new to both of us, I wasn't sure what to do without the usual distraction of things exploding or people always hammering on my door because something needed doing.

"Hungry?" Taz asked, stretching his arms up with a loud groan.

I bit my lip. "Yeah."

"Come on then. It's still early but no doubt we'll be in the thick of it soon enough."

I watched him sit up and pull his t-shirt on. I didn't want to get up at all but we'd run out of time.

"Are you taking Leo?" he asked.

I frowned, looking at the deceptively innocent-looking lizard currently snoozing on his back in the Y of two branches.

"I think he'll be safe enough," I decided. "If need be I can leave him in the conservatory to help protect anyone wounded."

Taz held out a hand and dragged me out of bed, hesitating long enough for me to grab fresh clothes and close my bedroom door behind me.

The bathroom was almost deserted, but I washed and dressed with anxiety roiling in my gut. I took my things back to my room, guessing Taz would appear if I didn't go looking for him first.

I busied myself checking Leo's side, the cuts from the Oricadae attack already healing over. When I was certain he wasn't injured, I held my satchel open for him.

"If you need to, I'll have you stay inside the conservatory and you can protect them. Help anyone doing the healing, do heavy lifting, okay?"

I had no idea if he could understand me, but he gave me a dismissive huff and slid into the satchel's main pocket as Taz appeared in the doorway.

"Ready to raise hell?" he asked.

I shrugged. "I tend to think of them as outings with your family now."

"Sounds about right," he said with a loud snort. "We'll both be careful today, extra careful. Not leave each other's side kind of careful."

I looked him in the eye then.

"We'll do what we have to and we both know it. But we're fairies, or Fae in your case. We'll find a way to twist the situation to our advantage."

He smirked as he walked into the room and closed the door behind him. He stopped right in front of me, one hand wiping my hair back from my face as I set the satchel and Leo back on the desk.

"There's my wicked princess, always one step ahead," he said. "No doubt the moment we left her office last night, Queenie was orchestrating some kind of devious plan. We just have to make sure she doesn't trick us into anything we don't agree with. Until then…"

He grinned and flopped onto my bed with his legs stretched out.

I frowned. "That doesn't look like 'raising hell' behaviour."

He lay back, looking perfectly comfortable with his hands held up towards me. I let him drag me down with him, not bothered in the slightest that we apparently weren't going down to breakfast anymore after all. But I couldn't stop the thoughts rioting around in my head, and he'd told me I should tell him everything I was thinking, so I did.

"When we get to your conservatory, do you think there'll be an actual plan?"

"*Our* conservatory," he said. "I want it to be a safe space for you too if you're ever there and I'm not around. Full access, unconditional."

I ignored the idea of gaining something and flicked the tip of his nose with my forefinger.

"You're not going to keep accusing me of nicking your things like usual as well as commandeering your safe spaces?"

"Nope, take all of it, as long as you accept that I come with it."

I sighed. "I guess I'll have to put up with you if I want the fancy conservatory."

"And the clothes. I'm going to run out if you keep wearing all my stuff."

"They're comfy," I protested.

"I think you just want to see me without any on."

My cheeks burned and my mind shot back to the Court of Illusions, recalling the maddening way I'd missed and wanted him over those few days. I shuddered, knowing it had been Kainen glamouring as him all along when I finally got what I wanted, or thought I had.

"Bad thought?" Taz asked, his voice instantly quiet.

I nodded and twisted so that I was lying over his chest, face to face. Whatever happened when we left the room, I didn't want to dwell on old stuff.

I let a fingertip trail from the tip of his nose over his face, his neck, his chest and down.

"Bad memory. But I want to make new ones."

His arm anchored around my waist, but I noticed the hesitant look on his face.

"Are you sure?" His cheeks flushed. "We can take more time. Don't get me wrong, you know I'm mad about you in all the ways, but you have to be ready."

I raised my eyebrows at him. "Scared?"

The taunt woke the dark in his eyes, but he tilted his head as if to acknowledge I might be right.

"There's only ever been you."

I nodded. "Likewise, but if you're worried that you'll suck at it…"

I squeaked as he rolled me in one swift movement, pinning me underneath him with his knees either side of mine.

"Wicked princess," he murmured.

The kiss that followed tasted of pure fire and longing, his mouth determined even as his hands curved around my waist, firm but gentle. His lips moved to my cheek and down.

"Not a princess," I managed to huff out a breathless gasp. "You abdicated."

His head appeared beside mine, his breath hot in my ear.

"I'm still a prince even if I'm not an heir. And we're anchored now, so that makes you a princess by right of Faerie law. *My* princess. Anyone moves against you now, the whole Royal court takes on the insult."

Daunting as that was, I couldn't ignore the sheer fairy temptation to taunt him just a little more.

"If *anyone* moves against me?" I folded my legs behind his back, pinning him tight against me and moving. Just a little. "Including you?"

This time as he claimed me with kisses, none of him was gentle. I might have gone beyond removing my hoodie and his, but a loud, insistent knocking filled the room.

Taz only growled and carried on. I went one further.

"GO AWAY OR ELSE."

"Yeah, sure." On the other side of the door, Ace sounded like he was trying not to pee himself laughing. "The whole war of Faerie is going to wait for you two to finish sexy time. I'm the gentle reminder that there's a meeting in the atrium in five minutes. Next reminder will be Petra and Queenie hauling you out by your feet, with or without clothes."

Taz collapsed on top of me with a frustrated groan, making me giggle.

"Risk it?" I asked, hopeful and in that moment utterly serious.

"Better not." He clambered off the bed and held a hand out to me. "But we're going into a fight, so I want you to promise me we'll resume this later. If you promise me, it has to come true and we'll return safe."

I took his hand and let him pull me to my feet.

"Okay. I promise the moment the battle is over, we'll resume this."

He grinned, his features flashing fully Fae and promising

devilry still to come.

As I grabbed my satchel and checked Leo was still inside it, although how he'd managed to drag his bag of dried crickets inside so quickly I had no idea, a thought struck me.

"So, last time we were in Egloriem fighting the Old King, when you called me your future queen… you weren't just saying that to taunt him?"

Taz swung his arm around my waist.

"Nope. If I ever have to put up with being a king, I'm dragging you down onto that throne with me. We can share it and you can sit on my lap to keep me entertained while we deal with the thousands of boring things running a court and a realm involves."

I grinned. "Apart from the thousands of boring things, I quite like the sound of that, especially if I'm the one with all your clothes by then."

"Wicked." He groaned quietly under his breath, dragging me down the hall toward the lift.

The atrium was full to bursting when Taz and I stepped out of the lift. We jostled through the crowd and found Ace, Milo and the others clustered near the reception desk.

Call-Me-Henry, Arcanium's stalwart Head Receptionist and Stationary Organisation Director, stood with his arms folded as he threw tight-lipped looks at Queenie who was standing on his desk calling for quiet.

A piercing whistle tore the air, calling all conversations to a halt. The moment I'd stopped wincing at the noise, I noticed Petra standing beside Call-Me-Henry and a wave of guilt hit me.

I haven't even checked in with her or caught up with her about any of the assignments.

As the atrium fell silent, I started wriggling through the crowd with Taz as a non-negotiable weight clinging to my hand.

"I'll keep this short." Queenie's voice filled the atrium, loud and strong. "Rumour will have reached you that the ancient Apocalyptians are once again roaming Faerie. They've captured the Queen's court and it's our job to go and defend it."

A brief murmur rippled through the crowd.

"Their powers are beyond compare," Queenie continued. "Reports say they can pierce through wardings like iron arrows, and ensnare minds as easily as breathing. The only advantage we will have is either trickery or strength in numbers. If we separate those overcome by the Apocalyptians' power, they should recover their right minds in time. That is your task, to bring those overcome into safe spaces that will be created on our arrival, and not be overcome yourself."

I caught Petra's eye and she raised one eyebrow at me.

Uh-oh, I'm in trouble now.

"Those I've spoken to already know what they have to do." Queenie slid down from the desk in one graceful leap. "Good luck to those remaining behind to defend our walls. For the rest of us, the lift shaft will take us to a safety zone within the Queen's court. May Faerie gift us all."

She blew a swelling breath toward the metal lift that led up to the human world and the door flew open, revealing a dark hole.

"So that's it?" Taz hissed over the growing clamour of the crowd. "Go in and try to rescue overcome people? She's not given us any instruction on what to do with the Selessium bottles, or where they are."

As the crowd surged toward the lift, I noticed Queenie and Petra waiting for us.

I grimaced. "If I'd checked in with my mentor like I should have done by now, we'd have been told."

I strode through the crowd to the desk, keeping it between

me and Petra.

"You're late," she said.

I nodded, aiming for meek apology. "I know, sorry."

"You've been through a lot lately." She sniffed. "So I'll overlook it. I'll be staying behind to protect the hub so you'll need to orb us updates. The first wave through the lift have the Selessium bottles, but you and Taz will need to go first to give permission for entry."

Of course, the conservatory, I should have thought of that.

I nodded again. "Thanks, Petra. We'll do our best."

She rolled her eyes and stepped back, as Queenie huffed in annoyance.

"Right, you two at the front. The first wave will follow you in."

I let Taz drag me through the waiting crowd, uneasy at having all eyes on us. I squeezed his fingers as we approached the lift shaft, and he dropped them a moment later to thread his arm tight around my waist. We might still survive this if we all kept our heads and worked as a team.

Together.

"Yeah, don't worry, you're stuck with me," he said with a grin.

I blinked. "You heard that?"

CHAPTER SEVENTEEN
Mind Whispers and Title Revelations

Taz frowned back at me. "What?"

"I didn't say anything, but you answered me."

"You said 'together', I heard you."

I stopped right at the mouth of the gaping darkness inside the lift shaft, turning my head so Taz could see my mouth.

I didn't say it out loud.

His eyes widened, lips parting in surprise.

What about this? His voice echoed in my head. *Can you hear this?*

"Yeah, I can." I glanced over my shoulder to see Petra and Queenie glaring at us. *But now's not the time to freak out about us apparently having telepathy for some reason.*

Taz nodded and together we stepped into the dark.

I closed my eyes to the subtle brush of air over my face and opened them again to a soft light streaming in around me. The usual scent of freshness I remembered from the conservatory was tainted by the scent of stale food, and looking around I could see several people clustered in various states of recovery and worry.

"Master Oakthorn! How glad we are to see you!"

Marthe appeared in front of us like magic, her wise eyes scanning him as he looked around the conservatory.

"Permission granted for all who follow me through the skip-way from Arcanium to enter," he announced.

I flinched when Marthe's burning gaze fixed on me next. A slight quirk hitched the corner of her mouth as she kept on staring.

What have I done now?

I tried to meet her eyes, but she was turning back to Taz before I could manage it.

"Most of the court are overcome, Master Oakthorn. The staff remain unaffected but we have only managed to rescue those you see here. We are unable to get anywhere near the Queen."

The first batch of FDPs appeared before Taz could answer her. I scanned the familiar faces, seeing Ace, Milo, the Eastwicks with Hutch and Harvey among them. And also a face I hadn't seen for a while.

I half expected seeing the girl in front of us to bring back bad memories, but I found a smile the moment Reyan left Kainen's side.

"This place looks amazing!" she said instead of a greeting. "Lord said you needed my help, although you could have called me yourself."

I frowned, aware of Taz ignoring Marthe now as Kainen came to stop a few paces behind Reyan, keeping a healthy distance.

"Would you have been able to come though?" I flicked a glance at Kainen.

Reyan followed my gaze, looking over her shoulder with a devilish grin.

"Well, you were given free reign of the Court of Illusions and, as far as I'm aware, that liberty was never rescinded. Short of him telling me not to obey, I would have had to do as you said."

I froze, memories swarming. Kainen *had* given me free reign of his court, but I'd assumed it was while I was there, as an apology of sorts for what he'd done to me.

"I'll rescind the privilege after this task is done," Kainen insisted. "But I thought it might come in useful if you ever needed it for the time being."

I couldn't bring myself to say thank you, but I nodded and focused on Reyan instead.

"I'm going to have to ask you to do your shadow thing," I said.

She shrugged. "Okay, what exactly am I shadowing to? Lord said we were hunting the essences again."

I bit my lip. I'd not had a chance to discuss this with Taz yet, exhausted last night and distracted this morning. I caught his eye and tried to send a mental message instead.

I didn't get a chance to tell you, but Reyan can shadow-weave. I think we can get your mother back here with her help.

He raised his brow, a tiny smile glimmering.

And how is she going to do that, princess?

I pushed aside the thrill mixed with trepidation at the idea of us sharing thoughts. Could he read mine whenever he chose, or only when I willed it?

She is going to use the shadows to cloak herself and find the Queen. When she's found her, she'll let us know and you skip to her with Milo, grab the Queen and skip back here.

He nodded. *Okay, you're in charge then. Also, you're cute when you're bossing everyone around.*

My cheeks burned and I was suddenly relieved we weren't having the conversation out loud.

Not the time right now!

He snickered, leaving me red-faced as I turned back to Reyan.

"We need you to shadow through the court to find the Queen," I said. "Once you've found her, we'll figure out a way of you getting the message back to us. Milo?" He appeared beside me in seconds. "I'm not sure how the whole you thing works but if Reyan finds the Queen, can you get to her the normal way, or will we need to tell you where she is?"

He nodded. "I don't know how it works exactly, but it's something to do with sense, so I should be able to intuit the location. Unless the Queen's court has wards against such things?"

Taz shook his head. "Once you're inside, you can skip or translocate to any of the public rooms. We'll just have to hope she's not locked in her bedroom, or it'll be a sneak upstairs and try to grab her by stealth job."

I really hoped the stealth job wouldn't be necessary and forced a determined smile to cover my nerves.

"Great. Okay, Reyan, I'm going to give you an orb to contact us on." I reached into my pocket, flinching when Kainen held up a hand.

"No need," he said. "Reyan will be able to reach me when she's found the Queen."

He snapped his fingers, summoning the sparkling black smoke. I let a warding creep up around me, almost amused when I felt it weaving itself around one already firm and solid.

Can you hear me through protections? Taz's voice echoed in my head.

I smiled. *Yeah, no escaping you now. Be interesting to see how far it stretches. You could be on the other side of Faerie and I'll be putting annoying songs in your head.*

Wicked. He blew me a kiss.

I sent one back. *Focus.*

Kainen marked something on Reyan's forehead with the black smoke caking his fingers. I noticed the subtle blush blooming across her skin, her chin dipped toward her chest.

I think she fancies him. Taz sounded intrigued. *Can't see why.*

I shot him a look. *Hush and get ready to go with Milo, he'll need you to get back in here with your mother.*

Reyan crept to the gap in the wall and the tapestry hanging on the other side that led to the rest of the court. As she stepped underneath the archway, she began to fade into the darkness, the vision of her dribbling to nothing as the shadows engulfed her. The slightest twitch of the tapestry suggested she'd slipped past it and was gone.

"Congratulations." Kainen's voice dragged my attention back.

I frowned. "What for?"

Taz appeared beside me, his arm around my shoulders and his face narrowed with warning. Kainen noticed and smiled sadly.

"On your anchoring. If we manage to survive this fight, I hope you'll be happy."

"She will be," Taz grunted.

I rolled my eyes, sending Kainen a rueful grimace. That's all the thanks he'd get from me, but I think he understood as he nodded and moved away.

"Still don't trust him, but I'll let it slide," Taz muttered.

"Not our problem. Focus on getting the Queen back here, and we might be able to use her power against the enemy. If she can change the weather and amend the court around her, we could find ways to separate the overcome people from the essences."

Taz chuckled. "Always planning. Alright Sparky, I'm ready whenever we get the summons."

We both noticed Kainen's head lifting. He turned to look at us, and Milo appeared with one hand ready on Taz's shoulder.

Warding up until I return, Taz insisted.

Okay. Be safe.

"Reyan says the Queen is in the throne-room, on the throne,"

Kainen announced.

I stepped back and reinforced my warding as Taz and Milo vanished, just in case as Kainen approached again.

"Call Reyan back," I told him.

Instead of waiting, I stalked across to Queenie who was marshalling the mass of FDPs into groups. The conservatory seemed to be swelling to accommodate the masses, but I guessed even the magic of the Queen's court would have a limit eventually.

"Taz and Milo have gone to fetch the Queen."

Queenie nodded. "Good thinking. We're grouping everyone in terms of skill to create mixed ability units."

I blinked, surprised that she was addressing me like an equal for once. For all of two seconds as her eyes flicked over me.

"You should invest in some proper Fae armour, or at least some appropriate attire for battles."

I rolled my eyes. "Not likely. This is comfortable so it'll do fine."

I flinched around as the sound of stumbling echoed behind me. Taz and Milo had the Queen between them, her head lolling and her mouth slack.

I let Queenie storm over first and a moderate fabric tent appeared in the corner of the conservatory a second later. Milo helped lead the Queen into it, but Taz was already seeking me out.

"What's the damage?" I asked.

He grimaced. *It's bad.*

I didn't push any further as he faced the room, all eyes turning to him.

"The Apocalyptians have lined the main hall with their thrones," he raised his voice so the announcement would reach the whole room. "They're using people as toys. Our only chance of saving more than one or two is to go in as a huge raging storm. They'll try to attack us but the swarm of emotions will disorientate them. We move in groups, a few to defend, a few to rescue. The moment you've got a couple of people, bring them back here."

He looked at me. *What have I missed?*

"Take time to rest if you need it," I added. "If any of your group gets overcome, retreat. The conservatory should let you in through the tapestry."

I looked to Taz and he nodded. "Readmittance permitted to anyone who has exited past the tapestry and means our side no harm, until the battle is over."

Hefty feet stomped across the floor toward us and I managed a weak smile as Sagar and Eldrich, the Queen's guards, bowed their heads to us.

"We are under servant oath," Eldrich rumbled. "The Apocalyptians have not overcome us yet, so we will be in charge of protecting you."

Taz's nose wrinkled. "I don't need protecting."

Sagar raised his shaggy black eyebrows, unimpressed.

"If the essences overcome you, your highness, we are responsible for getting you both back here to safety."

"We didn't arrive in time to save the Queen," Eldrich added. "We haven't been able to even get close, but we will not fail again."

Taz side-eyed me.

"Fine, but don't get in our way." He lifted his head to the group waiting behind us. "May Faerie gift us all."

I clenched his hand tight as we strode toward the exit side by side, him surging in front to pass underneath the tapestry. I couldn't hold in a gasp the moment we reached the hallway.

The carpet runner lay in tatters, the pantry door hanging from a single hinge and the kitchen door blasted clean off.

Taz powered past all of it, ignoring the sounds of people behind another door that was no doubt Lust's doing. I focused on Taz's hand in mine and dredged every remnant of my emotion to the front of my mind, letting it fill my body with roiling anticipation.

Fury will be here soon enough. I owe her.

Her volatility leapt up to play chase with my own anger, and I smiled. This felt more like it.

A quick glance over my shoulder showed the FDPs filling out the hall behind us. Taz stormed past the stairs and the oak tree still growing in its pot.

The last time I was here, I thought you were gone, I admitted.

He pulled me a few paces forward so I was alongside him.

The last time I was here, I threatened to kill several people, abdicated my title and called my mother at least sixteen names that she should have blown my head off for.

I had to smile at him, nerves fluttering in my gut. *You're having way too much fun with this.*

He shot me a spirited grin and kicked open the main hall door.

The Apocalyptians were on their feet, raising hands and sashaying toward us, but with the groups filling out behind us, we had the temporary advantage of surprise and scattered emotional targets darting everywhere.

Taz and I merged into the crowd as groups plucked people from the room, disappearing in a surge of coordinated units. I grabbed a Selessium bottle from Milo's hand as I dragged Taz past him, heading straight for a familiar face.

"Well now," Lust crooned, eying us both hungrily. "You two will be a delightful diversion. So much unsaid, so much to *uncover.*"

I darted sideways and flicked a shot of energy straight into her gut, holding it there to pin her. She flinched, her eyes widening as she doubled over. I could feel her power pushing back against mine, an instinctive defence, and gritted my teeth to keep her head lowered.

Just enough to…

Taz shoved the Selessium bottle against her lips before she could straighten up. With a feral snarl, she disappeared into the bottle. He grabbed my hand and I didn't even have time to blink before the swirl of grey nether caught me and the conservatory appeared around us.

"We got one!" I shouted.

Queenie emerged from the tent.

"Good." She swiped the bottle from Taz's hand. "We have three still captured, now four, but there are still six at large and four left roaming the court."

In the mayhem, I'd not seen what Apocalyptians we had still outstanding, but groups were piling back into the conservatory now with people in various states.

Some were listless and others refused to talk. Many seemed to be arguing with each other or fighting over meaningless objects. A couple were already falling on the food and scarfing enough to make themselves sick. I noticed Marthe hurrying past with large buckets, as if she'd been doing exactly this for years.

"It'll be mayhem until the effect wears off," Taz muttered. "What do we do, let them work it out?"

"I guess so." I shrugged and turned to Queenie. "Who's left out there?"

"Diligence, Greed, Gluttony and Sloth."

I frowned. "Do you think we can manipulate any of them? Sloth might be trappable if we move fast, and Gluttony we could trade a sip from the bottle for food-"

Queenie shook her head. "They'll see the Selessium and know what's going on, you can't trick them. You just need to be fast enough to get near them."

I started to pace, aware of Milo and Ace stumbling in nearby with an old man. The crowds seemed to be growing but I took the chance to grab Milo before they raced back out again.

"Is there any way to know how long it'll take the effects of the essences to wear off?" I asked.

Milo frowned. "There's a herb that might speed it up if we mixed it with some oia berry juice."

I flinched as Marthe bustled up, handing me a metal cup. I peered at the liquid inside, so dark purple it was almost black, the surface of the cup warm against my hand.

"It will give you strength," she said. "We know most herbs. And there is always oia berry juice, as it's Lady Blossom's favourite."

"Where are the Ladies?" I asked.

She stared at me for a long moment and again I had the uneasy feeling she was judging me somehow.

Does she not think I'm good enough for him or something?

I took a sip of the drink in case that appeased her.

"Lady Belladonna has defected." She sniffed. "She is now serving the traitorous whore who would call herself Queen."

I spluttered half my drink out.

"Quite," she continued. "Lady Rose and Lady Blossom are elsewhere for their own safety. What herb is it you need?"

Milo pulled out his orb-reader. "Ragwort, grown on the full moon. It's a poison technically, but-"

"This way then, please."

Milo shot me a hesitant look and I nodded.

She's not going to eat him or anything, don't worry. Taz's amused voice filled my head. *She's just a tad protective over me, but she'll grow to love you.*

I searched the room and found him emerging from the tent.

Oh yeah? She keeps squinting like she's inspecting me.

He grinned, striding toward me. *She is, but she gave you your strength draught before bringing me one, which means she accepts that your place in the hierarchy is higher than mine currently.*

I folded my arms as he stopped in front of me.

"How do you figure that one out?" I frowned up at him.

"I abdicated. You being princess consort in the eyes of Faerie means that even if I'm not in-line for the throne anymore, you technically are."

CHAPTER EIGHTEEN
An Unexpected Saviour and an Old Enemy Returns

"WHAT?!"

My scream startled most of the people languishing nearby, and probably most of the court outside as well.

Taz grinned. "I didn't know how to tell you, but now I realise it was actually really simple. You don't have to accept or anything."

His voice filled my head before I could argue.

If Marthe didn't accept you as mine, the other half of me, she would have probably ignored the etiquette on the basis that the Queen is clearly incapacitated. Nothing is certain. But she accepts you as part of the family.

I pressed a clammy hand to my forehead.

I can't deal with this right now.

"Then don't," Taz murmured. "It doesn't change anything. Which Apocalyptian are we targeting next?"

He knew me too well. Diligence, Greed, Gluttony and Sloth were still out there, but the only way to catch any of them according to Queenie would be either stealth or speed.

Ace and Milo appeared in front of us before I could answer, Ace supporting a young woman muttering to herself, and a red-cheeked Milo brandishing a Selessium bottle.

"We got Diligence!" he gasped.

I took the bottle for him so he could double over panting.

"How?" Taz asked.

"Milo was brilliant," Ace said with a grin, giving his

boyfriend an amused look. "He started arguing with me about some random library cataloguing method he'd invented and Diligence was so baffled by it, so distracted, I just whacked the bottle into her mouth from behind."

I didn't wait for Milo to recover to congratulate him, ferrying the bottle to Queenie.

"This one's Diligence. Only Sloth, Greed and Gluttony to get."

She nodded. For the first time since I'd met her, I could see beyond her stark glamour, the dark circles under her eyes visible and her eyeliner smudged.

"It won't be easy," she said. "Even once we recapture this lot, we have to lift the protection over the court and let the others come to us."

I nodded. "And they'll come with Elvira and her lot as back-up. We can only hope that they get targeted by the essences as much as we do in the confusion."

Queenie stalked off into the tent with the bottle and I returned to Taz's side.

"We've been thinking," he said.

I gave him a look. "Dangerous, but go on."

His eyes sparked deep green. *Meanie.*

"The lure and snatch technique is working," he continued. "So, who do we know who would be able to lure any of the essences we've not got yet?"

I frowned. "I take it this is one of those 'I already know the answer' things?"

"Yes, princess, I have all the answers." He rolled his eyes. "Not so sure about Sloth and Gluttony, but there's one person who could lure Greed, someone we know who wants the whole lot. Ambitious, ruthless."

"Who?"

"That would be me."

I span around to see Kainen standing a few metres away from us. He gave me a quirked look before turning his attention to Taz, who seemed to be struggling between hostility and admitting that Kainen was going to come in handy after all.

"You think you can lure Greed? How?" I asked.

He shrugged. "Let me worry about that. I'm ready when you are."

Taz took my hand and dragged me toward the tapestry without waiting. A wave of FDPs swept past us with several Fae that were overcome, and I wondered how many we had left to save. If we could get the Apocalyptians back in their bottles, we might have enough time for a reprieve before lifting the court's protection for the final fight.

We hurried down the corridor but apparently the Apocalyptians were erring on the side of caution, and we found the grand hall empty.

"What now?" Kainen asked.

I looked to Taz but he stood frowning at the deserted hall.

"Where in the castle would Greed go to feel safe?" I asked. "Do you have some kind of treasure room maybe, or something where things get hoarded?"

In truth, I was thinking of old fantasy stories when I said it, like the greed of dragons, but Taz's eyes lit up.

"Of course, the catacombs. Come on."

I squeaked as he broke into a jog and almost lifted me off my feet. I didn't look back to check if Kainen was behind us and didn't dare suggest we at least share a warding to make sure we didn't get separated.

Taz led us through a warren of corridors and down a dark set of stairs lit by lanterns on the walls. My cheeks burned with effort from keeping up. I almost got knocked aside as his wings flared, the firelight catching the golden tones of the feathers and making them look like rippling flame.

"Quiet," he whispered.

I did look back then to see Kainen right behind me, no shred of personal space left. Taz had our warding around us, but I knew the Apocalyptian would be able to feed straight through it even if Kainen couldn't.

I let Taz guide me under his arm so I was walking right beside him, curved inside the protective edge of his right wing. He led us around a corner and we came to a ragged halt.

The Apocalyptian Greed crouched in the middle of a vaulted underground hall, his tall form still graceful as he hunched over to survey something on the floor in front of him.

Kainen took out a Selessium bottle and crept past us.

Taz gave me a knowing look.

If he doesn't manage by stealth or he double-crosses us, be ready. We have to let the essence feed on him first if he fails, and no splitting up.

I nodded, every part of me thudding with fear as Kainen crept closer, inching up behind Greed. He lifted the bottle, only feet away, when Greed whirled around with a wicked smile.

As the Apocalyptian stood, he towered over Kainen, a sparkle in his eyes that was more gemstone than pupil.

"Now you are interesting," Greed spoke with the honeyed voice of a snake oil salesman. "So much you want that you can't have. But, you are the Illusion court's Lord, are you not? It was on your watch that Lust and Chastity were captured."

Kainen clasped his hands behind his back, walking steadily past Greed who rotated to keep him in view, putting his back to us.

Think ungreedy thoughts, like giving. I told Taz telepathically. *But not too many.*

I took a bottle from my pocket and we crept forward.

"That was unfortunate," Kainen said. "But several others were captured right here without any input from my court. It's the game we play."

Greed said nothing for a long moment as Taz and I inched toward him.

If this goes south, I thought to Taz, *turn into an animal with the bottle in your mouth and go straight for him.*

Taz's only answer was his fingers tightening around mine.

"We could easily give you anything you want," Greed continued. "You have the court, but under our power you could have your father's title, his powers, even the girl that haunts your dreams."

I flinched as Taz's foot kicked an old painting stood against a stone pillar. Greed whirled around, his eyes sparking on us.

Taz dropped my hand without any warning and morphed into a giant crow.

He grabbed the Selessium bottle from my hand even as I pulled another one from my pocket. Greed's eyes narrowed, assessing me as Taz swooped toward him with the vial in his claws. I yelled as Greed sent out a wave of power and knocked Taz off course, forcing him into one of the pillars. Sickness burned my gut and my throat, and I screamed again as Taz hit the floor.

He lay motionless and I sprang forward, but Greed's power held me in place, my arms and legs flailing on the spot.

"You have very little use to me." Greed sniffed. "You already seem to have much of what you want right now, and you have patience for the rest. Very inconvenient."

I stared at Kainen instead.

Why isn't he moving? He stared back at me and I realised. *He's considering it. What Greed offered him. He's been overcome.*

I tried to plead silently with him, but he stared back at me with no discernible emotion on his face. He took a step toward us as Greed pulled me closer with effortless, invisible power.

"Consider, young Lord," he said. "The girl of your dreams holding court as your Lady while you, the most powerful Mage of the new age, wield dominion over all you survey. These have always been your dreams, have they not?"

I didn't know what to do. Struggling was pointless. I couldn't see any movement from Taz and my gut twisted. Nobody even knew where we were. I wriggled my fingers, flailing in the attempt to get my fingers into my pocket. If I could reach my orb, I could at least get someone down here to take Taz to somewhere safe.

Kainen appeared beside Greed, his expression resolute.

He didn't even try to fight it. Anger burned inside me hot and spiky, but Greed only laughed.

"Fury will be happy to see you, girl. You're radiating part of her like a beacon. Once she is done with you, the young Lord here may take you as his Lady, or whatever he sees fit."

Kainen lifted a hand over Greed's shoulder. My insides crunched as I saw the flash of deep, brilliant blue.

"She's already taken sadly," he said.

The vial slammed against Greed's sneering lips. The expression stuck on his face, his eyes widening as the vial sucked him in. Kainen rammed the stopper in and held out the vial out to me on his open palm.

I forced myself to meet his eyes. I doubted I'd ever forgive him for the past between us, but for him to reject the offer of everything he wanted in order to do the right thing, I had to honour that.

"Thank you."

I grabbed the vial and hurried over to Taz, his human form slumped against the pillar. His breathing was ragged but still there, a small mercy, and I frantically searched for the right way to lift him.

"Taz, wake up, please." I tried shaking him.

He mumbled something and I almost cried out with relief.

"I think I might have to carry him for you, kitten," Kainen said, his tone rolling dark and soft.

I flinched, but he was looking at me with one eyebrow raised, amused.

"No way in *Faerie* are you lifting me." Taz's voice was feeble, but he opened his eyes. "And if you ever call her that again, or any variation of an affectionate name, I will have your title rescinded and your family in the forever mountains before you can so much as wink at her."

Kainen winked at me and it was everything Taz needed. He rolled onto his hands and knees, using the pillar to stand. I shoved my shoulder under his arm and cast a protection warding around the two of us.

Even after what Kainen had just done, I was still vulnerable to his gifts even if Taz wasn't.

"Come on, we've only got two left to catch now."

I led the way toward the exit.

Did he do anything to you? Even Taz's voice in my head sounded sluggish.

Apart from saving our arses? No. I'm not going to ask you to be nice to him but he made the right choice today, so maybe at least stop threatening his family. Once the war is over you can challenge him to a duel or something for the sake of your egos.

Taz snuffled a laugh and we focused on getting up the stairs and through the hallways to the conservatory.

"What happened?" Marthe popped up in front of us the moment the tapestry dropped.

Taz lifted his head. "I turned into a bird and got slammed into a stone pillar."

Marthe tutted even as he managed a wicked grin back at her.

"Well, don't do that again," she said. "I'll get you a tonic. Do you need another one, mistress?"

I shook my head, wondering when the appropriate time to tell her she didn't have to call me 'mistress' no matter what the law of Faerie dictated. Probably not in the middle of a war.

"You need to sit down," I told Taz.

I looked around for a chair, amazed when one materialised right behind him. He didn't seem to notice it had only just appeared, but he didn't hesitate to pull me down on top of him as he sank onto it.

Queenie appeared in front of us, disapproval scrawled across her face, but I held out the bottle.

"Greed."

She nodded. "Good. The Eastwick sisters managed to get Gluttony, apparently by challenging the Hutchinson boys to an eating contest, so there is only Sloth left. I've advised those who have been here since the beginning to take breaks while they can, and a fresh wave is going in search of Sloth now. Also, the Queen is much more herself and demanding to see you."

"Okay," Taz sighed. "Give me a minute."

Queenie shook her head. "Not you, she wants to see Demi. Although knowing you two it's much the same thing these days."

She swept off before either of us could comment, but I couldn't ignore the sinking in my gut.

"Your mum wanting to see me isn't going to be a good thing, is it?" I asked.

Taz shook his head with a ragged sigh.

Probably not, he whispered into my mind. *Give me a minute and I'll come with you. Don't agree to anything, I mean it. Tell her you need time to think and we'll use that to talk it through. Whatever she does ask of you will undoubtedly be some kind of trap, even if it's not for you. Don't let her separate us either, not for anything.*

I raised my eyebrows at him. *You mean they'll try to use me as bait again? Surely not.*

He growled softly at my sarcastic tone but didn't respond, tightening his arms around me and resting his cheek on my shoulder. I settled my chin on top of his head, soaking in those few blissful moments.

As we approached the Queen's tent a few minutes later, I prepared myself for the inevitable.

The Queen sat on an ornate, over-padded chair, looking immaculate with her honey brown hair pinned back by crystals and her peach gown draped without a wrinkle. She set down the delicate tea-cup she was holding and looked at us.

"You wanted to see me?" I asked, beyond politeness.

Even if this was my boyfriend's mother, and the Queen of my realm, she had used me and I wasn't done hating her for what she put me through with Taz's supposed death.

She nodded. "Yes. We are about to capture the final escaped essence-"

"*We?*" Taz asked, his voice dangerously calm. "That would be the royal we I take it? While Demi and I have been saving your court with our friends, what have you been doing?"

I didn't care enough to interfere. A sensation was irking me, the familiar prickle of anger climbing through my muscles, dribbling out of my bones and setting my skin on fire.

The Queen noticed, her gaze fixed on my eyes. Taz followed

suit and grimaced.

"Are you okay?" he asked. "Your eyes have gone red again."

I unclenched my jaw. "Happens when I'm furious."

A back entrance to the tent billowed. I almost crunched the bones in Taz's hand as the fabric separated and someone else joined us.

"Speaking of fury, hello my dear."

CHAPTER NINETEEN
The Truth is Finally Laid Bare

Fury deflected the shot of my energy gift without a single twitch of her body. I only just remembered to push Taz aside in time and ward him, splitting my gifts as I sent stream after stream of irate crackling energy at the Apocalyptian.

She blocked each one until smoke and the smell of burning filled the tent, the Queen putting out my fires. I didn't even know until then that I could use my energy to make actual flames, but that was the least of my concerns.

"You are dead," I snarled. "On my breath and my body, I'll kill you or die trying."

Fury was still batting off my attacks even as she took a seat at the Queen's table, supremely unconcerned.

"Tempting, but perhaps you should listen to your Queen first."

Dem, calm down. Taz punctured the maelstrom of my anger. *She can only make us angry and if we end up like that, we walk out. Hear them out, then we leave, okay?*

I glowered at him. *Why?*

I want to know my mother's plan, for one. That way I can protect us from it better.

I nodded and let Taz into my warding. It was probably pointless to keep it going now, but it gave me something to hang onto.

"Fine, talk."

Fury and the Queen exchanged a weary glance.

"How long has it been," the Queen asked. "The anchoring?"

Taz scowled. "A while, but that's got nothing to do with what's going on now."

Oh orbs alive, has it?

He gave me a warning glance. *No, you said yourself an anchoring can't be conjured or forced. Don't let their word-tangling mess with your head.*

"But it does have everything to do with you, Oakthorn," the Queen said. "On the day you were conceived, the enemy resurrected the Old King and the Apocalyptians with him. Your fate has been somewhat tied to theirs ever since. Faerie is only concerned with the balance, and where great power is tipped to one side, great power must also be created on the other."

Taz's hand tightened in mine but neither of us interrupted. I would hold my tongue indefinitely, and my assassination of Fury, if it got him the answers I knew he wanted deep down.

The Queen sighed. "We built Arcanium to watch over the enemies that I couldn't reach. Your aunt took over running it to keep an eye on you, as we knew you'd be too high a target if we sent you to the normal Fae institutions. Then I got word that you'd built a friendship group last year. I took great pains to have them investigated. A half-Fae fairy boy and a girl with no known Fae blood at all. But soon, Demerara, you were distinguishing yourself. This is as much your story as it is his, because he chose you."

I frowned as she used my full name, biting my lips together to stop from interrupting.

"Your lack of Fae nature came in very useful," she continued. "You were easy to read and your hatred of the Forgotten was clear from the beginning. I insisted Queenie give you assignments, test you, strengthen you. But it was evident that you two were growing too close too fast."

"That's what that me spending that season here was about?"

Taz growled.

The Queen nodded.

"To strengthen you both for this very moment. After the battle for Arcanium, in which you both performed beautifully, we showed our power to the enemy. Deposing the Old King forced Elvira's hand, forced her to bring the Apocalyptians into play. Which is where we find ourselves now."

I flicked my gaze to Fury, her gift spiking through me as she gave me that smug, self-satisfied smile in return.

"So what about her?" I had to ask.

"Fury owed me a rather large debt shortly before the I took the throne. I sought her out soon after Oakthorn was born and called in that debt, that she had to do whatever it took to ensure we succeeded in beating Elvira and driving the essences back."

"She almost killed your son!" I shouted.

Fury scoffed. "I merely scratched him a little, on purpose. It was necessary to heighten your emotions to draw the rest of *my* family to you. There was never any intention of killing him, or you'd be so turned to grief you might have ruined the wider plan entirely."

I pressed a hand to my forehead, uneasy as everything I'd been building myself on started to collapse. I knew the Queen had used me as bait, but the fact that Fury was involved in the whole thing, apparently from the very beginning…

"What about Kainen?" Taz asked my next question for me. "Was he in on all this?"

"Ah, poor Kainen." The Queen didn't look bothered in the slightest about 'poor Kainen'. "When he came offering to absolve himself of his crimes, and those of his family, he said he would do anything. His father was too far gone to pardon, but Kainen entreated me on behalf of himself and his sister."

I'd never even thought that Kainen's father would likely be

in the forever mountains now, but Kainen had made no attempt to see or mention him when we went there, or to ask Marten about him. I had no idea if he even had a mother to miss either.

"I explained that the situation would be dangerous," the Queen continued. "He would be expected to use his court for the purposes of tricking the enemy. He became our spy and our decoy of sorts. It was also convenient as his emotions were such that we could test Demerara's loyalty at the same time. For one joining the royal family-"

Taz laughed, the sound a sinister threat in the confines of the tent, silencing even his mother.

"Demi's my family now," he said. "Once the enemy are defeated, I'm severing all ties with this wretched household."

Um… okay, sure, but might want to consult me on that next time? I reminded him.

He didn't smile or reply. The Queen repaid the expression in kind, no shiver of hurt or emotion crossing her face.

"You are young. Anchored you may be, but you're both in the beginning of very long lives. Things change. People change."

Taz stood silent. I wonder if he was worrying the same thoughts I'd tormented myself with since we properly got together, that he'd tire of me, that things would change as we aged.

Except, I wasn't afraid of the future, not anymore.

"True." I shrugged. "But that's just an excuse people use to stop other people being happy. We'll grow together, or maybe apart, but we'll be doing the growing either way. As far as we're concerned, we'll be stronger together as one unit until we change our minds. For my part, I really don't think I will ever stop loving him."

Taz's head turned. He blinked at me, as if seeing me properly for the first time. I gave him a rueful smile.

Meant it.

He squeezed my hand. *Thank you.*

I faced the Queen and Fury once more, intention welling up inside me.

"So, you no doubt want me to do the whole thing again," I said. "You want me to play the pawn game one more time, do whatever puppetry you have planned for me. If I do this, you'll show us the courtesy of telling us what the plan is. No manipulations, no tricks, no pretending people are dead. Otherwise you're on your own."

The Queen's lips lifted.

"Spoken like a true princess of Faerie. I believe Oakthorn is still set on abdicating, which is his right, so you are technically now leading in his stead."

I held up a hand. "I'm not part of your family, nor am I anything royal. If he's abdicating, then you're not throwing his noose around my neck next. But you will give me the respect I've earned and tell me the plan straight, royalty or not."

Taz unfurled his wings, wordlessly standing by me. Perhaps he thought it was a show of strength, or he was planning to fly us straight out of the exit if something went wrong. Either way, I'd made this decision from the very first day I set foot in Arcanium, perhaps even the very first day I'd walked up Xavio's garden path, still not believing I could actually be anything other than a failure.

I would defend Faerie, my friends and my home, and I would give whatever I had to do it with.

Fury leaned slightly toward the Queen, amusement curling on her ruby lips.

"I think I may have given her a little too much me," she said.

The Queen actually rolled her eyes, looking so much like Taz in that moment I almost snorted.

"She's always been this stubborn by all accounts."

I ignored them talking about me like I wasn't there, waiting for them to concede and tell us what exactly was going on.

"The plan is simple," the Queen said. "When Elvira and the other Apocalyptians arrive, we must distract them long enough for the Apocalyptians to almost fully merge with her. They will take Elvira as a host, as that is the bargain she struck with them."

"But I will stay away," Fury added. "When the time comes, I will merge with my own host, one that will play to their powers. Together, we can nullify her and when my kin scatter to find a new host, they will be capturable."

Taz frowned. "How exactly will they be capturable?"

"I gave you your transmutation power for a reason," the Queen said.

"Xavio gave me that one."

"And who do you think ordered him to?"

Of course. The whole thing was orchestrated, us being nothing but puppets of the Queen's wider plan. I wanted to ask her if she even saw Taz as mindless collateral but now wasn't the time.

"So when the time comes, you want me to turn the Selessium into liquid and solidify it around them?" Taz pressed. "And who will be fighting Elvira?"

The Queen stood. "I will."

Phew. Taz and I both said much the same thing at exactly the same time.

Fury cleared her throat.

"Unfortunately not," she said. "You may have chosen Demi as your champion and rightly so. She has much promise in her. However, I gifted her and there's a part of my essence which I need to reclaim."

I froze as she turned to me, her eyes flashing as red as my own, the burning in mine answering her call.

"I decided I would keep you," she told me. "Now you know why."

"I refuse," the Queen said.

Fury raised her brow. "You offered me this trade and I asked for one unrefusable condition. This is it. It's Demi and I together, or not at all."

Taz glowered at them both and I thought he'd start shouting, but no words left his lips.

Talk to me, Sparky. You know you don't have to do this. We can try to beat Elvira the normal way, while others try to capture the essences.

I looked into Taz's worried face, my chest squishing. If I did this, if I succeeded, he would be safe. My friends could go home and not have to worry when going out on assignments. Elvira would be dealt with.

Talk to me, please, he begged.

I nodded. *We might have a shot the other way, but capturing them will be tough as it is, let alone during a battle. If they've gone to these lengths to manipulate us for this long, they must think it's our only hope.*

"Will I die?" I asked.

The briefest flash of emotion passed over Fury's face. I could almost imagine it was pity, the kind of sorrow that dwelt in anger for how unfair life sometimes was to good people.

"There are no guarantees," was all she said in reply.

Taz pressed a hand to my cheek and turned me to face him.

"Don't do it then," he said. "You've given more than enough. If we can't do it together then we don't do it at all."

This was why the Queen dealt in trickery. This was why she never told me he was still alive, never let him be awake until the right moment. This was no doubt why she stopped Kainen from being able to tell me the truth at the Court of Illusions. All because Taz would beg me not to do what they'd been training me for since my very first day. Or possibly even before then.

"Was I part of this before I came to Arcanium?" I asked. "Did Xavio know this would happen to me?"

The Queen shook her head. "He mentioned your promise in passing, but only as someone to watch for the sake of the court and the future. Then Oakthorn chose you, and you fitted the role to perfection."

"It was necessary," Fury added.

I nodded. "Perhaps, but that makes both of you as bad as the people we're trying to beat. You happily sacrifice people to fight your wars because you can't manage what you've been given to govern."

"You go too far now."

The Queen looked like she might lash out and hit me then, but I didn't care. Some part of me, some remnant of Fury's volatility or my own bitter anguish, wanted her to snap, wanted her to lose control as I had so many times recently because of her actions.

"Growth takes time," Fury said.

I snorted. "And yet you've both spent an age or more growing, but Taz and I already have more humanity and kindness than you'll ever feel in the lifespan of Faerie."

The Queen's cheeks flushed pink, the rest of her suddenly pale. Outside I could hear the steady rumble of thunder. I didn't care.

Let her strike me down if she wanted.

Let her be as torn and broken and tormented as I am for once.

"Tell us the plan exactly," Taz insisted. "Then we'll judge if

Demi's going to go through with it."

The Queen seemed incapable of words now, her fingers curled tight at her sides and her shoulders lifted rigid.

Fury stood up.

"The remaining Apocalyptians will arrive the moment the protection on the court is lifted, and Demi will need to be part of the crowd fighting," she insisted. "When all the Apocalyptians are freed except for me, they will merge with Elvira. They have no other choice due to the deal that was made when she freed us. But I will merge with Demi and together we will fight Elvira. The Apocalyptians will see the balance, and the strength of Demi's emotions, and join me. Only then can we defeat your enemy."

I frowned. "If there was a deal struck when you were freed, what's to stop you all joining with Elvira and screwing the rest of us?"

Fury smiled. "You are wise to be suspicious, but my prior debt to the Queen predates our awakening and therefore our debt with the Forgotten, so I am immune to that summons."

I guessed that was meant to reassure me, but I didn't bother asking if Apocalyptians could lie or not. They probably could but their powers were such that they wouldn't feel the need to lie or deceive except for fun.

"And how do we know once you've all overtaken me, you won't just keep me and skip off to ruin the whole of Faerie using me as your vessel?" I insisted.

"You don't entirely, that is a risk," Fury said with an airy shrug. "But when all essences are together, if faced with Selessium, we will be sucked into it and contained. When we are whole, we either rule or go to ruin. If encased in Selessium, it will be ruin. The very essence of it will suck all the potency from us, rendering us non-existent. We have been very careful in times past to avoid Selessium, and to hide its existence from the realm."

"But you'll be nullified too," I pushed. "Why would you be helping us essentially get rid of you for good?"

Fury's smile remained, but I recognised a subtle sadness in her eyes amid the flickering hues of red.

"When you live a long time, champion, longer than many ages of the realms, you eventually desire to see what lies beyond."

I couldn't answer that, mainly because all of my answers would risk Fury changing her mind. I didn't believe there was something 'after', unless it was some kind of Faerie heaven, but like most of us, I knew we returned to the essence of Faerie when we died. Our bodies went back into the earth, to Old Tara, and our souls dissipated into the nether.

We didn't have time for this, and if Fury had some kind of goal of 'heaven for all-powerful essences' in mind, I wasn't going to dissuade her. But I couldn't help asking one final question.

"So, if you're whole and you get encased, then your host dies with you?"

Fury eyed me for a moment.

"That is how it's always happened before."

CHAPTER TWENTY
The Breath Before The End

"Then it's not happening." Taz's snarl filled the tent. "You'd happily send her off to her death just to achieve your goals."

The Queen's eyes flashed, her shoulders rising as she grew, the air around her swirling hostile and bitter. Even as every pore of me begged to cower, I focused on Taz's hand still in mine and stood my ground.

"If Elvira merges with all fourteen essences, she will be unstoppable," she hissed back. "The pure evil eating her alive inside will grow until she is able to suck the very gifts from those around her. She will kill without feeling once the last vestiges of her emotions are drained. She will have no heed for anyone but her own desires."

"What makes you think the same won't happen to Demi? What makes you think I'd ever risk her, even for the fate of Faerie?"

Because you're the good one. I tugged on his fingers. *You told me that we would come in here, listen, avoid anger and walk out again. We can do that now. Say we need time to think it over, make a decision.*

You can't possibly be even considering it?!

I pulled a face. *I wish I didn't have to, but think about all our friends. If Elvira becomes all-powerful she'll go straight for them. It's the ancient 'one life to save millions' thing.*

He shook his head, anguish turning his eyes electric blue.

I won't do it. I won't use the Selessium. If you do this, I won't be the one to end you.

"It's rude to mind-speak in company," Fury drawled.

I gave her a hand gesture that told her in no uncertain terms where she could stick her company and she snickered.

If I don't do this, what are our options? I focused solely on Taz. *Elvira comes in, busts out the other essences or they escape, if not today then in two weeks, two years. She collects them, becomes all-powerful and the whole of the world turns to ashes.*

"Why not choose someone else?" Taz asked, turning to Fury. "Anyone but her, even me."

She sniffed. "You most certainly would *not* do. Demi has a part of my essence locked inside her. Without that, Elvira will be mostly powerful, but there will be no banishing her or any of the Apocalyptians."

"So merge into her now, take it and get the hell out again!"

Fury smiled sadly at him. "It doesn't work like that, young prince. Once Demi and I have merged, only a full merging would be able to leave a host body."

Any remnant of hope died as I realised what that meant.

"So you're saying either Elvira is mostly powerful if I do nothing, and potentially all-powerful if I go along with your plan and don't succeed. And the only way to succeed, is for me to sacrifice myself as a host body, because Fury was too dumb to choose someone who could actually pull this off?"

Fury's lips twitched. "Beautifully put. Together, your rage and my power would be a force to be reckoned with."

"But why can't you merge with Demi, get what you need, then merge with Elvira and I'll trap her instead?"

Taz tugged at his hair with his free hand, tears pooling in his eyes. I couldn't remember the last time I'd seen him cry.

"Because you would not as much as get near her," Fury huffed, irritated. "She knows of your gifts and you will be her first target. With the power of all the essences at her fingertips, she will be able to pierce your wardings, dominate your mind and you'll beg for mercy before the end. There's also a high guarantee that Demi would not survive the severing of me from her body if I tried to join the others in Elvira."

I wiped my face, the sight of Taz's tears now raining down his cheeks all but destroying me where I stood.

"How long have I got?" I asked, my voice sounding very far away. "Either I'm done by you leaving me or done by being encased, so how long have I got left?"

The Queen seemed to have regained control of her temper and sat back down.

"Once Sloth is caught, we'll release the protection around the court. As soon as Elvira and the rest arrive it will be time to make our final stand."

Taz turned his face to me, his eyes swimming and his mouth moving without emitting any sound.

Don't, please. I don't care about anyone else. We can run away, go somewhere, the human world even.

I shook my head. *Trust me?*

What? He dried his eyes roughly on his sleeve.

If they merge with me and I become all-powerful, and I'm going bad, you have to stop me. I have a plan but it's risky. I also need to spend this time giving our friends every gift I can think of. But the transmutation of the Selessium, that has to be you okay? I can't trust anyone else.

He took a deep breath. I'd asked him to trust me, but this was mad even for me. Without even asking what I planned to do, Taz nodded. I faced the Queen and Fury, determination rising.

"I have things I need to do," I said.

The Queen actually glared at me. "You'll do it? You'll follow Fury's plan?"

Fury's plan, not her plan.

Determined to raise hell, just in case these really were my last hours, I looked her up and down. Slowly. Curled my lip a little.

"I'll do what needs to be done to save Faerie."

Her eyes narrowed as she assessed the woolliness of my statement. Without waiting for her to reply, I turned on my heel and dragged Taz out of the tent. I half expected her to haul me back or scream after me but she didn't.

The moment we reached a secluded spot behind a cluster of tall plants, Taz turned me to face him, wrapped his arms tight around my waist and pressed his face into the crook of my neck.

Talk to me, now.

I gulped. *When Fury merges with me, she's going to try and draw the other Apocalyptians into me. If she succeeds, she's hoping that my balance will be better than Elvira's, less toxic and volatile. That way, when you lot try to attack me with the Selessium, I won't be as much of a threat.*

"How does this benefit you though?" he growled into my skin.

When you encase us in Selessium, make it liquid. The essences are nullified by coming into contact with it, but if you make it liquid, I can still keep my nose above the surface.

"That's it?" He pulled back. "That's your plan?"

I nodded. "Yeah. If I merge with Fury at all, it's all the way or nothing. If she leaves me without the others, I die. If they all leave me for Elvira, I die. But if I'm surrounded in Selessium, it kills them. If I'm still breathing, it might be the only way."

"It's too risky."

"The alternative is damning Faerie forever. Damning the human world too in time. I won't do it. Even if we hide the essences we have and keep part of Fury inside me, Elvira will still become more and more powerful. She'll be near to unstoppable with a few of them, let alone all of them."

Taz bit his lip. "If it looks like you're suffering, or like you're going to die, I'm going to pull you out. Even if you end up being all-powerful, I'm not going to let you die."

I pressed my forehead to his shoulder.

"Fair enough," I placated him. "You have to be prepared for me not being myself once the merge happens though. Don't let me be the reason people get hurt."

It was easy to lie to him. I was a dead woman walking anyway, and apparently one little lie wasn't going to be what killed me. Sure, there was a tiny chance that keeping my nose above the surface might be all I needed to survive, but I had no hopes for that. I also didn't expect to be myself once Fury overcame me. Once all the Apocalyptians merged with me, I doubted I'd even be a person.

Taz stroked a strand of hair back from my face. In the darkness that now hung outside the conservatory, illuminated by hundreds of little torches and candles hanging in jars, I could see the tears still shining in his eyes.

"What do we need to do now?" he asked, his voice shaky.

I took a deep breath. "I need to see as many of our friends as we can trust. I need to gift them all with as much power as I can. If everything goes wrong, they'll need to be fighting on your side, giving you time. I'll protect you with a gifted army, if I can't do it myself."

Taz kissed me, my hands shaking on his shoulders as his lips trembled against mine. I clung to him, crying tears of my own that mixed with his, our cheeks soaked.

I don't ever want to let you go, I told him, refusing to break away.

He pressed even closer, deepening the touch of our mouths

with agonising intent.

I won't ever let you go. His voice was fierce in my mind. *Ever. You're mine, always. I will save you from this somehow.*

I had to lift my head, dizzy and unable to breathe for weeping. Taz wiped my cheeks with his fingertips, turning the water to air so my cheeks dried in seconds. He didn't bother with his as he turned and walked away, his voice harsh enough to splinter wood as he called for Milo, Ace, Beryl, Hutch, any and all of them that would hear him.

I clutched my arms around my middle. I would have to ask Ace to look after Leo until Taz was ready. I pulled Leo from my rucksack, amazed he'd managed to snooze through the whole thing, although he'd eaten most of the dried crickets he snuck in with him already.

He crawled up to my shoulder, anchoring his tail around my neck. I rubbed the top of his head for something to do as Taz returned with our friends.

"No easy way to say this," I announced, my voice raw. "I'm going to have to do something rash and really, *really* dim. I want to leave you guys with every bit of protection I can, so start thinking up what gifts you want. Not sure how many I can give, or how strong, but I'm going to do it anyway."

Beryl stepped up in front of me first and I wondered what she was going to ask for.

"You're going to sacrifice yourself, aren't you." It wasn't a question, but I nodded.

I couldn't bring myself to look in Ace's direction, or respond to Milo's horrified gasp.

"Well, it's been an honour to serve alongside you," Beryl continued, completely serious.

I dredged up the last remnants of my humour, trying for their sake not to crumble right there on the floor.

"You're not going to bow or anything, are you?"

She snorted. "Someone's got a mighty high opinion of herself. You may be a princess of Faerie now, but you're still one of us."

She might as well have thrown her arms around my neck and hugged the life out of me herself.

"Is there anything we can do?" Hutch asked. "Something that might twist the decks?"

I shook my head. "Not by the sounds of it. My card's apparently been marked for a while. So, who wants what gift? We don't have long."

I forced myself to go through the process of gifting my friends with anything we could think of. Increased speed, agility, night-vision, foresight, knowledge, rhythm. We worked a rotation system, and while I gifted each of them in turn, they'd rush off and test the new gift. We figured out that I couldn't gift elemental abilities, like Meryl's ability to manipulate metal or Beryl's vocal rock-shattering, but I could gift enhancements to natural abilities, like speed or sight.

Taz refused to join in, standing with his arms folded and a brooding, distant scowl on his face. I guessed he was trying to think of another way out of this, but we both knew it was pointless.

"Take a break, Dem," Ace insisted after a while. "We're powered up to the hilt and you should take some downtime while you- well, have time."

I nodded, watching them all drift away until it was just Taz and I hidden behind the plants.

What are you thinking? Taz asked.

I hesitated. *About all the things I won't get to do.*

Marthe appeared with strength tonics for both of us, serving me first. I knocked mine back in time to put my cup back on her tray but Taz hung onto his.

A spark of reckless mischief twisted through my mind as he took a long sip, his hooded eyes fixed on me.

Also didn't think I'd end up dying a virgin.

Although he was about two metres away, the spurt of liquid he coughed up almost hit me. The hysteria rose, bursting out of me until I wasn't sure if I was laughing or crying. Taz seized my face in both hands and kissed me without letting me up for air, as if making me pass out would keep me from facing what I had to do.

"I need to orb Petra," I mumbled. *I need to thank her and say goodbye.*

Taz nodded, his eyes sketching over my face. "I'll give you a few minutes. Then we'll discuss the whole 'you not dying a virgin' thing. They can wait a while to lift the protection."

I doubted the Queen would be willing to wait around for that but I didn't say it. The moment he was out of sight, I pulled out my orb.

"Petra?"

Her face appeared instantly, her eyes wide.

"Holy shit, Demi, Queenie just told me the whole thing. She translocated back here to check in and she's absolutely fuming. She said, and I quote, "I'll pull that brat off her throne by her hair", and Call-Me-Henry threatened to write a petition to have her deposed."

I blinked at the pearly grey image of her magnified in front of me. I'd never see her in colour ever again. Never spar with her or have her tell me that she thought I was showing promise in my training. I bit my lip hard to stop the tears welling up, but it was a moment before I felt safe enough to speak.

"Queenie didn't know?"

Petra shook her head. "She knew about Taz not being dead,

but she had no idea that Fury had targeted you or that the Queen had been planning this for you all along. I swear, if she's still Queen after all this is over, she's going to have a massive revolt on her hands."

"Petra? I'm scared."

I couldn't voice my fears to Taz, knowing he'd use them to coerce me into not doing this, but Petra was like the big sister I should have had growing up.

Oh god, Mum. I didn't even think about how this will affect her.

"I want you to listen to me very carefully, Demi," Petra said. "There are always choices. You're choosing to do this right now, and it's your choice to make. But remember, when you do whatever it is that you're meant to do, you're still you. You're *always* you. Remember that, and your human side, and they won't be able to take it from you."

I blinked. She made it sound so easy, but I doubted I'd be able to hold onto any memory of myself once the Apocalyptians took over with all their bountiful power.

Taz appeared in view a short distance away. I could see the Queen and Fury behind him and noticed the sudden watchful hum of a murmuring crowd behind them.

"It's time," I said.

Petra sighed. "Be strong, Demi. Remember who you are. Everything I've done is to train you for this, and it's been an honour to train you, even for this short time. Besides, I'm not even half done with you yet, so you hang onto yourself until I can get you back."

I sniffed, aware of the tears leaking free again. Petra looked like she was crying too, but we both managed a smile for each other.

"Thanks, Petra."

"I'll see you back here after the war is done," she said.

I wiped my face with my sleeve as the vision of her disappeared and put my orb back in my pocket. I then took several deep breaths, none of which helped.

With my chin set, I walked toward Taz. He took my hand in his, then dropped it again to slip his arm around my shoulders, holding tight as he walked me toward the others.

"Once I lift the protection, it might be instant or there might be a wait," the Queen said.

I nodded. "Whatever comes, let it come. My friends know what to do."

Again that slight narrowing of her eyes, as though she didn't quite trust me.

No, that wasn't it. It wasn't a lack of trust as much as a curiosity. She was wondering if I'd thought of something she hadn't.

I let the others cluster around me and Taz as the Queen lifted a hand and whispered a bunch of words I didn't understand.

I'll never get to learn the Old Faerie language properly.

I didn't realise I'd thought it to Taz until he answered me.

Not missing much, princess. I'm not going to let you die though, so if you really insist on learning it, Milo probably has a book somewhere.

I choked a laugh, letting him hold me close. I shut my eyes and memorised the feel of his hands on my back, his cheek against mine, the smell of the apple shampoo he used.

I visualised every single inch of Arcanium in those moments. The broad maroon beams of the atrium. Trevor grinning up on the despatch platform with Moss hanging from his rickshaw. Old Tara's willow branches swaying in the breeze. My room. Taz's room. The bathroom. The halls. The library. Milo glaring at people for making even a single decibel of noise. The canteen with all the clashing and clanging and amazing smells. Queenie's office, where so many parts of my life had gone horribly wrong and also totally right.

I could feel Fury's essence sticking inside my skin, tugging at me like an invisible rope. I pushed it down, dredging every single last second of this moment out as much as I could.

A loud banging filled the air.

As Taz swore, I knew my time had come.

CHAPTER TWENTY ONE
The Fight Begins and the Darkness Beckons

The Queen stood marshalling those gathered around us, FDPs and warriors, many of whom I'd never get to meet properly now.

I clung onto Taz. He would be okay after I was gone. Not okay, but alive. He'd have our friends protecting him now and consoling him after. He'd live.

The Queen had a satchel of ancient brown leather hanging over her shoulder and I heard the familiar clinking coming from inside. So many Apocalyptians encased together. Did she plan to set them free and hope they all drifted into Elvira? Or was the plan to get Elvira's essences into her before we released our own?

I had no idea. Now the time had come to be brave, my entire body was shaking.

"Dem?" Taz kissed my cheek. "We're going out there now, and you'll have to fight alongside me. Are you ready?"

I nodded, even though I wasn't. Fury appeared beside me.

"Remember how it felt to lose him," she murmured so only I could hear. "Don't let it happen again. Remember that rage driving you, keeping your mind sharp and relentless. Embrace it. That is why I chose you."

"Because I'm angry?"

"Because you've been angry all your life, and yet you controlled it. Do that now. Make it work for you."

If we don't get rid of them, I'm going to kill her. Taz's voice snarled in my head.

I managed a weak smile. *If we don't get rid of them, I'm*

joining you.

Together?

Together.

We reached the tapestry and burst out into the hall. Gifts were flying back and forth already, zapping the stone walls and exploding into paintings. Taz and I had our warding up against the enemy, but I could already sense the Apocalyptians' power radiating from the throne room.

As if he sensed it too, Taz dragged me in that direction. We ran, and I saw Queenie zip in out of nowhere. She glowered at us and I flinched in surprise. A moment later, the Queen raced past us and I realised Queenie's hostility was for her, not us.

We followed them into the throne room with several other FDPs at our backs, all charging into complete carnage.

Elvira stood on top of the throne, her sharp eyes sending random attacks of seemingly invisible power through the room.

She's merged with them already!

Taz grimaced. *I know. Don't leave me, whatever happens, however it happens.*

I couldn't promise him that, but I sent a jolt of energy sizzling toward someone aiming for him. Their attack bounced off our warding but my attack hit them in the chest, felling them to the floor.

I froze as the Queen lifted the satchel and Fury appeared to snatch it, throwing it high in the air. With a wave of her hand, Fury sent it flying toward Elvira. The satchel landed in Elvira's outstretched hand. With a cruel smile, she opened the flap and peered inside.

Turned the satchel upside down.

And her laughter crackled off the marble like a death toll.

The vials rained against the marble floor, the Selessium shattering into an explosion of blue shards. I could just see the various hazes as the essences escaped, wavering on the air. Elvira sucked in a deep breath like a wolf about to blow on the houses of pigs, and the essences sailed into her open mouth.

I saw Taz's mouth open too, his eyes wide as he started screaming something I couldn't hear.

The burn behind my eyes spasmed before I could get my head close enough to hear him, building up to a violent crescendo of pain. Pressure tightened around me like a vice, binding my limbs, my chest, turning my nerves numb.

"Hello my dear." The words came out of my mouth, but they weren't mine. "I'll do the talking for the moment."

I could feel my hand lifting, turning back and forth. My gaze drifted down to admire it.

Not mine. Fury's.

My body felt like a flu hallucination, a product of my mind that wasn't really there.

But my mind is *still here. She could have warned me this would happen but she didn't. She could have told me this merging would give her control of me, but she chose not to.*

Petra's words filled my head and a burning scent filled my nose.

"NO." The word forced past my lips. "It's…" I fought the sensation trying to drag me down. "My body. You're a… passenger."

I could feel Fury inside me, fighting me for control. Angry claws scratched inside my skin, tearing to puppeteer my arms, my legs. But I fought her. I focused on memories, how it felt to hug people and forgive them. What it meant to apologise, to accept that some things just weren't worth the hassle.

The jittering in my limbs dissipated, the sound of fighting rushing back to me a second later.

I could still feel Fury's essence inside me, but she was

simmering on low, ready for when I needed her. I guessed she had yielded to me for now, but could rage against me at any time.

I scanned the crowd and saw Taz a few paces away, staring at me. I didn't need to check myself to know that my eyes were going to be glowing red.

Can you hear me still? I sent the thought out to him.

A lengthy beat. Then, *Oh, thank Faerie. It is really you? What's my favourite drink?*

Cherry bubble juice, especially if you take a mouthful, tip your head back and throw a couple of Jelly Babies in with it.

He actually grinned, as if this was suddenly something we could fight, could beat. Even with Fury merged inside me, her anger a well I could draw from when I needed it at the risk of it possibly consuming me entirely, I knew this wasn't going to be a fight I walked away from.

But I couldn't tell Taz that. I smiled back at him, finding it easier to force the pretence now. I had other more important scores to settle.

I faced Elvira, still merrily swiping down the crowd whenever they surged near her. Even the Queen got thrown back, powerful though she was.

That's got to hurt the ego. I could have sworn I felt Fury sniggering in reply through the rippling burn that seared behind my eyes.

Determined to do what I'd come here to do, I resurrected my old motto from the day of Taz's supposed funeral. Here in this very room, I'd sworn it.

Make it hurt. Make them pay.

Elvira was so focused on the Queen's attempts to reach her that she never saw me coming. I sent a jagged flash of invisible energy through the air, solidifying it around her in a wall of agonising pain.

The burn increased inside me but instead of fearing it, I let it fill me. The power crackled from Fury's essence into my gift. Elvira raised both hands, shoving them down in a violent motion that forced my gift toward the ground. As she shot her own wave of power at me, I pulled my energy around myself as a wall of protection instead.

I stumbled back, fighting against the onslaught trying to sweep me aside. Elvira knew she needed me, or at least needed not to send me away until she managed to sever Fury from my body, but she would have to subdue the Queen first.

I had little else to fight her with other than my energy gift, but being part-Apocalyptian had the benefit of increased power. I translocated behind her as she sent another wave toward me.

Over her shoulder, I could see the fight between the FDPs and the Forgotten continuing, but their eyes were partly on us. Loyalties would be tested, broken and forged based on what side triumphed today.

Even as Elvira spun around, I sent another attack, this time right to her head.

"You are rotten," I seethed, pouring every awful encounter I'd had with her into the malice behind my words. "There is no balance in you, nothing good, no kindness, no humility. You are poison without antidote. You're a disease that will eradicate everything, the good, the bad, all of it."

She pushed off my attack once again, her eyes flashing different colours, but I translocated behind a pillar before she could try to sweep me away again.

I chose my natural voice gift next, sending it out as loud and as clear as I could so that everyone would hear and know.

"What good is power, if there's nobody to be more powerful than? What good is relaxation without effort? What good is kindness, without strength to know when you're being taken advantage of?"

I eyed the Queen, letting my eyes flash molten orange.

"What is the point of being patient if you can't act when the situation calls for it? Without emotion, physical attraction is meaningless."

On and on I went, attacking each and every Apocalyptian I could remember, reminding them of their balance. Each time Elvira found me, I moved again, my voice singing out stronger and stronger into the now almost silent hall.

"But you, Elvira, you are rotten. You fester. You can't ever achieve balance because there's no good in you. You will erase the world, the Faerie realm, and you will delight in being the only soul in the ruins. Is that a world worth fighting for?"

I froze even as Fury tried to force me forwards. A shimmering haze of pale pink burst like droplets from Elvira's shoulders, closely followed by pinpoints of carnal red from between her hips.

The essences shone out of her like a rainbow painting a sky, mingling and melding as they drifted toward me. I could see Taz straining, the Queen holding him back by his arms. He wanted to try encasing them so it was only me and Fury left.

Don't. I sent him the plea. *They all need to be caught together inside me. Remember our plan.*

The plan I'd lied to him about, the plan which wouldn't give me any hope of surviving afterwards. He kept struggling against his mother but I could see his eyes locked on me. He wanted to be free, to be ready.

Promise me you'll come back to me. He shouted in my mind. *Promise me, and then you can't die.*

It was a desperate attempt, and I was going to die anyway.

I promise.

The essences danced around me, but I was more entranced by Elvira's shaking body. Her skin looked pale now and grey, leeched of life. Her skin was cracked with tiny wrinkles as though she'd been drained of all moisture, and her eyes sockets were sunken to the bone. She fell to her knees and I heard the cracks through the silent hall. Soon enough, that would happen to me.

I let the thought fill me up, forcing myself to think logical, sensible thoughts.

No, not my thoughts.

The light grey essence, almost silver, had permeated my forehead. I had been diligent in my planning. Taz would be safe, if heartbroken. My friends had many gifts to protect them in whatever inevitably came after this battle. I had said farewell to Petra.

The essences sank into me, soothing like cream onto parched skin. Perhaps Elvira had felt this blissful union when they merged with her. It was exquisite, like being born, becoming whole when you had only been one part before.

I was whole though. The thought irked me, even as the feelings inside me begged me to let the pesky idea go.

You're still whole. A familiar voice filled my head like thorns, pressing against the comforting security of my newfound cocoon. *Demi, Sparky, my wicked princess, come back to me. We're not whole without each other.*

The weight of the anchoring slammed into me and drew a savage scream from my lips. Anger fired through my chest, soothed moments later by a sensation of kind affection and a stern voice counselling patience.

I'm not whole without him.

Again, the wave of anger hit me. I had the vaguest sensation in my knees, something hard and unforgiving. My palms, and my fingers, were cold.

Demi, stay with me. Open your eyes for me. Look at me.

The soft cocoon of emotions wouldn't like the light, I knew that. But they *were* my eyes, whatever the cocoon said.

"My… eyes…" I ground the words out of a mouth that felt very far away. "My… body."

I focused on the surface beneath my knees, the cold beneath my palms. I forced my eyelids up.

Light blinded me, but I refused to close my eyes. The cocoon roared, voices merging as one until the instruction, the command, made no sense.

My vision wavered, but lines and colours were becoming clear. White marble and many thin golden lines. The throne room at the Queen's court. The Queen.

Taz.

I lifted my head. Met his eyes. His turquoise eyes drowning in tears.

Do it now, I commanded. *While I'm still me.*

If I focused on him, I could drown out the essences trying to overcome me. I was doing this for him. For my friends, although I couldn't risk drawing my gaze away from Taz for a second. I was doing this for Arcanium. For all the other fairies who needed to find a place to belong like I had. For Faerie.

A wave of excruciating pain hit me from the side, washing over my skin like scalding needles. The voices inside me roared as one collective, overpowering me. I felt my hands slipping and sliding. My face hit the floor. I had to close my eyes. The darkness of the cocoon opened wide, the sensations drowning me as Taz was drowning them.

Anger swirled in my gut. Caution echoed in my head. Aching throbbed in secret parts of me as much as it did in my heart.

I'd never see Taz again.

Never even told Mum goodbye.

Never got to explore all the places in Faerie I'd heard about.

Never learned everything I wanted to.

Didn't help my friends enough.

And it was my fault. If I'd trained harder, or been as good as others who came before me, if I'd not been so defensive to people.

If I'd… If…

She won't stop fighting us!

What choice do we have?

The Selessium burns!

We can return to the previous host, quickly, before we are too weak.

I could hear nothing except the warring voices, the scrape and burn of Selessium becoming a dull diffracting of my cells as the Apocalyptians fled my body. Each desertion left a part of me numb, weightless and drifting in the dark.

Silence fell, everything around me still.

I peered into the cocoon without opening my eyes, my senses peeking through that endless darkness.

Who am I? The silence seemed to shout. *Who are you?*

Who was I? I knew exactly who I was.

"My name is Demi Darcy," I told it. "Princess consort of Faerie and FDP of Arcanium. Taz's anchor."

And Queen of Holly and Essences… the voice whispered back. *As the light of Faerie brings life of the body, the dark of the nether brings renewal of the soul.*

The darkness quivered as an endless sea that began to wave with the memory of colours. It swirled and twisted in graceful shapes until I could recognise the outline of something familiar. Something I hadn't seen since…

"A Christmas tree?" I asked.

The darkness of the nether drew me toward the vision, or drew the image to me, I couldn't tell. But the scent of frosty air and fresh, sweet boughs swirled around me so strongly as I noticed the corners of presents, the red flash of ribbons and the twinkling silver of baubles on branches.

I reached out for the tree, my fingers forming in my line of sight and wavering right through the nearest branch.

As much as it was in front of me, the essence of frost and warm fires, of sparkles and warmth, was also part of me. I recognised it, recognised familiar stamps on what these items truly stood for. The gifts, the care and attention to the decorations on the tree, the warmth of home.

"This is Xavio's gift, isn't it?" I asked. "The one he passed down to me was the gift of giving? "

The nether was silent and still once more, but the sense of anticipation around me suggested it held its breath, urging me on to the realisation.

The gift Xavio had passed to me when he died was manifesting as Christmas, but I felt it older than that, the ancient sensation of kindness seeping right through to my bones.

The Queen of Holly and Essences has the power to overcome them and their host, the nether whispered. *Snare them the humanity they have never understood. Show them how a fairy wields her kindness.*

"I will. But how do I get back?"

How did you get here? The nether asked.

I looked down at my arms and turned the insides of my wrists up. Taz's artwork, the fiery orb of feathers, sat on my left wrist. The Queen's marking of my loyalty to the court, the colour-changing tattoo of Leo, on my right.

The Queen was how I got here. She used me like a piece of kitchen roll, and I'm bloody furious. My kindness might not be very obvious to her.

The nether might have laughed if it could. I could sense it swelling around me, echoing sentiments.

Sometimes the kindest thing a person can give is a lesson to be learned.

Okay, now the nether was definitely being feisty and I had a war to get back to. Scratch that, I had a war to win.

I searched my senses to prepare myself for the return, assessing myself and my feelings the way Petra had taught me.

Petra, who had told me to remember who I was.

I would owe her many things in the coming days, my life the very least among them. But among the humbling revelations, I was glad to realise that not a touch of Fury's volatility remained. The anger inside me was all mine, as was every other emotion and morality I possessed.

I smiled.

As the nether smiled back, I opened my eyes.

CHAPTER TWENTY TWO
The Holly Queen Rises

Fractured scrapes of sound tore into my ears, making me wince against the unyielding marble floor. From where I lay, I could see Elvira surrounded in a whirling maelstrom of blue. I twisted my body and saw Taz wielding the Selessium with a look of pure devastation on his face. He thought I was dead and it had broken him, but he was doing what he knew I'd want him to.

Elvira was trying to break through the liquid swirl, but I could see flashes of the essences trying to escape, their haze punching into her body and out again just as quickly in their panic.

As I tried to get my hand underneath my head to lift myself, my fingers snared against something tucked into my hair. I looked down into the reflection of the marble and found a smile.

A holly crown was woven into my messed-up curls, the red berries fetching against the dark with the shine of the usual oil-slicked colours.

The Eastwicks will tease me rotten about this.

I found my strength and pushed myself onto all fours, a deep fire of intention lighting in my chest. I heard Taz's whimper shoot across the room but didn't have time to check whether he'd noticed me getting up or was simply mired by grief.

A quick look down at my hands and I saw fiery flickers underneath the ice-white skin sprinkled with frost. In that moment I became the snowballs of a Christmas morning, the warmth of a winter night's hearth, my emotions pure fire trapped under the surface of an iced lake.

Xavio's gift had claimed me at last, and had also manifested with what felt like an arsenal of untapped power.

Taz dropped to his knees, his hands still out as if his control of the swirling Selessium around Elvira was on auto-pilot without any intervention from him. I surveyed the crowd, irked when they started copying him.

Perhaps they're taking their lead from him, thinking I've been reborn as something 'other'.

Even the Queen, eyes like chips of ice, dipped her chin a minute amount. I would deal with her later.

I felt the jagged blast of power from Elvira before it reached me and threw up a hand. A wall of frost and ice solidified in front of me, deflecting her attempt to wipe me off my feet. Even with the Apocalyptians shattered and her own worn state, the effort should have knocked most of the room to their feet, but my ice wall stood firm.

A volley of wooden arrows fired against it, chipping through the delicate weaves of the frost. I concentrated on the gaps and threw out flames that burned them to glittering ashes.

I pushed against the power emanating from her side of the room, feeling it sneak through the Selessium barrier. Elvira dropped to her knees as the essences pulsated, frenetically fighting to stay part of her, or flee, I couldn't be sure.

"I should show you mercy," I told her as I advanced. "I could give you a chance to repent, to change. I've learned a lot about giving in the last few days."

I would give her exactly what she wanted, for that was the balance of this gift. I could give her good or bad and tilt the meanings in whatever way I chose. I ignored the heady rush of power as she sneered at me, defiant to the last.

"Then again…" I pretended to be thinking about it. "I am however a fairy of the royal court. The first ever proper fairy of the royal court who isn't Fae, that I know of. And fairies never do play fair."

She lurched to the side but I formed a hand of ice to hold her in place. She seethed at the bite against her skin, but I wouldn't relent.

I noticed one of the essences veering away from her body and getting caught in the whirl of the Selessium. A second later, a solidified block dropped to the ground. I watched as the next essence was caught the same way, then a third. I couldn't make out which ones they were, but I held a struggling Elvira in place.

As the essences tried their last desperate attempt to flee, the Selessium bound around them with artful effort, and I knew Taz was with me, working to separate them so that there was only Elvira left.

I lost count, but suddenly the Selessium surged and fell, dropping to the floor in a splash that turned to particles of glimmering blue sand. I held Elvira still as Sagar and Eldrich trotted past, collecting up the blocks around her. She tried to reach for one of them, but I twisted an icicle into her shoulder until she was forced to focus on me.

"You are too weak to harm me," she sneered. "Too human to truly damage me. What'll it be, a clean death or a miserable incarceration? I have endured and overcome both before."

I waited until I was leaning right over her, strangely unafraid as my gifts forced her to still beneath me.

"I will give you the very worst thing you can think of," I crooned, wickedness in every single note. "Kindness and mercy. Because after that you belong to the Queen. I doubt she's as forgiving as I am, and I imagine she has had many centuries thinking up ways to torment Fae like you. Or rather, you in particular."

I noted the subtle widening of Elvira's eyes and the hitched freeze of her breathing for a single moment. That would be all the vindictive victory I'd be given, but it was enough.

The Queen swept past me and leaned down, casting a hand over Elvira's face with lightning fast reflexes. Before Elvira could so much as snarl, she dropped to the floor.

"Is she asleep?" I asked. "Or did you, you know…"

The Queen looked at me then, her eyes blazing into mine. I saw the dance of several centuries reflected in their depths, timeless events ever rolling. The hall was silent behind us, but I couldn't tell if that was her doing or just the hope of a whole army of fairies and Fae wanting to hear every word.

"There has long been an imbalance," she said quietly. "As summer matches winter, as the old ways balance the new. The tales tell of oak and holly kings, but perhaps there will be a balance of Queens. Summer and light alongside winter and darkness. Did the nether name you?"

I blinked at her, only realising then the seriousness of what had happened to me.

"Queen of Holly and Essences."

She nodded as Sagar and Eldrich appeared to take Elvira away, along with what seemed to be an escort of at least eight guards. I expected the Queen to say something, anything, even if it was just 'don't get too many grand ideas' or 'this doesn't make you special'. But she turned and stalked away without another word.

As if she'd taken every element of my previous power with her, I felt the last vestiges of strength leave me. As if I'd run myself from full power to zero battery, I stumbled onto my knees and let my arms buckle underneath me. Rolling onto my back, I decided lying down was definitely an improvement to standing up.

I'd never noticed the Queen's throne room had a vaulted

ceiling before. I stared at the arcing beams for a moment, bemused. Then two flashing points of stormy turquoise broke my inspection and my insides fizzled with elation.

"I'm terribly sorry, but I don't think I'm able to get up yet," I said conversationally.

"Has she gone, you know, in the head?" I heard Beryl hiss nearby.

I grinned wider, probably not helping disprove her assessment of me in the slightest.

Droplets of wet hit my chin and I sagged as strong arms dug underneath my shoulders to flop me up like a rag doll. The fleeting scent of apple and sweaty skin hit me as I pressed my face into Taz's neck.

I'm going to... he hesitated. *Okay, I can't kill you, but I'm seriously pissed off with you right now.*

I grinned. *Love you too. Your voice saved me, helped to keep me myself.*

When he started weeping, it set me off too.

"Right, show's over." I heard Queenie a fair few paces away. "Get that scum rounded up and off to the forever mountains, or you'll be next. FDPs help our injured back to Arcanium through that door there. And you, my dear sister, are officially in deep shit."

I couldn't control the wild flailing of my emotions, laughter spilling out even as I tried to dry my tears on Taz's shoulder.

I managed to raise my head, enough to see that the gathered crowd were shaking themselves in the hubbub that followed Queenie's command. Sagar and Eldrich were flanking the Queen, and several of our friends and fellow FDPs had begun the task of checking on each other.

I pulled back so I could see Taz's face, gaunt and tormented and still as beautiful a sight as I had ever seen.

"Stay there," he muttered. "Like literally don't move. I'm going to find Marthe and get her to give you something to help you feel better. Then I'm going to yell at you. A lot."

I didn't bother replying as he struggled to his feet and stormed off toward the doors to the hallway. I looked down and found myself surrounded by sparkling blue shards, so fine they were like sand.

"Mistress, thank Faerie you survived." Marthe appeared beside me, holding out a huge cup. "Drink this please. Have you seen master Oakthorn?"

I nodded. "He went looking for you to get one of these." I lifted the cup to show her before draining it. "What's even in this stuff?"

She smiled then, the first time I'd ever seen her properly smile at me.

"You don't want to know."

I drank it anyway. The tonic seared down my throat and into my gut, filling me with renewed determination. I tested my arms, bracing my hands against the floor. The muscles ached and groaned but I managed to clamber to my feet. Marthe patted my arm and pointed to the refilled cup.

I drained it again in a few huge gulps and guessed now would be the ideal time to ask another question.

"Can I ask you to do something for me?"

She took the empty cup out of my hands. "If it's in my power to grant, mistress, of course."

"Can you not call me mistress please? It freaks me out. My name is Demi. Taz would probably prefer it if you just called him that as well."

Marthe's eyes twinkled. "I can't call you both Demi. But, seeing as you are the saviour of Faerie today, I suppose I can grant your chosen names to you. Although, perhaps not in front of her majesty. I'll check the conservatory, see if master Oakthorn has gone looking for me there."

I nodded, relieved that something was finally going my way. Although I guessed being crowned Holly Queen by the very fabric of our world was meant to be a good thing too.

I would have to find my friends and thank them all, make sure they were all okay. I would need to ensure everyone made it back to Arcanium safely and that the Queen had no more crazy ideas for my future. I had to find out what happened to the Forgotten as well, and what would happen to them in the coming days.

But first, I had a promise to keep. Not the desperate one I'd given Taz before the Apocalyptians took me, but one from much earlier in the day.

Or was that yesterday? I couldn't remember.

I lifted my gaze from the blue-marked floor at my feet and caught sight of Taz across the room. Now I looked properly, he had a deep cut on his neck that would likely scar, and stood with his weight tilted over one leg like he was hurting.

Then he gave me a broad smile, relief mingled with exhaustion. I grinned back, delighting in the need to be frivolous and carefree. To be wicked a while.

I made you a promise, I reminded him.

I drew the last dregs of my connection around me and translocated. He didn't flinch as I materialised beside him and grabbed his hand, content to follow me wherever I intended to go.

"Conservatory, people can go out but they can't just go back in, right?" I asked.

He nodded as I started towing him along. "Yeah, why?"

I didn't answer, dodging those still lingering in the hall. I could see the tapestry to the conservatory ahead, and spared a thought for Taz lagging behind.

"Any part of you seriously injured?" I flicked a glance at him as I lifted the tapestry.

He ducked under. "Just cuts and bruises, I think. I have some of Marthe's healing balm still in my pocket for my neck. Are *you* okay? You look like you could go another ten rounds now."

You have no idea.

I dragged him into the fading light of the conservatory. Marthe hurried up to us, but although her eyes were on Taz, she was just checking him over.

"Marthe, is anyone seriously injured in here?" I asked her.

She shook her head. "No, mistr- Demi. We've moved everyone into the healing hall for the moment, and those able to leave are doing so from the throne room. I'm on my way back there to assist now."

"Good, thank you."

I let her tut and fuss over Taz's neck for a moment, still amazed to see the dark purple balm closing up the wound on his throat. I didn't want to wait, but I needed him as healed as possible and fast. I rotated back and forth to survey the room, checking for anyone who might have been left behind.

The moment Marthe was gone and Taz's neck had scabbed over, I pulled off my hoodie.

"Dem, what-" Taz stopped as I held up a hand.

I eyed the doorway, covered only by the tapestry. If I really was a Queen now in the eyes of our world, then perhaps this would work.

"Nobody's to bother us," I called out.

A moment of stillness.

Then a door slammed into existence across the doorway. Outside, I heard a suspiciously familiar voice that sounded a lot like Keesley.

"No unauthorised visitors!"

I turned to face Taz and found him gawping at me.

"Woah." He eyed me up and down. "The house is obeying you. It doesn't even obey me, or my sisters."

I thought of the chair that had appeared behind him when I needed it to earlier in this very room. But that was something we could contemplate another day. I smiled and moved closer.

"Forget that. I made you a promise," I reminded him. "And I'm not talking about the one in the throne room."

His hands landed on my hips, his eyes swirling dark with flashes of green. His lips curved up.

"You did," he murmured. "I didn't actually mean right after, but this works so much better. We need to talk about what happened, but not tonight. I don't think I can face… I finally understand why you were so mad at me when you thought I was in on the whole me dying thing."

I winced, still not okay about it. "We have some healing to do. Which starts with the promise I made you right before we left Arcanium."

His cheeks turned pink. "Are you sure? Are you well enough? Are you ready?"

A memory inched into my head, of desire, rocky walls and dark corners lit by flame. But this wasn't Kainen's court, and this was most definitely Taz in front of me. I could tell in the way his eyes flickered over me, checking for doubt or pain.

The daylight fading around us now was being replaced by starfire and a luminous moon, a soft glow that made this whole situation entirely separate from the trickery I'd suffered from before. I banished the old memories, let them wither away with the remnants of the war.

I curled my fingers around Taz's neck, my thumb lining his throat just underneath his cut now almost healed over and scarring pink.

He gulped and that hint of anticipation made me bolder than I think I ever had been. I pushed him back and a bed appeared behind him, one that the house had conjured from my imagination. I leaned over him, fizzling as I saw the hungry glint in his eyes and felt the wisp of his fingertips tracing my sides.

"Dem, are you sure?" he asked again, his impatience twisting on the edge of his mouth.

"You talk too much. Yes, I'm sure."

I spoke right against his lips, my insides on fire as he pulled me down over him, then under him. Words vanished quicker than clothing, but by the end I wasn't sure if the stars dazzling in my eyes were outside anymore, or just my reaction to him as we lay together, exhausted and calm.

"My wicked princess," he whispered. "My Queen. My everything. I will always be yours, and hopefully you mine."

I had no flowery words for him in return, my head still spinning. But I stared back at him and conveyed every single sentiment into the one word.

"Together."

Taz collapsed beside me and I fumbled around by our knees until I found enough of a fabric lump to haul covers over us.

His eyes were dopey, the darkness sated and the turquoise colour tinged with gold from the light of candles around us. I nestled against him, my head on his shoulder and his arm around my waist, legs tangled together. It amazed me how unphased by the whole situation I was. I'd always assumed there'd be awkwardness and anxiety, at least the first time. But this was Taz.

When you know, you know.

Taz had no intention of thinking such deeply profound thoughts.

"We're never leaving this room again," he said with a grin. "No more war, no more assignments, no more clothes."

I giggled at that. "The Queen would rescind your conservatory-"

"-*our* conservatory."

"Fine, ours. She'll take away our court privileges."

"Queenie will send someone on assignment to get us," he joined in.

I laughed as he peppered kisses over my face, but he was already half asleep on the pillow.

"Petra will take the court down brick by magic brick to get me back into training." I added. "I owe her too. Her advice guided me in the end."

He yawned. "She's your mentor, it's her job. But if you owe her, then I owe her too. Sleep a bit. If we stay here long enough our friends will find a way to realm-skip in to fetch us."

"Milo's probably already able to." I watched Taz's eyes close. "Love you."

He smiled. "Love you."

While he all but passed out, my mind circled a while longer. The darkness of the nether had called me the Queen of Holly and Essences. That probably wasn't even a thing but I quite liked the sound of it. I wouldn't tell anyone, not yet. I doubted with Taz's abdication that I'd ever be a real queen of anything anyway.

But I'd succeeded. We won.

Of all the Fae in Faerie, it was the fairy that saved Faerie in the end.

Taz nestled closer to me with a quiet grumble.

"You think way too loud. Can't sleep?"

I shrugged. "A lot's happened. Stuff mended, stuff broken. My heads still full of stuff. Is everyone okay? I should have asked before jumping you."

"Yes." He chuckled. "Although, you can jump me any time you like. Milo had minor injuries, Ace has a couple of wicked cuts on his arm that might scar, but he'll be happy about those as badges of honour. Some woman tried to turn Harvey to ice and Beryl went absolutely mental. She even called him her boyfriend."

I grinned. "Brilliant, he'll never let her forget that, even though she'll deny it to the high hills."

Silence descended for a moment, until I had to ask.

"What do we do now though?"

Taz shrugged. "We go back to Arcanium. We help build Faerie up in the wake of everything that's happened. We're still FDPs, no matter what happened here today. Um, Dem?"

"Yeah?"

"What did happen here today?"

He wanted to know what had happened to me. And I owed him that explanation. Even as he drew breath, no doubt to reassure me I didn't have to tell him if I didn't want to or wasn't ready, I let it spill out.

"When I was overcome and in the Selessium, they were fighting me. I could hear them and feel them. Then there was nothing. Except it wasn't nothing. The nether stared back at me. It asked me who I was, so I told it, and it named me."

"What did it name you?" he asked, his tone hushed with reverence.

"Queen of Holly and Essences. Then it showed me Xavio's gift, the one I couldn't use or find. It was the gift of giving. I think we've been given a chance to start again by the powers that be. Although I don't have any idea how to do that, and this whole queen thing is probably not even anything serious."

Taz was silent for a long moment.

"That's a lot to take in," he said eventually. "But it changes nothing with us. Whether you're a queen or a princess consort, an FDP or not, a fairy or anything else, you're mine."

I grinned, but then another thought hit me.

"Did you mean it, about disowning your family?"

He shrugged. "I don't know right now. I'm not willing to speak to my mother yet. Maybe not ever. Queenie will deal with her, but there might be a time where I'm in the right frame of mind to forgive her for what she's done to us. But I'll never forget that she tried to use you. Never. You're my family and Arcanium is our home."

I stifled a huge yawn, as if that reassurance was all I needed to finally wipe all wakefulness from my mind.

"Oh, before I forget," I mumbled, closing my eyes. "Marthe said she'd call us by our names from now on. She said it was because I was the saviour of Faerie, but I think that's going a bit far."

Taz snorted. "Never mind the saviour of Faerie. Orbs alive, Sparky, you've gotten the house to obey you, Marthe to drop the titles and my aunt to swear at my mother. You're basically the most powerful person that ever lived."

But at least I did live. I smiled into the darkness inside my mind. *Queen of Holly and Essences. I wonder if there's any way to get the Book of Faerie to record that.*

CHAPTER TWENTY THREE
Arcanium Chooses a Side and Milo Goes Way Overboard

Taz and I woke late the next morning but lingered in the conservatory until I'd told him in better detail all about what I saw in the darkness, what Xavio's gift meant, and his mother's words to me when Elvira was being carted off.

I had about three seconds of worry that the whole thing might change how he felt about me, but he insisted that he was used to dealing with irritable royalty so my newfound 'Holly Queen' status didn't alter a thing for him.

After that, we said goodbye to Marthe and realm-skipped back to Arcanium. Everyone else wanted to tell their battle stories, so Taz and I set up camp in the common area on the residents' floor.

Although I felt physically recovered, Taz was determined to milk every situation for all we were worth. Soon plates of food and drink were mysteriously appearing on the common area table. I didn't want to say it out loud, but if the Braunees were able to magic stuff up from the canteen to us without actually having to leave their kitchen, they could make a killing by offering room delivery for a price.

Queenie found us there that afternoon. After managing to scare off everyone else except our friends, she insisted that measures were being put in place to eradicate any trace of all old evils. She also mentioned that the Queen was looking into suggestions to educate the Fae population and weave more human moralities into the culture. Given the look on Queenie's face, she didn't think it would go down well.

It would be a blessing for the Queen's rule to reach out to those who might have been forgotten by the courts, and I said as much, thinking of Reyan and her father, of Milo and his uncle.

She asked Taz if he had any plans to speak to his mother, and he said not at present. The moment she was gone, I told him telepathically that I'd support him either way, but perhaps a rift wasn't in the spirit of things right now. He called me a name in retaliation, so I found the sensitive spot on the ridge of his wing that drove him crazy. He dragged me back to our bedroom and we didn't bother to get up until the next morning.

"I've been thinking about what you said." He sighed while sitting on my bed with Leo on his lap. "About my mother and not creating rifts. I don't want to let her think what she did is okay, or forgiven, but I reckon we should talk to her one last time. Then we go on with our lives here, and if she happens to feature in our future, then so be it."

I raised my eyebrows at him. "Very wise of you. I'm sure if you spoke to Queenie, she'd have your mother in her office in a split second."

Taz groaned. "You mean do it now, don't you."

"No time like the present, and once it's done, it's done. Come on. If you do this, I'll let you take me up to the human world and we can have doughnuts for breakfast."

I tried not to laugh as his eyes lit up. For a boy raised on the finest Faerie food, he was absolutely obsessed with human sweet stuff.

People smiled at us, nodded, or exchanged the odd word as we walked through the hall to the lift. Once inside and whistling upwards, I ran my finger over the golden carvings on the gate.

One of our common area visitors when we first got back had been Marvin, Arcanium's head healer. He said that after what happened to me, it would be normal to start finding amazement and relief in tiny things, which was apparently part of the after-effects of the shock. He also said I'd likely wake up crying a lot too, but I was already used to that.

We ambled down the hallway to Queenie's office, me resolutely ignoring the still patched-up parts of wall. I didn't want that reminder of the time I thought Taz was dead, because then I started thinking about how he must have felt thinking I might die in the Selessium, and it would start the whole mental spiral off that I was trying not to face up to just yet.

Not all in one go anyway.

We stepped into Queenie's office after I insisted we knock first, only to find Taz's mother already seated on a spare chair at Queenie's desk.

"I would like you to reconsider your abdication," she said, without greeting.

Taz stiffened beside me.

This was a mistake, he thought to me.

I squeezed my arm around his waist. *Say your piece, then we're done.*

"Fine," he said, his tone steely. "No greeting, no 'sorry using you both like lab rats', just 'here's what I want'. Okay, we'll do this your way: no. I'm not reconsidering, and Demi's not taking it on as princess anything. We do however have some conditions that we want to put forward now that she is Queen."

We'd discussed this late into the night, what we would do if anyone actually took my newfound royalty status seriously. I hadn't thought however about how *he* would take it seriously, which I should have been smart enough to factor in.

The Queen raised her brow, but said nothing.

"The forever mountains will be overhauled," Taz continued. "Most folk there have committed terrible crimes, but some of them are merely there because of sleights against our family. Even outcast Fae deserve the basics."

"You would have us pamper our enemies?" the Queen asked.

I shook my head, forgetting my reluctance to speak in my irritation.

"They're your enemies because you keep them that way," I said. "Why not build new methods in the wake of what's happened? Treat everyone as people, not just those in your favour."

She frowned. "I'll consider it. Anything else?"

"Yeah." Taz nodded. "Every kid, fairy or Fae, gets a gift on their sixteenth birthday. Whether they come to Arcanium or not, no matter how influential or low-key their family is. Even if they don't have a family to stand for them. Every kid gets that chance. Possibly even judge the gift based on their personality, their ability to do good with it."

His mother covered her astonishment well, but I could see Queenie trying not to smirk.

"I'll look into it. Since you brought it up, we also have Demi's new... *role* to consider."

I raised my eyebrows at that. "Does it come with a job description then, this queen thing?"

"No." She pursed her lips at me. "But you will be expected to form a court, allow people to join or seek sanctuary in exchange for their service. The nether chose you, so there's little we can do to reverse it."

I hadn't thought of actually forming a proper court, although clearly the Queen had been thinking about any way to get me out of the responsibility.

She doesn't like to share. But if I did have a court, would anyone bother joining it?

Taz gave me a playful look one eyebrow raised as his voice

echoed in my head.

We'd need to actually find someone who'd want to join your court first.

I'd get him back for that later, even though it was exactly what I'd been thinking myself.

"There are also some matters which apparently haven't been managed as yet, outstanding matters," the Queen continued. "Xavio left you his cottage in his final instructions with the hope you would continue to allow other juniors to be trained there."

I didn't even need a second longer than it took to process to agree to that one.

"Of course, if it's needed. I guess certain types of Fae wouldn't take kindly to me using a cottage for a royal court anyway."

I wondered how Petra would feel about training juniors, and decided I would ask her when the time came. As much as I loved her mentoring me, if she wanted to help others she would be perfect for it. She'd come to see me the moment we got back and we'd had the most awkward of hugs, but the sentiment was there. Then she'd sniffed loudly, said I had three days grace before training started again and hurried off.

"What state are we in?" Taz asked. "The courts and Faerie? Does anyone know about Demi's new appointment?"

The Queen nodded. "There are those who weren't at the battle."

"Emil," Taz's tone turned dark. "And why would that be I wonder."

A flash of a present echoed in my mind, the wrapping torn and the box open. Inside, a Russian nesting doll. I clenched my eyes shut and shook my head until the image was gone. When I looked again, the other three were staring at me, but I knew what the vision had meant.

Enemies inside enemies inside enemies.

We'd once thought the Old King was our enemy, but Elvira had been pulling his strings. Now I had to wonder, if Emil had avoided the battle, was it out of fear or had he perhaps been pulling Elvira's strings all along?

The Queen nodded at me. "The visions will become easier to manage. I'm assuming that's what the constipated look on your face was."

Wow, not pulling any punches.

I shrugged, veiling the hurt inside. Even if she was my equal in status now, she was still my boyfriend's mother and I had this alien urge for her to think well of me despite everything.

"Emil isn't stupid, he's proven that much," I said. "If he is a threat, he needs to be found and dealt with. But what of the rest of Faerie? Are the Forgotten massing anywhere? Is there anything we can do?"

Taz's mother didn't reply to that, but it was Queenie who stood, drawing everyone's attention.

"We watch, we listen and we learn. If we do still have an enemy to fight, they will reveal themselves soon enough. Until then, I think we'd best take a short journey downstairs to the atrium. Is there anybody here who can't... oh, Taz, you can't translocate so you'll have to take the lift."

I ignored Taz's resigned eye-roll and the flicker of amusement on the faces of both women as they disappeared into thin air.

I grabbed his hand and towed him out of the office. Just because I could already translocate like they could, didn't mean I was going to.

"Any idea what this detour is about?" I asked as we got back into the lift.

He shook his head and jabbed the button for the atrium.

"Not a clue, princess." His expression brightened immediately. "Or should that be your majesty? My Queen?"

I elbowed him in the ribs, laughing when he hugged me to him with one arm.

"I think I always preferred Sparky most of all," I admitted. "Although now it'll be you having to sit on my throne and entertain me apparently instead of the other way around. Which is still completely nuts."

We arrived at the atrium and Taz slid the grill aside without responding. Perhaps he thought my new status was nuts too, but I knew he'd be at my side whatever title I had or didn't have.

Taz's mother and Queenie stood a little way away, the people in the atrium just finished bowing. Even as they rose to their feet, they spotted me and went back down again.

Taz started laughing as I groaned under my breath.

"I'm not going to get anything done if everyone keeps doing this," I muttered.

"Tell them to get up then," he teased.

"Oh no, do I actually have to?"

Luckily, most of them got up of their own accord and I could ignore the mortification burning its way across my skin. I turned my attention to Queenie instead, who pointed behind me.

I swivelled around and my mouth dropped open.

Climbing the walls of the atrium amid the ivy and the butterflies were new leaves. Shinier and brighter in colour, with sharper edges. Red berries nestled amid the green and the fluttering dashes of colour the butterflies provided.

"Everyone knows that Arcanium has always pledged allegiance to the royal family of Faerie," Queenie said. "Such is the protection we wove when it was built. Now it appears to have accepted you in that as well."

I could have cried. Nothing, not a new title, my increased

powers or even the knowledge that Faerie was now relatively safe could have compared to this.

Arcanium had chosen me.

Faerie itself had chosen me.

It was no doubt Old Tara pulling the strings, or vines and branches in her case, but where Arcanium had once bent to Taz's will as it was built to protect him, now it pledged loyalty to me.

Taz took my hand in his and squeezed. He alone knew exactly what this would mean to me, that not only did I see this as home, but the home actually wanted me in it.

"Nobody deserves this more than you," he said.

I turned back to Queenie, meaning to ask what exactly this meant in terms of practicalities, although at that point I really didn't care. The moment she had my gaze, she slid downward, landing on one knee.

"Arcanium will serve and protect you, as you have served and protected us. As Director, I can offer this to you as a location for your court, if you wish."

I blinked at her, aware of the Queen's sharp intake of breath nearby. I should say something. Anything would do. But any words I might have had in my brain wandered off.

Taz helpfully nudged my chin to close my gawping mouth, but I still couldn't say a single word.

Sparky? Take it this charming silence is a yes?

Even in our telepathy I had no words. Some Queen.

The sharp spike of self-deprecation shook me from the shock and I rubbed a hand over my face.

"I- um, yeah. Thanks. I mean yes, absolutely, definitely would love to have my court here. Although I doubt anyone would want to actually join it, but as like an honorary club-house type thing it'd be great."

I trailed off as Queenie's expression descended from one of anticipation into resigned, withering despair. She rose to her feet and eyed the atrium, full of suspiciously busy people working hard to pretend they weren't listening to every word.

The effect was somewhat spoiled by Milo bursting out of a nearby lift, the biggest wad of paper I'd ever seen flapping in his hands.

"Demi!" He puffed toward me, cheeks flushed and eyes bright. "I hope you don't mind, but Ace said you'd be struggling with this whole new Queen thing, so I wanted to help."

I opened my mouth to fend him off, guessing he hadn't noticed Taz's mother standing haughtily behind me, but his excitement beat me to it.

"Now, I've done some research," he continued. "And I've penned a basic draft of a manifesto of sorts. There will need to be meetings, but I've set up a process for waiting lists, and also a list of courts you need to speak to. I should probably make a list of the lists-"

"Um, Milo…"

"I made Ace ask around, even though he sulked *a lot*, and apparently at least half of Arcanium are already declaring for your court as it is, and you haven't even said anything to them yet! We'll need to deal with the animosity that might come from there now being two Queens, and I doubt she-"

I cleared my throat loudly and his eyes flicked up.

His mouth froze halfway through a word.

I was trying hard not to laugh at the stunned goldfish expression as he noticed the Queen behind me.

"Oh." He went from pink to burning red. "I, um, with the-I…"

I took pity on him. Something told me I'd need someone who actually cared about my court in the coming days, even if I hadn't started to process any of it yet.

"Could you do me an overview?" I asked. "Somewhere else maybe?"

He nodded, almost dropping his papers in his haste to get away. He mouthed something soundless that might have been an apology and directed it over my shoulder before fleeing back into the lift.

I managed to hold in my laughter somehow. Taz didn't bother, his amusement rolling loudly across the atrium. Even Queenie looked like she was trying to reign in the smirk twitching the edges of her mouth.

"We'll carve out a space for your court over the coming days," she suggested. "While we serve, our most important function is the smooth assistance we provide to Faerie, and by extension you."

"Can I continue on as an FDP?" I asked.

She nodded. "Yes, but perhaps for more diplomatic matters. Although with your track record, maybe we should take each assignment as it comes."

I choked through a laugh, but it was all flying over my head now. I could continue to be an FDP *and* hold my court here as Queen. Nobody would want to join anyway, so it was probably not going to be too much of a stretch. No doubt Taz's mother and Queenie both imagined a united front and some placation would be enough to control me and convince me to side with whatever they decided. Boy were they going to get a surprise if they tried. But for that moment, I let myself sink deep into the roots of my future.

"Well, *her majesty* is still recovering," Taz said with a huge grin, no doubt aware of all the eavesdropping ears. "If anyone wishes to join her court, they can let Milo know. *Her majesty* will have audiences at a later date."

I stared at him, alarmed despite the annoying expression on his face that suggested he was teasing me and revelling in it.

Will I really have to hold audiences and things? I asked him. *Urgh.*

I realised that his words were as much to annoy his mother as they were to tease me when she lifted her voice so that the whole atrium would have no trouble hearing.

"It can be a difficult adjustment for one untrained to such responsibility and power," she warned. "You would do well to heed the advice of those around you."

I knew she would still be smarting from the indignity of having another Queen around. Milo's unerring loyalty to me probably hadn't helped with that though, Faerie gift him.

I also knew that it probably hurt to see her sister and her only son championing a sixteen-year-old girl instead of backing her. But she and I weren't friends, and I still had the marks of what she'd used me for in my head.

I made a show of shrugging my shoulders, as if her warning had no consequence at all.

"That's what's gotten me this far." I lifted my voice just as clearly. "I learned early on who to trust. Look, I'm not here to play war games or have an ego contest. I've got too much stuff to be getting on with as it is. But I will use this status to make sure that Fae and fairies alike are treated fairly, and that any mindless cruelty of the past is destroyed."

Her eyes flashed the bruised purple of a sea-storm. Seconds passed. Even if I had all this power now crackling around inside of me, she had centuries of experience wielding hers.

"Is that all?" she asked.

Taz caught my eye. *Go on, have a parting shot. You've earned it, and I'm pretty sure she won't vaporise my girlfriend. Mostly sure anyway.*

He was right. I'd earned my fun.

I smiled at the Queen, lifting my head high.

"For now."

I turned toward the lift that led to the human world, Taz striding beside me. We waited until the doors were shut and we were on our way upwards before bursting into laughter.

"I think this power is going to your head," I told him. "Getting me to face off against your mother, telling people I'll be having audiences. I am *not* having audiences. If people want stuff they can ask by shouting at me in the halls or the canteen or the bathroom like normal."

Taz smiled. "Ah, you'll get used to it and remember, you promised me a throne to sit you on. Ace also collared me in the bathroom and mentioned something about me asking you to go see Milo and look at charts for court colours?"

I groaned loudly and pressed my face into my hands, peeking through my fingers. Even with what now felt like the peril of my new appointment hanging over me, I smiled to see 'Trev woz 'ere' scratched into the wall, like this was a totally normal human-world lift and not a portal to a magical realm.

"You okay though?" Taz asked once he'd stopped laughing. "As much as can be expected? I know we haven't talked as much about the serious things."

I nodded and dropped my hands to my sides as the lift stopped.

"I will be. I've got you, and friends, and home. I'll be absolutely fine."

We walked along the barren corridor with its flickering halogen bulbs and through the door that led to the arcade.

The machines flashed and pinged around us, but the place was deserted. Deep down, I secretly thought it was the smell that put people off, like mould and stale alcohol. Perhaps, given that there was an entrance to a secret world there, that was no bad thing.

Taz led me out of the arcade and into dazzling sunshine. After a few moments of lifting my face to the warmth, I watched people going about their business. A kid screamed as his parents dragged him past the ice cream hut without stopping, dog walkers aimed for the pier and the scent of fish and chips mixed with the determined cry of the gulls squabbling over a nearby bin.

"It's weird to think that with everything that's gone on, the human world doesn't have a clue," I said.

Taz stood beside me. "That's why we do what we do. We keep Faerie a secret and the nightmares firmly in the world of dreams. And you're Queen of Faerie now."

I snorted. "What does that make you then?"

"Whatever role you choose to give me, your majesty."

I recognised a vein of seriousness in his tone then, hidden behind the sparkling eyes and easy, humoured smile.

I glowered back at him. "Okay, any more 'your majesty' stuff, and I'll do something really awful to you, like banish you or something."

I ignored his laughter, both of us knowing that didn't count as an outright lie. I could banish him, but I wouldn't.

I'd miss him too much. But can I lie now that I'm Queen?

I didn't want to think about things like that right now and shook all thoughts of seriousness away. By the sounds of it, the seriousness would be coming at me in everlasting waves, so I was determined to take every single opportunity I had to be silly while I still could.

Taz caught my hands in his, entwining our fingers as he stared at me, waiting.

He wanted me to give him his role, I realised. Let him know

where he stood.

If I told him he was simply my boyfriend, he'd accept it. If I sent him to the other end of Faerie, he'd tantrum *a lot*, but he'd do it simply because I asked him. Not as a queen, or even his queen, but as me. Because I was his girlfriend and he loved me. That was pretty much all I needed to know.

"You once said you'd never be king." I left it hanging there.

He nodded, his easy smile never faltering.

"I said I didn't want to be *crowned* king," he amended. "Being the only regent sounds kind of lonely, and I've seen my mother do it for far too long that way. But it might not be so bad if I were your king consort, supporting you rather than ruling alongside you."

I grinned. "Then that's what you are, but I'll probably get you to do the icky stuff I don't want to do, like audiences."

I giggled as Taz slid an arm around my waist and pretended to throttle me.

"That could technically be seen as attempted regicide," I told him. "But I'll let it go this once. Where are we going anyway? Doughnuts?"

He shrugged. "Wherever you want, Sparky, as long as it's you and me."

"Deal."

I still revelled in it whenever he said things like that, and smiled wide, wrapping my arms around his neck and pressing my chin to his shoulder.

"Do you want to get chips and sit on the pier for a bit?" he asked. "Then doughnuts for afters."

I nodded. "In a minute."

He laughed and I knew he'd stand there and wait for as long as I wanted. His ego probably thought it was because I wanted to keep hugging him, but I was more absorbed in staring over his shoulder.

A dilapidated amusement arcade doesn't seem a likely place to find a portal hub to Faerie. But sometimes it's in the most unlikely of places and people that you find the deepest magic of all.

ACKNOWLEDGEMENTS

Huge thank you to every reader who has joined Demi and Taz and friends on their journey! To those who've shared on social media, done ARC reads or just given me compliments about the book to keep me going.

To my family and also my writing family as always, your support means everything to me – Anna Britton, Debbie Roxburgh, Samantha Williams, Sally Doherty, Marisa Noelle, Emma Finlayson-Palmer, Katina Wright, Alison Hunt, the amazing ARC readers Maria Oliver, Loz Doyle, Estelle Tudor (who have caught so many printing blips it's not even funny...) writing Twitter, Rebecca Kenney for the stunning covers, everyone who joins #ukteenchat, the WriteMentor crew, libraries and schools who took a chance on this series, shops that are still stocking these books and giving this indie author a chance to reach more readers, and to the readers who will find these books in the future.

THANK YOU!

ABOUT THE AUTHOR

While always convinced that there has to be something out there beyond the everyday, Emma focuses on weaving magic realms with words (the real world can wait a while). The idea of other worlds fascinates her and she's determined to find her own entrance to an alternate realm one day.

Raised in London, she now lives on the UK south coast with her husband and a very lazy black Labrador who occasionally condescends to take her out for a walk.

Aside from creative writing studies, an addiction to cake and spending far too much time procrastinating on social media, Emma is still waiting for the arrival of her unicorn. Or a tank, she's not fussy.

For the latest news and updates, check the website or come say hi on social media:

www.emmaebradley.com
@EmmaEBradley